CONSTABLE'S RUN

CONSTABLE'S RUN

LAURIE MOORE

Five Star • Waterville, Maine

Published in 2003 in conjunction with Merry Laureen Moore.

Set in 11 pt. Plantin by Myrna S. Raven.

Printed in the United States on permanent paper.

Library of Congress Cataloging-in-Publication Data

Moore, Laurie.
    Constable's run / Laurie Moore.
       p. cm.—(Five Star expressions)
     ISBN 0-7862-4641-3 (hc : alk. paper)
     ISBN 1-4104-0120-0 (sc : alk. paper)
     1. Police—Texas—Fiction. 2. Policewomen—Fiction.
   3. Romanies—Fiction. I. Title. II. Series.
   PS3613.O658 C66 2002
    814.6—dc21   2002026618

Dedication

To my parents, who thought I should practice law; to my sister, who told me to do what made me happy; and to my daughter, Laura, who always believed in me when I said I would be a published author.

Acknowledgements

For Hazel Rumney and Russell Davis of Five Star, thank you for your confidence in me; for retired Tarrant County Constable Jim Palmer, the lawdog who carried my peace officer commission and the barometer by which all Texas Constables should be measured, many thanks for giving me the opportunity to witness the insanity of Cowtown politics; for my friends and colleagues at the DFW Writers Workshop, who laughed along with my stories; and for my wonderful family, a slave-driving lot who inspire me to be a better person.

Chapter One

Sirens from emergency vehicles pealed out, and traffic crawled past the warning flares. Beyond the nasty wreck and the rubberneckers, three lanes opened up.

Thank goodness.

Raven checked her watch.

Fifteen 'til five.

Her stomach clenched as she floored the loaner car's accelerator. The circa-sixties Lincoln with gangster-tinted windows and suicide doors lurched forward and died in the center lane of Fort Worth's Loop 820.

Shouldn't have tried to conduct personal business on company time, she thought. Old Judge Masterson signed a Writ of Attachment to remove a child from the mother, and Jinx Porter, Tarrant County Constable, expected his deputies to accompany him when he served it. Including her.

With the bald tires still rolling, she popped the gearshift into neutral and cranked the ignition. The wicked dog-vomit beige machine backfired like a LAWS rocket and belched a cone of blue smoke into the ozone.

Drifting into the slow lane only made matters worse. A blaring white streak sheared past. Any closer and they'd have swapped paint—not to mention provided her the opportunity to reach out and yank the passenger's upraised finger out of its socket. Rotten mechanic, keeping her car a whole week before telling her he never picked up the part.

Something about refusing to deal with *furriners*.

She cut her gaze from the roadway to a scrap of paper on the seat, then grabbed the cell phone from its place on the console and stabbed out the number for Al's AAAA Aard-vark Import Auto Salvage and Repair.

Dumb bastard. Starting with "Al's" meant he had thirty-seven junkyards ahead of him in the Yellow Pages listings. A tone purred in her ear and a man answered in a clipped foreign accent.

That explained it.

Raven cleared her throat. "Yes, hello, I'm the one who phoned earlier about a window motor for an old BMW, re-member?"

"No. I did not speak with you."

A gangrenous Mustang that must've had a Porsche engine conversion whizzed past, seemingly without a driver. Either that, or the maniac's head didn't reach the top of the steering wheel. The car cut in front of her and she braked hard, nearly giving the pony an enema with the Lincoln's hood ornament.

"SORRY SONOFABITCH."

The phone went dead in her hand.

Oh, good grief. The salvage yard guy must've thought—

She pressed the redial button.

Heart racing, she stiffened against the seat. Good thing she wasn't paranoid. A nut case might jump to conclusions that Ichabod Crane deliberately tried to force her off the road.

A jingle of tones, and again, the foreigner.

"I'm so sorry." Words geysered out. "Please don't hang up, I'm in traffic. There was a bad wreck. I'm trying to get to your shop before you close. I need that motor."

"We close in fifteen minutes."

The man—Iranian, or maybe Pakistani considering his inflection—sounded pleased at her distress.

"You don't understand. I have to have this motor."

Lazy-assed mechanic should be the one scrounging parts. "My car's rotting in the shop."

"We close in fourteen minutes."

The click of a dead connection stung in her ear.

The Lincoln slumped heavily down the highway. She angled closer to the exit ramp and filed in behind the official pace car—a cancer-infested old pickup—chugging along at a warp speed of twenty-five. Nuzzling up close enough to kiss the bumper turned out to be a bad move. The Lincoln disappeared inside a whirling cornucopia of yellow exhaust, and in no time flat, fumes blasted through the air-conditioner vents with the vengeance of the showers at Treblinka.

Disgusted, Raven slapped the off-button. The knob ricocheted off the dash panel and pinged to the floorboard. The radio blared and the fan stuck on high. Dark hair blew back from her face at a cyclone windspeed. Over the rush of air, the voice of Yana the Mystic from the drive-time talk show gave a caller the low-down on his future. Raven derived a modicum of pleasure hearing his sad, sorry tale—apparently she wasn't the only one in Fort Worth, Texas, whose planets were auguring in. She turned off the radio, mashed the A/C vents closed, and tapped the phone back on.

The foreigner again.

Her eyes flickered to her watch, then to the bottleneck of traffic up ahead. "Please, have mercy. It's been a horrible day."

Think Jinx's cheating on me.

Two A.M. phone calls.

Jerk takes 'em in the bathroom.

"It is bad day for many. World hunger. Persons become skeletons each moment we speak. In Middle East, there is much bloodshed. In Africa, Hutu warriors engage in the

11

slaughter of Tutsi tribe. Ebola breakout in Gabon."

"You don't understand."

"I understand perfectly. It is you who do not understand. Have you no regard for crocodiles?"

"What?" She pulled the phone from her ear long enough to stare at it.

"Such a situation wreaks much havoc on our ecosystem. Tutsi people tragically perish beneath the blade of the Hutu. Discarded bodies—thousands—float downriver. Crocodiles in Rwanda gorge themselves until they flip, belly-up, like goldfish." He clicked his tongue, tsk-tsk-tsk. "It is most dismal future to the environmental balance, having not enough crocodiles."

Thanks for the food chain bulletin, Walter "Achmed" Cronkite.

Steam rose from the blacktop and a light mist coated the windshield. Raven flicked a lever and the sluggish wipers squeegeed against the glass. The second swipe picked up speed. The third struck metal with a frenzied whack, and by the fourth, the left wiper shot across the highway, leaving the one on the right hovering above her line of vision like a Turkish sword from the Ottoman Empire.

For no good reason, the pickup braked. She dropped the phone and gripped the steering wheel in a two-handed death grip. Swerving sent the Lincoln fishtailing inches from the guardrail.

Damned cardboard cutout behind the wheel.

Ought to have his driver's license revoked.

Never glanced in his rearview mirror, not once.

Too bad she wasn't in her patrol car, she'd cite him.

She pulled in a cleansing breath. Retrieved the phone from the seat. "You don't understand."

Shitty day. Found out this eff-ing gypsy I arrested put a con-

tract out on me. Don't know whether to take it seriously—

"Thirteen minutes."

"I NEED THAT PART."

Eff-ing mechanic didn't pick up the motor—eff-ing foreigner intends to lock me out. Can't take any more of this shit.

"You must hasten or I shall be forced to secure my doors."

"Don't you dare close up on me." An erratic pulse throbbed at the base of her throat. Ahead, flickering taillights slowed to a bottleneck. Another minute and she'd blow a gasket. "Look, Mister, I'm doing my dead-level best."

"Twelve minutes, now."

"I'm begging you, wait. Please don't let me down."

She winced at the Golden Gloves groveling. Cops were supposed to be in control and she hadn't been in control of anything all day. Not to mention having to take guff off a junkyard guy—a member of a profession that ranked near the top of the list of people she'd just as soon put a price tag on and buy 'em, for God's sake—all because he had the only BMW window motor in the Metroplex.

"You are aware, yes, the number of calls from ingrates who promise they are already to be here?"

"I'm not like that. I never told a lie in my life."

A disembodied chuckle. "It appears you have just done so."

"Listen to me. You can take my word to the bank."

"If only I have a coin each time I hear this, to deposit in your great financial institutions," he said wistfully.

"I'm calling from a cell phone. I'm driving as fast as I can."

"This I do not know for certain. You will be sure to organize much better your time, on your next trip to my business establishment."

She didn't care for the traces of homeland in his voice. Especially the way the towel-head trilled his "R"s.

"Don't fuck with me." Words spewed out before she could stop them. "Please. I'm under a lot of pressure. My boss informed me somebody took out a contract on me."

"I wish you much luck with your contract. May Allah will that you accumulate much wealth. Unfortunately, there are now only eleven minutes."

"You don't understand. A contract is a hit."

"What is *hit?* Somebody punch you? Or this hit is like hit movie, hit record, baseball hit, take a hit off my reefer?"

"He's trying to kill me."

"Your boss is trying to kill you? Perhaps you should quit your job."

"Not my boss. Some gyppo. I don't know whether it's a hoax, but a confidential informant who's Hungarian or Rumanian, overheard at Gypsy Feast how the head gyp put a contract out on me." She sat up sharply, wondering, Why am I spilling my guts to this moron? But she knew.

"Why he is hungry? You just said they feasted."

"Not hungry, Hun-gar-i-an." She enunciated each syllable.

"Do not talk down to me. I speak perfect English. It is you who do not talk correctly."

"I'm not talking down to you—"

"Ten minutes."

The countdown scalded her. "Look, Mohammed, the mountain's coming. But you can't expect me to appear like a genie. Have you looked outside? The streets are slicker than cow snot on a doorknob."

"I see you are—how do you say—pulling my foot? I am looking through the window. The ground is dry. Much like an elephant carcass bleached by the sun."

14

"This is Texas. Weather changes at the drop of a Stetson. Not to mention, I've had a raincloud dogging me the last ten minutes."

"This is so? For ten minutes? That is one minute more than you have to arrive in."

"Yeah? Well, right now, I don't care if a gypsy does kill me, I just want that motor for my window so I don't die of heat stroke."

The pickup pulled into the exit lane and slowed to a crawl. She punched the accelerator, blasted the horn and zeroed in so close the truck's license plate disappeared from sight.

Around mile marker forty-eight, Raven climbed out of denial and accepted the reality of her situation. Jinx Porter might be worried about his reelection campaign as constable, but that wee-hour phone call wasn't business. She set her jaw and bitterly concluded that the world had two kinds of women—those Jinx had slept with, and those he intended to.

The immigrant compounded her misery.

"Perhaps you should alert police to your gypsy problem."

"I don't need to call the police. I *am* the police. What I need is that motor." She took a deep breath to calm herself; she couldn't afford to piss the guy off. "Listen carefully. I need the right passenger window motor for a 1983 BMW 318i—"

"I know what you want. I am not ignorant. I may not be from this country but I speak very excellent English."

"I'm not saying you don't." Her voice trailed off. Expecting the Shah to post another time check, her eyes flickered to the speedometer. It seemed to be hung on ninety-three miles per hour, putting her true speed in inverse proportion to the gauge.

"You are declaring to my face that my English is no good? That is final insult. I will not speak further to such a person. Find another dealer for this part. Good day."

He hung up.

Raven's police radio crackled to life.

Jinx. "What's your ETA? We're standing by, ready to go, and you're not here."

Raven thought fast. Only a mile from the salvage yard. She could still get the motor without Jinx knowing. Dating the boss didn't mean he wouldn't document infractions in her personnel file; Jinx was a stickler for policy. But she'd come so close it didn't make sense to abandon her mission when she could make up the time exceeding the speed limit without compromising the writ.

She did what she had to do.

Picked up the handie-talkie and keyed the mike.

"Ten-nine? You're cutting out." She banged the radio against the dashboard. "I can't hear you. Repeat."

In the middle of Jinx's transmission, she pressed the off-button.

Simple as that.

She returned the police handheld to its place on the seat, choked the steering wheel and stomped the gas pedal.

The Texas Rangers Ballclub was looking for a left-handed pitcher and Constable Jinx Porter knew just where they could find one. The Mexican who delivered the morning newspaper at five-thirty lobbed Friday's edition over the second story balcony of his apartment in what he gauged to be a ninety-five-mile-an-hour pitch, judging by the explosion of shatterproof glass.

Almost twelve hours later, Jinx concluded that having to

board up the window and lock the Siamese cat in the bedroom until maintenance arrived turned out to be the best part of his day.

Raven had him hopping mad.

Executing a child writ was dangerous business, and he wouldn't do it with less than four deputies; two at the front door, two at the back. He and Raven would take the front the way they always did; Mickey and Dell could guard the rear in case of escape.

But after a day serving papers, Raven hadn't returned, and he let Dell and Mickey con him into going for burgers during the wait. Now he'd have to pay his deputies overtime, and the commissioner's court would bitch to high Heaven at their next meeting. Not that he gave a rat, but they did have the authority to tinker with his budget, and he was already operating on a shoestring.

Anger pinched the corners of his mouth.

If Raven had been on time, the four of them could have been long gone from the windowless crackerbox the commissioners expected him to run a law enforcement agency out of, and he would have missed Evan Rainey completely. The high-dollar attorney wouldn't give Jinx a campaign contribution, but he didn't seem to have any problem inconveniencing him on a Friday afternoon, five minutes before quitting time. As soon as the cowbell clanged above the glass door, and Fort Worth's oiliest lawyer—Mr. Slick-Fifty, himself—barged in wearing a custom tailored suit, Jinx wished he'd already thrown the deadbolt and called it a day.

Especially when he found out the shyster came with divorce papers for Eleanor Thornton. Rainey expected the Constable's Office to drop everything and get his rich client's soon-to-be-ex-wife served.

The lawyer rattled a Temporary Restraining Order at Jinx. "This has to be done tonight."

Jinx gave him a practiced give-a-shit look. "Why's that?"

"Because Eleanor's spending my client blind. And this TRO will put a stop to it."

Except for people in comas, everybody in the Lower Forty-Eight knew Alexander Thornton III decided to trade the old Rolls Royce in for a late model Lamborghini. And everybody in law enforcement knew that on the advice of counsel, Mrs. Thornton took up residence in Beverly Hills in an attempt to make service of process more difficult, and give the old coot time to come to his senses.

Sniffing a campaign donation for his dedication, Jinx jumped on the opportunity like a rat on a Chee-to. "We can serve it tomorrow."

"You work weekends?" Rainey, incredulous.

"We will if we have to."

"Well, I don't. Eleanor's here for the ballet's opening night performance of Swan Lake. Trey offered to vacate the estate for the weekend so she could fly in and make a big splash. She's a big patron of the arts, you know."

"You don't say," Jinx deadpanned. Stitches from last Thursday's hemorrhoid surgery still throbbed, making Rainey even more of a pain in the ass than usual.

"Eleanor thinks Trey's in New York. She plans to be back in California by the time her picture runs in Sunday's society section."

"How nice. Your client tricked her into coming here."

Rainey brightened. "Isn't it great? She has no idea. That's why it has to be done now. If Eleanor gets wind of this, she'll split. It's happened before."

"Not with me."

"Which leads me to why I'm here."

18

"It'll have to wait. We're about to run an emergency child writ. Why don't you take it to one of the other constables? I'm not the only one who can do this, you know."

Rainey torqued his jaw. "You're the only county employee who actually works until five on Fridays. And you always seem to get people served, even the difficult ones. And difficult is a euphemism for what Eleanor Thornton's going to be."

And I have an opponent in the upcoming election and you can't even donate to my campaign?

"Get your cop car and meet me at the Thornton mansion. But don't park near the estate. Wait one street over and I'll drive you. She'll open the door for me."

Jinx squirmed uncomfortably against the inflatable donut. He rose, reached for his jacket, and wrangled into each sleeve. With Thornton's divorce papers tucked safely inside his pocket, he grabbed the rubber donut and looped it through one arm.

Might as well knock out Alexander Thornton III's divorce papers and reassemble after Mickey and Dell finished dinner.

The cowbell jingled as he shooed Rainey out. While he turned off the lights and locked the door, his gaze lingered on the crescent of reverse-image letters stuck to the glass entry. Letters proclaiming him Tarrant County Constable Jinx Porter.

Letters scraped off in a heartbeat if he lost his bid for reelection. Jinx let out a hard sigh.

Fifty years old and all washed up.

Where the devil was Raven, anyway, and what the heck was taking so long?

The instant he threw the deadbolt, the telephone pealed out its annoying ring. He made what he considered to be a sound executive decision.

Screw it.

Anyone who called after five on a Friday afternoon didn't deserve to get an answer.

Raven picked up the cell phone and pressed the auto-redial.

"Al's AAAA Aardvark. We are closed."

"No, you're not. I still have eight minutes."

"That is what you think."

The connection went dead.

She winced, then slammed the base of the phone against the dashboard so hard it cracked the brittle vinyl.

With one hand, she jerked the steering wheel hard right, jumping the bloated Lincoln off the freeway, over the shoulder, down a grassy hillside, through a foot and a half of muddy water. The barge floated down the asphalt stream with the grace of a Naval aircraft carrier rocking in the swells. It drifted past the broken stripe on the frontage road where posted signs warned that the lane was about to play out.

She pressed the redial.

"Aardvark."

She spoke in a hyperventilating rush. "You're mad because you think I insulted you, but you misunderstood. I didn't say you don't speak well, it's just that my connection's bad and the cell phone battery's about to go." She glanced in her rearview mirror. Thank God, no cop cars in sight. Gray eyes misted in a great salt lake of sincerity. "I'm stuck in this God-awful traffic and you're about to close, and you have the only part in the whole city, and if I don't get it I'll be without my car another week."

"Eeeeeeerrrrrrrr—" His rusty-hinge distress signal

pealed all the way down her ear canal. "—It is the crazy lady who shouts insults to foreign persons."

"I only wanted to clear this up."

"You have no soul."

A lump formed in her throat. "You're wrong. People love me. They beg me to be godmother to their babies. I send money to that-that-that—" The name escaped her. She felt the lightheaded rush of someone whose brain wasn't getting enough oxygen. "—Third World adopt-a-kid program. I have nine pictures at the office of emaciated children I've never met, hanging on my wall."

"You hang children from your wall?"

"What? Of course not. Their photos. Snapshots."

"Perhaps you should seek the Nobel Peace Prize."

He was fucking with her.

"I attend church," she blurted in a shameless ploy for sympathy. "Not every Sunday, okay? But at least twice a year. I'm the designated driver for the world. Drunks adore me. I'm welcome at River Crest Country Club, for God's sake. I'm sorry-sorry-sorry for the misunderstanding."

"I tell you again. I have this. Why do you torture me? I will sell to you the part. You must arrive before closing and we will surely pull it."

"Please just pull it now."

"This we cannot accomplish until arrival. It is policy."

Unbridled panic surged through her extremities. "How long'll that take?"

"Twenty, perhaps fifteen minutes."

"I'm begging you. I have to drive clear across town and my boss'll kill me if I'm late." She clenched the steering wheel, braced hard, and forced the foot-feed all the way to the threadbare mat.

The Lincoln bucked beneath her. Followed by a sick-

21

ening crack and the distant clink of floorboard chunks falling away. She glanced down. Pavement rolled underfoot with conveyor belt speed. A couple of twitches, and the speedometer dropped to the twenty mark.

"Please make an exception. I have to meet my boss, Constable Jinx Porter. . . ."

. . . who's also my "insignificant other"—intend to get to the bottom of his philandering tonight—bastard can't seem to keep his dangling participle in his pants.

"I feel it is my duty to remind you," the man said cheerily, "five—no, please to pardon—four minutes."

"Listen to me. My boss is the constable. We're supposed to serve a writ and I have to be there. Jinx goes ballistic when I'm late."

"Battle stick? What is battle stick?"

"Please just pull the damned motor because I cannot take any more stress." Traces of spit glittered against the backs of her hands.

"We must first see money."

"I have it." A bespectacled old hunchback crossing against the signal glanced up in time to see her careening toward him. Wild-eyed, he jumped for the gutter. She found herself aiming for him. "Swear to God, I'll be there if I have to steamroll everything between us. Just do it."

"Did I not say it will be done? When you arrive."

In the distance, a string of traffic lights dominoed into red connect-a-dots.

Time to pull rank.

Take up this conversation with somebody with clout.

"I don't seem to be making headway with you. Let me speak to the manager. What's his name?" A name skidded across the Teflon lining inside her skull. "Chuck?"

"I would be most pleased for you to unleash such rabid

madness on my manager, so it is with much sadness that I must report—" He hissed out a punctured-tire sigh. "— Mister Chuck is in the yard."

"THEN, GET ME THE OWNER."

"Speaking." Then, "Three minutes."

"How much is the motor?"

"Ten thousand dollars."

"WHAT?"

A belly-laugh. "The price is seventy-five dollars."

"Seventy-five dollars?"

"You do not want part? See you later, alligator."

"Don't hang up." Turban-headed terrorist. If there was a God, she'd get a chance to arrest this smart-ass. *After* she got her motor. "I want the part. I only meant that seventy-five dollars—"

"This seems to you, excessive? Enjoy finding this part elsewhere."

"You don't understand—"

Three warning beeps, and she lost the signal.

Raven howled loud enough to curl the ceiling liner.

She'd wanted to tell Attila the Hun seventy-five dollars was jim-dandy. Cheap, even. Especially when the asshole-y mechanic would've charged her out the wazoo if he'd had to drive out to stinking Egypt, in the stinking bumper-to-bumper traffic to pick it up. Infuriated, she groped for the electric window gizmo so she could fling the latest in communication technology out the opening.

No response.

Rat-mangled, sorry piece of shit jalopy. The phone torpedoed to the floormat with a thunk.

Now what?

She'd hung up on a pissed-off Arab-Turk-Iraqi-Whatever, and best she figured, had three or four minutes left before the Sheik said "up your leg" and threw the deadbolt.

The mobile gas chamber skidded into the parking lot in front of Al's AAAA Aardvark Import Auto Salvage and Repair, scattershooting pea gravel across the sidewalk. Bolting from the vehicle, Raven tried to make an entrance worthy of Cindy Crawford at a Calvin Klein showing. A golden web of lightning lit the gloomy skies. A bowling ball rumble reverberated through the atmosphere. The first drops of what promised to be a gullywasher came down in splats.

Inside, a bronze-skinned man seated on a stool in front of a computer paused long enough to look up from beneath the cap set jauntily on his head. Dark, smoldering eyes flashed contempt.

"You are the one hung up in my ear, yes? You look as imagined, Miss Hotshot."

Raven took a deep breath. No need for street theater, just pay the Emir for the part and vamoose.

"The phone battery crapped out. I apologize, okay?" She whipped out her checkbook and dug for a pen. "You've got my part?"

"Most certainly."

He slid off the stool, strutted over to a pile of dusty parts, fished out a chunk of plastic with wires porcupining out, and held it up like he'd discovered the Ark of the Covenant. In horror, she stopped the hasty scrawl long enough to poise her pen in the nightmarish angle of a dagger about to be plunged into a sacrificial heart.

He gave her a cheesy grin. "Here is your mirror."

"My motor," she said dully.

"Mirror."

Staring past faint lettering that warned OBJECTS ARE CLOSER THAN THEY APPEAR, she not only felt her face contort into a grotesque mask, but got to watch it happen.

She felt her vital signs drop dramatically. "Motor, not mirror. I said 'motor.' I want a window motor for my Beemer."

His brows fused above his nose to form a long, hairy rope.

"You said mirror."

"Window motor." She enunciated each syllable, the way she had over the telephone before the camel jockey lashed out to let her know how great he spoke English. "So the glass will roll down."

She lowered her sunglasses enough to peer over the top. He needed to see the murderous bent in the eyes of someone who opposed immigration.

"You said mirror." He spoke the trigger words that brought out the hysteria lying dormant during the ride out.

"I said motor, Habib, or whatever your name is. You said, 'Don't talk down to me, I speak perfect English,' and I said I wasn't talking down to you, I just wanted to make sure you knew what part to pull for my BMW. And the part I want is a motor, not a mirror."

She checked her watch.

Ohgod.

Jinx would be white-hot.

Omar shrugged off the temper tantrum with the universal "who-gives-a-shit" symbol. The palms-up, shoulder-lift kind of gesture unique to junkyard employees, roofers, convicts, and people who didn't speak English as a first language and didn't intend to learn.

"There is grave possibility we do not have."

"You have it. Find it."

"If Allah wills it."

Allah? So far, Allah had been a real hands-off guy. She

lost her composure. "Do you mean to tell me I drove—"

She didn't see who tackled her from behind. But the blow knocked the breath out of her, and her knees buckled under the impact of a great weight.

Middle-Easterner eyes snapped open like rollershades. The countertop moved away in slow motion and the room tilted on its side. Her purse skidded beyond her reach, scattering the contents across the concrete.

With an attacker firmly on top of her, Raven tasted the floor. Her .38 Smith & Wesson pinwheeled away and came to rest near the wall. With her lungs burning from oxygen deprivation, she writhed to dislodge him in her struggle to breathe.

Angry words, hissed directly into her ear, sent a chill through her heart. "Die, *gadja*. I curse my dead mother and dead father if I don't succeed."

Chapter Two

Parked under an inadequate shade tree a block from Alexander Thornton's estate, Jinx squirmed against the inflatable donut and waited for Rainey to show.

He volumed the car radio down low and took stock of his career. It wasn't as if there was a market for defeated elected officials.

And there you have it, he thought.

Fifty years old and all washed up.

Too young to be put out to pasture, too old to get another cop job, since he exceeded the age cutoff for any decent police department by at least ten years. He allowed his mind to free-associate on mid-life career change possibilities before settling on one he liked.

Ranger baseball scout.

He could tip off the Team Manager about the undiscovered talent masquerading as a newspaper deliveryman. Unless the Rangers had a fixation with accuracy, the wild-pitching Mexican might even get a tryout.

Fifteen minutes went by.

Just when Jinx decided to leave, a champagne-colored Lexus purred up next to the patrol car. The tinted window slid down, revealing Rainey's unsmiling face.

The lawyer hollered over his music. "You ready?"

Jinx set his jaw. "You're late."

"Couldn't be helped. Hop in." Rainey produced a small plastic box and waved it. "I have the opener to the security gate, and I paid off the maid."

Jinx hitched up his pants, ran a thumb over the holster

snap securing the long-barrel .38, unplugged his cell phone from the charger and stuffed it into his jacket pocket.

Inside the Lexus, Rainey opened his mouth to speak, and the highball on his breath telegraphed the reason for his delay.

"Couldn't help noticing the rubber donut when you opened your door. Hemorrhoids?"

"Not since last week's surgery. Mine were long enough to tie into bows."

Rainey wore the smirk of a younger man, in tiptop shape, who didn't have a clue. But that didn't keep Jinx from hoping Thornton's lawyer took lots of reading material into the bathroom each morning. By the time Rainey jerked the Lexus away from the patrol car, Jinx wished him a similar fate—telephone pole-sized obstructions worthy of formaldehyde and a museum shelf in *Ripley's Believe It or Not!*

Reflexively, he felt his back pocket for the tin of Copenhagen and wondered how Rainey would react if he took out a pinch, then dusted his hands off over the pristine seats with their new-leather smell.

Not that Trey Thornton's attorney made it easy to sniff the car's interior.

Since Rainey's cologne smelled bad enough to choke a goat, Jinx figured it must be his car, his thick glossy hair, and the hand-tailored suit that made the women at the courthouse stick to the seats of their chairs when he sauntered in. Jinx glanced down at the front of his own jacket, the one that started out a cheap imitation of Rainey's but ended up with a certain mohair quality, thanks to the custom shredding from his seal-point Siamese, Caesar. Probably ought to quit layering his sportcoats over the dining room chairs, maybe make it more of a challenge for the kitty to climb them by hanging them in the closet.

He caught the lawyer staring.

"Say, Porter, aren't you up for reelection?"

"Yeah." Acid churned in his stomach. "And this time, I've got an opponent."

"Who's running against you?"

"Rudy Castro."

"Never heard of him. What's he do?"

"He's a twenty-four-year-old kid in junior college."

"He can't beat you," Rainey predicted with confidence.

For an instant, reality suspended and Jinx's hopes soared—and came crashing down like the *Flying Wallendas* without a safety net. With a campaign treasurer like Skeeter Clinkscale, who acted as if raising money was beneath him, a truculent employee out on indefinite suspension, and Georgia, the office secretary, who thought sick days and vacation were interchangeable, he didn't have a Chinaman's chance.

He squirmed against the seat cushion and dropped a hint the size of a Texas cow patty. "Somebody's bankrolling Castro. And since he's unemployed, he's got all day to fraternize with people. I'm operating my campaign on a thread, and I've still got an office to run."

"You've been around, what? Fifteen, twenty years?"

"Sixteen."

Rainey pursed his lips and let out a low whistle. "Your retirement's not vested until you put in four more years?"

"That about says it."

"Does the guy have any law enforcement credentials?"

Jinx shook his head. Big shakes.

A sadistic smile crossed Rainey's face. "You act worried."

Not worried. Scared shitless.

Rainey rolled up to a formidable brick wall with an electric gate, and activated the remote control device. Imposing, wrought-iron spikes slid open like the sleepy eye of a Cyclops.

"Does Mrs. Thornton know we're coming?"

"She knows I'm coming."

The Lexus passed an electric sensor and the gate swung closed.

"Jesus H." Jinx took in the view.

Thornton's house turned out to be a slightly smaller version of the Parthenon. Winged cherubs peed into fountains that eventually formed a massive waterfall, and seven-foot bronzes of Greek gods and garlanded goddesses dotted the manicured grounds.

Trey Thornton could give a donation.

Could probably finance the entire campaign with a week's worth of lunch money.

Rainey slipped the Lexus into park and unsnapped the electric door locks. Onyx eyes, blank and fathomless, surveyed the perimeter.

"Let me do the talking," he said.

"Suits me."

"She's not expecting this." Rainey quickened his gait as they strolled toward the door. "She thinks I'm here to get her to sign off on a stock trade."

"Why all the cloak and dagger stuff? This lady's a blueblood. Why not just phone her up? Tell her to have the chauffeur drive her down to the office and pick up the papers without all the hoopla?"

Rainey's eyelids fell to half-mast, fluttering like the American flag for a dead president.

"Surely, you jest." He stabbed the doorbell with the tip of his Mont Blanc. "Do you think Eleanor wants this divorce? She actually believes Trey'll tire of his little distraction, and once he gets the girl out of his system, he'll amble on home and be the delightful companion he's always been."

The massive door swung open and a uniformed maid with sad eyes welcomed them inside.

"Hello, Beatrice." Rainey dug in his pocket and pressed a wad of bills into the domestic's hand. "Buy yourself something nice."

He motioned Jinx to follow him upstairs, leaving Beatrice to skulk away with her thirty pieces of silver.

Jinx stepped onto the marble floor and took a visual inventory. His gaze tracked a cantilevered staircase that wound up an oval entry bigger than most homes. Fresh flower arrangements decorated gilded pedestals and Italian Provincial antiques, and he welcomed any scent that overpowered the fireball breath fermenting in Rainey's stomach. Overhead, a crystal chandelier the size of his bathroom almost blinded him with its illumination.

At the top of the stairs, Rainey gave a wall textured to resemble classical ruins a slight tap.

"*Trompe l'oeil,*" he whispered with reverence.

Whatever the hell that meant. Jinx lifted an eyebrow and continued to scope out the surroundings.

"It's French. It means, To deceive the eye. This isn't a pillar, it's a door. Designed to resemble an ancient column, yet it's part of the wall." Rainey appeared to be channeling the spirit of a dead museum docent. "Even the cornices at the top are *faux*. That's French for 'fake.' Very clever, don't you think?"

"Nice." But he was thinking, Donate to my political campaign, Shithead.

The wall moved. A hatchet-nosed matron the size of the

bronze Zeus on the steps of Thornton's stone pavilion stood before them in a snug silk chemise. Enormous breasts merged with her thick waist.

"Evan, Dear, you're early." Adoring eyes crinkled at the corners. Skin collected in folds around her neck and she had her big, white, Texas hair lacquered to the high gloss of spun glass.

She spotted Jinx and her grandmotherly smile vanished. Eyes became slitted and shrewd. Her face melted into fear.

"Eleanor, this is—"

Rainey never got to finish.

Jinx stepped through the opening and whipped out the petition. "Eleanor Thornton, I'm Constable Jinx Porter. . . ."

She recoiled, retreating to a bed larger than some tropical islands, to a stockpile of shoes—Italian, most likely—and began launching them, grenade-like, across the room.

". . . and I have divorce papers for you."

A stiletto heel whizzed past his cheek, imbedding itself in the wall momentarily before dropping to the carpet with a thud.

"BENEDICT ARNOLD." A leather torpedo spiraled toward Rainey. It hit the door with a clatter. Paint shrapnel flaked to the floor.

Jinx took another step, arm outstretched. "You're hereby served—"

"Don't come any closer, you bastards." Enraged, she fired off another pump, grappling for reinforcements with her free hand.

Jinx ducked.

"Evan, you little piss-ant, how could you?"

Whack. A Staffordshire dog disintegrated.

"Your mother and I are friends, you snot-nosed vermin."

The whistle of an incoming round propelled Evan Rainey into a gazelle imitation. He hightailed it through the fake wall, leaving Jinx to dodge another high-heel.

Splat.

"Come back here, you pinch-faced weasel. I'm the one who made Trey give you your first job."

Thwack.

Rainey's ratlike shriek pierced the outer rotunda.

Jinx inched closer. Eleanor Thornton blitzed him with a fistful of flats. A flicker of recognition flashed in her glittery eyes.

"Aren't you Dan and Kamille Porter's son?" She grabbed another shoe and held her pose. "Your mother's my bridge partner, you son of a bitch."

Ka-Bam.

Plaster cracked.

Eleanor Thornton went for the gunboats.

Bang.

With the impressive presence of an unhappy Statue of Liberty, she held up a discouraging spike heel. Her eyes sparkled like bottle rockets.

Jinx tossed the papers on the California king bed and backed out of the line of fire. "You know, Mrs. Thornton, I always thought you were high class. But you're acting no different than Rosita Martinez down on Hemphill Street the day I served her papers."

Eleanor Thornton relaxed her fingers in defeat. The last missile dropped to the carpet. She flung herself across the empty bed, clutched a down pillow to her face, and allowed her grief to roar out.

Jinx shook his head. With a disconcerting thought, he stepped onto the mezzanine and closed the door behind him.

Raven had a saying.

No matter how hard you try, some days just suck.

He hoped Alexander Thornton III might remember him fondly and make a generous contribution when Rainey told him Eleanor had been personally served.

If not, he'd just found the Rangers a left-handed pitcher.

Chapter Three

Raven knew instinctively she'd been jumped by a fiend.

With her .38 snub-nose beyond reach, she drew up an elbow and jabbed blindly. The crunch against bone signaled contact. A banshee song hit a midrange note, shrieked up the diatonic scale, and hung in an eerie, anguished wail. She cocked her head in time to catch a distorted glimpse of pointy-toed spats and baggy pants.

"My gun," she screamed.

The salvage baron gave her an impotent blink.

A rubbery vise with hairy knuckles gripped her ankle and dragged her across the cold concrete on her belly. She clawed the floor in a feeble attempt to stop.

"Gimme a hand," she shouted.

The Ayatollah clapped.

"No, you idiot—HELP."

"I am for peace."

Gandhi.

The weight of an anvil fell across her. She rolled the fleshy mass off and body-slammed him while Omar, King-of-the-Junkyard looked on, wide-eyed, behind the safety of the counter.

"At least—" she pinned the stocky shoulders against the floor "—call the police."

Drawing up a knee, she planted it in the middle of a gelatinous belly.

"But already you have said you are the police."

"Dial nine one one," she cried.

Instead, he glanced at the wall clock. "Two minutes."

"ARE YOU INSANE?"

She stared, dumfounded, while a stubby fist pummeled her ribs. She grabbed what appeared to be a hairy coconut jutting out from an oxlike neck and put it in a headlock.

"In one minute we are closed. Please to be finished with your wrestling by then."

Raven inched over to the Lady Smith. A foot hooked around her leg. Tried to climb her like Jack-in-the-Beanstalk. She tightened the stranglehold.

Flailing flippers went limp. The flabby torso deflated. She unhanded him. Lunged for the gun. Stuck the one-and-a-half-inch barrel up the snout of—

—a troll?

She blinked several times but the corpulent, greasy-skinned midget didn't grow any bigger. He backed away on all fours, unfolded his legs and stretched to his full height—

—a yard at best guess.

Then again, it was hard to take a visual measurement sprawled out on the floor with her skirt hiked up, her legs splayed, and her panties showing.

"You're under arrest," she panted, breathless. "Assault on a peace officer." In disbelief, she shook her head. Patted the floor for her badge case. "Holy shit, you're tiny. A runt."

Her gaze flickered to the reincarnated Prime Minister Nehru. "I'd better hear fingers punching nine one one. Tell them 'Officer needs assistance' and give this address."

"Do not talk down to me. I speak most excellent English."

Raven's quarry twitched a hand. She cocked her piece. Rumpelstiltskin froze. His stubby fingers lingered near the purple mouse puffing out beneath one watery eye.

Without taking her eyes off her attacker, she groped her

bag for handcuffs. "Who the hell are you?"

"I am Balogh."

"What?" The guy's mother must've been clearing a phlegm ball from her throat when she named him.

The squatty man with the pock-marked face and slicked-back "do" flashed a sheepish smile filled with marbled-gray teeth. "Cousin to Ivan Balogh, Prince of the Gypsies. He sent me to kill you. To regain the family honor."

This was the best they could come up with?

"Just how tall are you?"

The assassin stood erect. "Five-one."

"You're not that tall." Raven rose to her feet. With her fingers looped through a set of handcuffs, she towered over him. "You're about four-eight."

"I'm five-one. And three-quarters. Almost five-two."

"In elevator shoes."

"It is true."

"Get out of here, Thumbelina. Four-six if you're anything."

"I am tallest of my brothers and sisters."

"You'd need a step stool to take a leak."

"My nickname is Treetop."

"Root-Cellar, more like."

"You are unkind."

"And you're delusional, Peter Pan."

A voice sang out from behind the computer. "She is very rude to foreign persons."

Raven scowled.

Seething indignantly, Balogh stared through milky green snake eyes. "You can see my driver's license. The height of my family is the envy of the clan."

He felt for his pocket but she stopped him with a lively *"Hup!"* and a flick of the pistol. She leaned close and plucked out his wallet, herself. Flipping it open, she read his vital statistics.

Blgh, Estv.

One vowel in the whole stinking name.

"What sort of monkey business is this?"

"That is me. Steve Balogh." He grew half an inch.

She smacked the wallet shut. AFIS, the automated fingerprint index system for law enforcement, would resolve any identity question.

"We'll see about this when we get you down to the booking desk, Atom Ant."

The gypsy lifted a noncommittal shoulder and let out an unamused chortle. "What's in a name? Names are a casual affair. For the *gadje* world, I am Steve Balogh. For gypsy use, well, you will never know. You are gadja."

"And you are about to be locked up."

The sand-flea walked over to the door, snapped the bolt and flipped the OPEN sign to CLOSED.

A shot of heat went through Raven's stomach. "What do you think you're doing?"

"Business has ended."

"Let me understand this," she said archly. "This guy just tried to kill me, you haven't dialed nine one one, and I still don't have my window motor?"

The Middle-Easterner gave her a blank stare. He stood close enough for her to read the monogrammed oval on his shirt.

Ali.

Al.

Al's AAAA Aardvark Import Auto Salvage and Repair.

The only thing missing to possibly add to the terror was if Al switched on the TV and forced them to watch Myron Kandel's financial report while they waited for the Tarrant

County Sheriff to arrive.

"Gimme the damned phone." She dialed the call herself.

To Balogh, she said, "If you so much as flinch, you're going to leak like the transmission on an eighty-three Beemer," and to the foreigner, "The cops are on the way. I want that motor."

Stalled in one spot with his jaunty cap askew, he stared back through kerosene soaked unignited coals.

"In this country, businessmen serve their customers," she snapped. "An American shop owner would want the referrals."

"I am drug-free."

"Not reefers, Ali Baba. Re-fer-rals. Don't women in your country buy things?"

"In my country, we do not allow them to speak, much less to trust with money."

Perhaps there was another way to generate enthusiasm. "Do you have any idea the damage a stray bullet can do?"

Fear evidently brought out a touch of humanity. He dashed out a set of saloon doors and disappeared into a boneyard of wrecked cars.

She looked Balogh over and said, "What did I ever do to you?"

He cast his evil eye on her. "You know."

For a fleeting second, he had her convinced she should.

"You're gonna do hard time for manhandling me."

"I speak for the entire tribe of Balogh when I say we will reclaim the family honor." The gypsy balled up a miniature fist and shook it. "I curse my dead mother and dead father if I don't succeed."

She still didn't have a clue why a tribe of people able to survive Nazis, masters of harassment who didn't even officially exist except on police blotters and in FBI dossiers, would want to exterminate her. But the threat was as serious as a lying gyp could make.

Worse, she still had to deal with that problem with Jinx. She glanced at the clock, narrowing her eyes to note the time. With any luck, the two-timing, double-dealing cheat would still be at the office. She should call him. Let him know that the gypsy he warned her about had his stinger out for her. Just when things were becoming orderly, the body-snatcher quality that began on the drive out resurfaced.

She picked up the phone and dialed Jinx's cellular.

Chapter Four

Scorched to the gills and dripping sweat, Raven trudged past the vehicle infirmary at Sonny's Auto Hospital. She powerwalked up an oil-stained pavement that oozed rivers of antifreeze and iridescent puddles of dead gasoline, only to find the CLOSED sign dangling and Sonny motoring off in the opposite direction. Unlike the car he loaned her, his actually ran.

She stamped her foot hard enough to leave an imprint in the hot asphalt. Lazy-assed mechanic promised he'd wait on that part. She whirled around to run after him and ripped the heel clean off her shoe.

Damned grease monkey, shutting down before she had a chance to beg another loaner car, considering the Lincoln gave a death rattle some three blocks away. Made her have to hitch the rest of the way, pinching a ten-pound window motor between the aching fingers of one hand, and a dead police radio in the other.

With her brain sizzling, she raked her hand through the fringe of indigo bangs drooping over her forehead and seared Sonny's name onto the short list of people she'd most like to sic a Rottweiler on. At the corner pay phone, she patted her pocketbook for coins. Down to the last quarter, she limped a few more blocks toward a convenience store.

She didn't give a rat that two fire engines—one with AUNT SUSIE stenciled on the driver's door, and the other with QUICKSILVER—screamed past with a couple of grim-faced firefighters dangling from the sides like chimpanzees;

nor did her curiosity peak when they groaned to a stop in the vicinity of Sonny's dog-puke Lincoln.

Raven had her own troubles.

She turned long enough to squint past a cloud of black smoke billowing into the sky, hoped the victim was insured, and kept plugging in the direction of the stop-and-rob. With any luck, she'd catch Mickey or Dell at the office and hitch a ride.

The day's events left her snot-slinging mad.

And for more reasons than Jinx's infidelity.

She hated child writs.

Kids went into hysterics. Parents never failed to contribute to the melee. Worst of all, she had yet to meet a deputy who left the scene knowing for sure whom to believe. Usually, Jinx's office got writs for recalcitrant fathers who refused to return their children at the end of visitation. But this one was different.

They were taking a kid away from the mother.

Unless the child had black and blue marks on her, the deal just seemed wrong on its face. Not that she'd ever have any kids of her own, Raven thought, but if she did, she'd be hard-pressed to release hers to some lawdog, even with a court order.

In an Ex Parte hearing, the judge heard only one side of the story. One thing for certain: from this day forward, she'd be willing to accept as gospel one particular premise, and draw on it when it came time to make crossroads decisions.

Men lied.

Even good men.

Northeast of Downtown, and a block south of the targeted house, Jinx nosed his unmarked patrol car around the corner. Dell Teague and Mickey Van Slycke must be plotting strategies; they yin-yanged their patrol cars close enough to speak through their windows. He eased the cruiser's front pushbars against Dell's bumper and gave it a gentle tap.

The brooding Goliath glanced in his rearview mirror. He mouthed something from a set of humorless lips and Raven's head popped up like a jack-in-the-box. When she twisted in her seat and flashed an insincere, beauty pageant smile, Jinx suspected she'd been pawing through her briefcase again. Raven had a rabid habit of staying abreast of the Texas Family Code and the Penal Code, and she kept current editions close by for easy reference.

Not that anyone in Tarrant County gave a shit, least of all the judges. Certainly not Dell—or Mickey, a modern day Wyatt Earp gunslinger type who still wore corduroy jackets with leather patches on the elbows and kept his salt-and-pepper hair long enough to ride him about.

And Dell. Nobody in the office could eke more than ten words a day out of him; but pair him with Raven and she'd have him chattering like a parakeet.

In short, though Dell and Mickey looked like a couple of hired killers, they were good ol' boys who unofficially competed for the Departmental Citation with their efforts to harass Ivy, the only other female deputy, into quitting. Along the way, Jinx's men figured out all they had to do was serve whatever papers came in from hire-date to fire-date or retire-date. It wasn't their business to ask why. Ivy and Raven actually read the Codes, but only Raven routinely tried to predict the outcome of Tarrant County's judicial wisdom.

Jinx gave the *Westward Ho* motion with his hand, then broke the seal on the tin of Copenhagen with his thumbnail. The cruiser lurched into the lane of traffic and the three units roared up the block trailing plumes of exhaust.

In less than a minute, Dell and Mickey wrenched their Chevys into park, bolted from their seats, and sprinted to the rear of the house to seal off escape. At the cyclone fence, Mickey tried out for the Olympic groin-pulling event. Having hurdled a doghouse big enough to shelter a family of immigrants, he groped his bulge and howled in a gut-churning bellow of the damned. Dell, pepper mace in hand, stared out from Aryan features, unlatched the gate, and disappeared from sight.

Jinx caught the fragile scent of Raven's perfume even before she slipped up behind him. He appraised her in a glance. Unlike her usual immaculate grooming, her hair looked like she took the radio into the shower, and her clothes looked like a haunted house. Dirty jacket, ripped sleeve, wrinkled blouse, easy to see, *Lucy had some 'splaining to do.*

They exchanged awkward glances.

Jinx positioned himself to the right of the door. "Top o' the mornin'. What happened to your clothes?"

"Let me understand this. We're taking a baby away from her mother?"

"It's a court order."

Raven huffed out a sigh. "This really bites."

"Part of the job."

"Still sucks."

"Let me do the talking." He hammered the doorjamb with his fist.

Footfalls sounded, the door opened a sliver, and a large blue eye peered out.

"Miz Sanders? Dana Sanders?" Jinx asked innocently.

"You got the wrong house." The crack narrowed.

"Wait." Jinx touched a hand to the knob, insurance she

44

couldn't slam it shut. He pretended to stare at the writ, then oscillated his head as if he were scanning the porch for a house number. "This isn't five-oh-eight Linda?"

"Uh-huh. But nobody named Dana lives here."

Jinx moved in for the kill. "You're not Dana Sanders?" She shook her head, the way he knew she would. "You sure? Tell ya what . . . would you mind producing some ID? Show me you're not Dana Sanders so I can verify what you're saying, and we can be on our way?"

"Sure."

The lady narrowed the opening to a slit. He waited until he heard her feet pad away before pushing the door wide enough to see inside. Barefooted and wearing a diaphanous skirt that silhouetted her slim legs, she glided over to a shoulder bag slung over an armchair and returned with her driver's license.

Jinx studied the photo. Then her date of birth. Barely more than a kid herself.

He cut his gaze to Raven and read aloud. "Ann-Jeanette Rice. What do you know? You were telling the truth."

In one fluid motion, he pushed his way inside the dimly lit interior and slapped the writ into the hand of a woman no larger than a twelve-year-old.

"Top o' the mornin', Miz Rice. Where's the kid?"

The kid, seated at a tiny school desk, peeked up expectantly, but the quaking papers in the hands of her mother brought the tot streaking safely behind the woman's legs. In the time it took Dell and Mickey to explode through the back door, Jinx found a wall switch and flooded the untidy room with light.

Raven shot him a disapproving glare. "We're from the Constable's Office. This is a writ to temporarily remove Marina from your custody until the hearing."

The words struck like blows. The lady's face ran the gamut of tortured contortions.

Ann-Jeanette Rice—identified in bold type as the Respondent—let out an anguished wail and backed away with the little girl wrapped in her skirts, and a stoic quiver on her small chin.

Ann-Jeanette's mouth hung open. What started as a moan screeched up several octaves and rolled through the stuffy den in invisible waves, then blended in disharmony with the unanswered ring of a distant telephone.

Not one to kowtow to theatrics, Jinx advanced. "Ma'am—"

"You can't take my baby."

The devastated woman dropped to her knees. The child hurtled forward and clung to her mother's neck. They exchanged ghastly looks before sobbing into spun-gold clouds of each other's hair.

Jinx rocked uncomfortably on his boot heels. "We've got no choice. It's a court order, signed by a judge."

Raven's eyes filmed with tears.

"Let's not make it worse for the girl," he said.

"Oh, my God, ohmygod, ohmygodohmygod." Pencil-thin arms wrapped her offspring in a clumsy embrace.

Jinx set his jaw and steeled himself. Sure enough, the kid tuned up like a piccolo. He looked to Raven for help.

Stupid Jinx.

She was biting her lower lip, a signal he was about to have three screaming Mimis on his hands.

Damned hysterical women, who needed 'em?

He sharpened his glare enough to shape Raven up. She floated down on one knee and touched the kid's mother. He checked his copy the way he always did when he felt the knot twist in his gut—the one that told him that Raven hit

46

the bullseye, that taking kids away from their parents really did suck—the one that made him not want to commit their names to memory, or see their faces in his sleep, just stay totally detached so he could do his job.

Ann-Jeanette Rice's name loomed large on the court order. With a little luck and some aversion techniques, he'd blot out these unfortunate ragamuffins by bedtime.

The incessant prattle going on around his knees pulled his attention from the papers. He felt the magnetic pull of the whimpering tyke's face and avoided her gaze.

"I'll help you pack her clothes," Raven whispered, her voice falling and weary.

Miz Rice dropped her copy of the order and clutched Raven's hands. Amazingly, Raven let her. Any other time, she'd have knocked somebody's block off if they tried to touch her uninvited.

This time Raven squeezed back until the shaky fingers whitened. "Let me understand this. You say your ex-husband hasn't seen this baby in four years?"

"Not since she was a couple of months." Sniffles turned into hiccoughs.

"Then why would he want her all of a sudden?" Raven released her grip, as if she could plot better unencumbered.

"How should I know?" Ann-Jeanette's voice climbed to an anguished howl. She pleaded with upturned palms. "We never heard from him 'til now."

"Mommeeeeeeee."

Hiccoughs turned into the choking gasps of an invisible ligature.

"Mommy, don't cry." The hysterical tot ran a finger across her mother's tear-streaked face.

The drama rose to the level of a Greek tragedy. Jinx wanted to grab the kid and get the fuck out, but Raven seemed hell-bent on public relations.

"Listen to me, Ann-Jeanette . . . may I call you Ann-Jeanette?" She enunciated each faint word. "I'm Raven, and I'm going to do whatever I can to help you get to the bottom of this. But right now, we don't want Marina to be afraid to go with us. You can make it easier."

The shaking mom stopped keening.

Mother love, Jinx supposed.

That, and the fact that Raven's refusal to speak above a whisper seemed to have the soothing effect of a library visit, or the numbing of a funeral. Jinx ducked his head enough to peer over the top of his bottle-lens wirerims. Even Dell and Mickey shifted on their feet at the awkwardness of it all.

"I don't know what Marina's father said to the judge, but I think maybe we should pretend it's a vacation. You know, Seaworld? Six Flags?"

Marina leaned close. A liquid prism rolled over one fiery cheek, but her sniffling stopped. Mother and child assumed the lethargy of drug addicts after a fix.

"So, when we go on vacation," Raven continued, her voice uplifting and childlike, "we give Mommy a little break, don't we? That way, Mommy gets all kinds of stuff done at home before Marina comes back."

The mom's mouth hung limp as a sling. The whites of her eyes had turned fiery red. She had no words, only a resigned sigh.

"We'll want to take our dolly on vacation, of course." Raven rose slowly. She pulled the lady to her feet and scooped up the tot in her arms. "And pretty things to wear."

"I got new shoes," Marina said helpfully. A twist of honey-colored hair hung limp against her forehead.

"Do you now? What do they look like?"

Dell and Mickey stared impassively at the office magician, seemingly spellbound by the hypnotic voice of their colleague.

She walked toward the kitchen with the child's mother in tow, a veritable Pied Piper. When they reached the table, Raven grazed her hand across a hardened pizza, still in its box. She breezed past the refrigerator, momentarily touching the top before swaying out of sight. The deputies followed, lemminglike, until the glint of the knife Raven placed beyond Ann-Jeanette Rice's reach broke the spell.

Jinx tapped his pen on the tabletop.

He knew good and well if he let Raven out of his sight longer than a fraction of a second, she'd give the sobbing mama the phone number of that ass-wipe attorney friend of hers. What'shisname? The one who turned all her referrals into pro bono cases—which left the rest of his deputies digging a finger under their Resistols, wondering why anyone in their right mind would agree to handle legal hearings for free.

Even for an old friend.

Unless. . . .

Intuitively, he watched Dell and Mickey. Opening the kitchen's screen door to arc out a wad of spit, Jinx came to an unsettling conclusion—idiots worked for him.

He stalked past the table to the bedroom door. Without so much as a backward turn, Raven shut it in his face. He stared at the doorknob with bonechilling cold, and listened.

"*We have to take her*—" Whisper, whisper. "—*Court order. But I'll see to it*—" Whisper, whisper. "—*She won't be scared on the ride over. You have my word.*" Followed by more whispers. Clandestine whispers, quieter than Hasidic Jews unrolling the Torah.

Made him mad enough to bust a blood vessel.

Unexpected giggles filtered through the walls.

When the three females strolled out of the bedroom, all smiles and tear free, Miz Ann-Jeanette Rice having just deeded over her pride and joy to Miss Schmoozer, Jinx came to another unsettling conclusion.

The woman ought to be in politics.

Chapter Five

Witnessing the stages of grief never ceased to amaze Raven, particularly when they all took place in the same rollercoaster time period; and Ann-Jeanette Rice had run the gamut of emotions in less than a half hour. And since domestic crisis had a way of blowing Jinx out of the saddle, the writ convinced Raven he needed to keep her around.

She and Jinx headed for an industrial area several miles away. With Jinx at the wheel, Raven on the passenger side, and Marina belted in the back seat, they hadn't traveled an entire block when he set his jaw. A RUDY CASTRO FOR CONSTABLE yard sign sprang out of the ground and into view like an unwelcome dandelion at the Lawn of the Month judging. She took a couple of shallow breaths. The mention of his unworthy adversary was enough to set him off the rest of the night.

Her gaze flickered across the seat and she caught him wincing. Neck veins bulged like garden hoses. His thighs stiffened and he seemed oblivious to the fact that a boot ground into the floorboard accelerated the car way beyond the legal speed limit. She tensed against the seat and reminded herself his campaign wasn't her problem anymore. Once she had proof Jinx couldn't keep his pants zipped, she'd gladly remove herself from the equation.

She twisted in her seat. Beckoned Marina with an outstretched hand. "Hop over, Baby. I'll show you how to work the police radio. You want to push the siren?"

Jinx shot her a wicked glare. "Kid needs to be belted in while the car's in motion."

At the snap of metal, Marina vaulted into Raven's lap.

"You watch TV?" Raven patted the limp bow that gathered all but the loosest tendrils curling at the nape of the child's dewy neck. "Cop shows where they catch bad guys?"

A slow nod.

"Touch this button."

Out came the finger, reaching.

Jinx issued a subtle warning. "That's enough."

Marina shifted her gaze to Raven.

"Go ahead, he'll let you." The siren yipped. "Once more."

Jinx's jaw muscles tightened.

Spoilsport.

"You excited about seeing your daddy?" She kept the singsong lilt in her voice while checking out cars whizzing past. Three expired inspection stickers in a row, each needing a ticket. Drivers whining, How come you're not out doing something important? She'd tell them because the really important stuff sucked.

Two miles from the house, Jinx wheeled the unmarked cruiser into a deserted parking lot in the warehouse district.

Maybe it would be all right.

Perhaps the mother lied.

Conceivably endangered her child.

Basic police academy teachings showed abused children always gravitated to the abusive parent. That could explain why the dad showed up out of the blue with a writ. With discretion, Raven lifted Marina's shirt, inspecting for bruises.

None.

She had almost convinced herself they'd done the right thing when five men and one grisly woman straight off the stage of *The Jerry Springer Show* bailed out of a beat-up sedan.

Her instincts went on point. "Keep going."

Jinx killed the engine and popped open the electric door locks. "Don't worry, it's the father."

"There's been a mistake."

"No mistake," he answered bluntly. "That's him."

She snatched the legal papers off the seat and inspected the signature page. "I know Henry Masterson. He teaches Sunday School at my church. He'd volunteer for a brain transplant before he'd turn a baby over to this riffraff."

"It's legal."

Her breath went shallow. "There's a mistake, I'm telling you. We need to call the court."

"This is Tarrant County. Everybody leaves early on Fridays. Maybe if you'd been on time—"

"Don't start."

Mickey and Dell pulled into the lot. Jinx popped open his door and swung out a leg. He inched off the donut to the edge of the seat, where he straightened, pale and clammy, to his full height.

Raven checked the last page for the name of the petitioner's lawyer. She closed her eyes and groaned. Denver Steeple. Steeple got better deals than a casino. The entire judicial system, not to mention every female eligible for induction into the Junior League, was in bed with Denver Steeple. The Fort Worth high roller masterminded political orgies, for God's sake. Rudy Castro loved him so much he made him his campaign treasurer.

Jinx appeared at her window.

He opened the door and she stepped out of the car, pried Marina's arms from her neck and shoved the little girl at him. He instinctively recoiled, but caught the tyke as she slid down his side and hooked a thigh over his service revolver.

"What're you doing?"

"Deal with it," she said crisply.

"This isn't my fault."

"We could've called the judge at home."

"You're laboring under the misapprehension I have his unlisted number."

To Marina, she said, "Want to be a Baby Deputy Constable?"

A nod.

"Terrific. This is the constable. He'll swear you in. Raise your right hand, no—the other one." She glared at Jinx. "All yours."

Jinx heaved the disgruntled sigh of a bad sport. "You promise to be a good girl and tell the truth at all times, and—"

"Tell us everything that happens while you're gone? Say 'I do.' "

"I do." The girl stuck her thumb in her mouth and hooked a finger over her nose.

Raven forced a smile. "One more thing—don't be scared."

" 'Kay."

"Okay." She planted a loud kiss on Marina's cheek. "Congratulations, you're our Baby Deputy."

To Jinx, she said, "Give me two minutes alone with him," and walked away with purpose in her step.

Instinct told her the mongrel with the fuchsia reindeer snout, the one who looked like he topped Chivas Regal's Christmas card list—the kind of guy no respectable funeral parlor would cremate without three or four fire trucks on standby—had to be the culprit.

She stared into a jack-o-lantern smile of tobacco-stained teeth and stood toe-to-toe. "I have her momma's phone number. I promised Marina if she gets scared, all she has to do is give it to you and you'll dial it up so they can talk."

"Whatever." Cornpone and insincere.

She lanced the man's chest with a finger and sensed Jinx's powerful glare drill the back of her head. If she'd heard him rant about civilians with video cameras once, she'd heard it until her ears were ready to slough off.

"I don't understand how you left this girl and all of a sudden you show up four years later with an Ex Parte writ."

The guy bowed out his chest, peacock-pleased, as if he wished he had lapels to thumb. He coughed up smoker's phlegm and spat near Raven's shoe.

Undaunted, she squared her shoulders. Lifted her chin in a dare. "Ms. Rice said you once took a swing at her—put a red mouse under her eye. Over a saucepan of mashed potatoes that didn't suit you."

Behind her, Mickey's raspy whisper carried like autumn leaves on a breeze. "If it was them instant ones, I dunno but what she mighta had it comin'."

Raven cut her eyes to the deputy. Neutralized him with a glare.

A chortle erupted from Marina's daddy.

She jerked her head so close she could smell his nasty cave-breath. "You think that's funny? And what's this about posting a set of rules in the house?"

"Crazy talk." He swiped his nose with the back of his hand and looked everywhere but in her eyes.

"House rules," she snapped. "Dinner will be served no later than thirty minutes after arrival."

"Wonder could we get a set o' them rules?" Mickey to Dell.

Raven extinguished Mickey's smile with a look. Dell was doing his pinball machine imitation, letting his eyes dart around like steel balls.

"I don't see anything amusing about this at all." She reached into her purse.

Behind her, Jinx sucked wind. Later, she'd be sure to inform him that she was not, repeat, not fixing to draw down on the guy—although, at the moment, it struck her as a jim-dandy idea. She dug out a scrap of paper and rummaged for a pen. Dirt devils Mickey churned up, peeling out of the parking lot, lingered heavy in the air.

"I bet the judge never even laid eyes on you, else I don't think he'd have signed this." She wagered to herself that Marina's father descended from chicken thieves and bootleggers. "I don't have anything against the poor but this is just abject filth. You're enough to scare this baby. Gimme your phone number."

She jotted it down, then made him repeat it to make sure he hadn't pulled a fast one.

Raven glimpsed Jinx stepping forward, tight-jawed and stiff-necked. No doubt he thought she'd gone berserk. She reminded herself that a minor complication such as intimacy wouldn't stop him from jerking her peace officer commission. But this time, the good guys were on the wrong side, and she seized the moment to get in a few last licks.

"Here's how this works." She laid down ground rules, one two three. "Marina gets to call home whenever she's frightened. And even when she's not. Agreed?"

Without waiting for a response, she cast her gaze on the cherub in Jinx's arms and felt the tightness in her features soften. Jinx looked fitting with a kid-attachment. The dagger in her heart twisted.

She steadied Marina's quivering chin with a finger.

"Hear that, Marina? Your daddy's going to let you call Mommy anytime you want. And you know what?" The angel stared in rapt adoration. Poor baby, trusted her completely. Well, she wasn't about to let her down. "Your mama's going to stay home until it's time for you to meet the judge, so there's not going to be a problem getting through."

"Now, wait a minute."

"I'm not done. I'm showing up at the hearing next Tuesday. If Marina says you didn't let her call, the judge'll hear about it."

Wordlessly, Jinx handed over the girl.

Raven's skin tingled with dread. She drew in a deep breath and fixed the man with the practiced scowl of unmitigated hatred.

"You done, now?" The deadbeat dad seemed cocky and self-assured.

"*Well* done."

One might even say burned to a crisp.

Chapter Six

On the drive back to the office, Raven rode with Dell. He stared impassively through the windshield, his eyes shaded from the tangerine sunset by a pair of wicked wraparound sunglasses. He knew enough to keep quiet, to give her space while she simmered in the passenger seat. When she cut her eyes in his direction, he bore the eternal countenance of a Sphinx cat, and she knew by the way he lowered his shades just enough to barely peer over the top that he had spoken to her.

"Pardon?"

"I asked if you were gonna be okay."

"Always." She reached over and slipped a pen from his pocket to fill out the return portion of the writ.

"You can do better." He refocused his attention on the road. "Jinx signs my paycheck so I have to get along. But Raven, you're a Reserve Officer so you're working for free. Any honcho in law enforcement would kill to carry your police commission."

"It's more complicated than that."

"We all know. We've known right from the start." His quiet voice emanated strength. "But Jinx's standing on your neck to be taller."

"You think he pushes me around? You're wrong."

"He's got the opportunity to meet people. We all do." Dell swallowed hard. "Women. They call the office a lot. He disappears in the afternoon and doesn't come back until closing time. Make whatever you want of it."

Lightheaded, she rested her cheek against the window

and tried to ignore the knotting pain in her stomach.

"He runs a law enforcement agency, Dell. He can't campaign on company time, so he has to do everything after hours. He's still getting fallout from that bum rap the media gave him—back when the State shut down Green Meadows Care Center and he had to evict all those old people. Dealing with an opponent's bad enough—he can't afford any more bad publicity."

"He's gone a lot, Raven."

Dell didn't know. Neither did the others. Jinx had asked her not to say anything about how he was finding homes for the elderly.

"I know what you're thinking, but you're wrong. Out of ninety displaced residents, Jinx found other nursing homes for fifty-five of those folks. Thirty went to live with relatives. That leaves five who still need housing. Of course he talks to other women."

"Jinx did that? Found places for those people to live?"

"Reporters only focus on unpleasant aspects of the job." A sad memory came crashing back. The previous Christmas, a landlord brought in a court order for an eviction. Jinx and Dell removed the family of migrant farm workers. Afterward, Channel Eighteen ran a series of hard luck clips that bordered on tearjerkers, and featured the tenants. A few days after the move-out, the dad overinflated a tire on their old station wagon, and it blew up. The press had a field day with his obituary. Raven said, "Remember those Mexicans—the ones y'all evicted with nine kids?"

"Yeah, that sucked." Slow headshake. "The press dogged us for days, trying to get a comment for the six o'clock news."

"Jinx has a good heart. A lot of people who dislike him shouldn't." Intuition told her Dell thought otherwise. "I shouldn't discuss this . . . we went to the Union Gospel Mission when the story broke. He left the mom an envelope with money in it. He really does care about the people in his precinct."

Silence grew long.

Dell steered the conversation back full-circle. "If you're waiting for him to slip a ring on your finger, pack a lunch. The only ring you'll ever get from Jinx is on the phone." He glanced over and gave her a sly wink. "Or in your bathtub."

"I don't want to marry him. I don't even want to be engaged. I just want a nice diamond to wear around." Huge lie.

"I think you get what you settle for."

"What's that supposed to mean?"

"You can do better." Soft. Compassionate. "Plenty of men would give their eyeteeth to pamper you, but you can't see it."

"Like who?"

"I'm making a point."

"No, you said guys want to go out with me, so give me names."

"Figure of speech."

"So, nobody wants to go out with me?"

"Will you just listen a minute?" Dell avoided her stare. "Lotta guys would go bald and be nearsighted to have you light up the way you do when he comes in the room. But they're scared to make a try with all the Jinx Porter vibes you put out." He let out a weary breath. "I'm saying—if you keep blinders on—you could overlook the perfect match."

Jinx was wrong. Dell Teague wasn't a mental midget. For the rest of the drive, she relaxed against the seat back and tried to assess her predicament through Dell's eyes.

You get what you settle for.

A few minutes after eight o'clock that evening, Raven thrashed her way past the secretary's jungle of plants. She moved aside a couple of Virgin Mary icons—Georgia, a sixtyish grandmother, trotted out her religion with the vigor of a used car salesman—and cleared enough space to enter the writ information into the computer's databank.

Across the room, Dell sat at his desk, filling out an over-time sheet. He spoke without looking up from the blotter. "Are you afraid of the gyps? Because if you're scared to stay by yourself—"

"I'll be fine." Fingers flew over the keyboard.

Her pager vibrated. The mechanic's telephone extension popped up on the digital display. After plugging in the last of the writ information, she stabbed out his number with the eraser tip of Georgia's number-two pencil and waited for the tone to trill out.

Sonny answered.

His gravelly voice thundered. "What the hell did you do to my car?"

Lazy-assed cretin.

Raven outshouted him. "You've got a lot of nerve. I ought to be the one raising Cain. I got the window motor, no thanks to you. I want to know when my Beemer's going to be ready."

"What the hell'd you do to my car?"

"You call that four-mile-per-gallon guzzler a car? How come you left me with an empty tank? You made me late, having to stop at the filling station. And you owe me a new pair of shoes. I want my vehicle."

"And I want mine."

"Then sprinkle holy water on it and buy a wreath. It's dead, three blocks over."

"Cremated, you mean. What the hell'd you do, set fire to it?"

Images of AUNT SUSIE and QUICKSILVER returned. Surely those fire engines weren't—

No way. Nobody's luck could be that bad.

"I nursed it to the curb and locked it," she said hopefully.

"Car killer, that's what you are."

"Hey, if you'd repaired my Beemer a week ago none of this would've happened. Besides, you said you could fix anything."

"Not if it's torched."

"Torched?"

"Who the hell are you, anyway? CIA?" A car horn blared in the background. "Just a cotton-pickin' minute, Sons-a-bitches," he bellowed.

"I beg your pardon?"

"Not you." Sonny carried on a profane monologue without bothering to mute the mouthpiece. Then he returned. "I shoulda figured. CIA people're always gettin' cars blown up. No small wonder you forgot to tell me you had assassins stalkin' you." A backup whistle chirped in the background. Sonny shouted, "I don't give a good goddam where you tow it. Just get it outta my sight."

He refocused on her. "I babied that car. She was my peach."

"Peach pit, more like. That car's a piece of shit."

"Used to be a piece of shit. It ain't every night I get my dinner interrupted by an arson investigator. Woulda got to me sooner, he said, but they had trouble trackin' me down, the license plates being so melted you couldn't read 'em.

Finally got the VIN off the engine block and ran the number. I hope to hell you got insurance."

Raven's heart leapt to her throat. She had a visual of Sonny, beaded in sweat and frothing at the mouth, his tanned, oiled face as weatherbeaten and cracked as an ancient hide.

"Alls I can say, it's a damned good thing for you they got witnesses. The bartender down the street saw a couple of brats tear out when the damned thing went up in flames."

She looked at Dell, at the frown on his face. Aqua eyes pulsed knowingly.

Maybe they weren't kids.

Maybe they were dwarfs.

Maybe she had an idea who was behind the charred Lincoln.

Balogh.

She returned the telephone receiver to its cradle. "I need a ride over to Jinx's."

Now, she was scared.

Chapter Seven

By the time Jinx wheeled the unmarked cruiser into the Château Du Roy Apartments' pothole-infested parking lot, the Mexican revolution that had been trying to catch up with him since lunch finally did.

He wedged the patrol car in between a junked Yugo and a red TransAm belonging to the limp-wristed twins in the apartment below his. He hated the Munsch brothers and their queer Scarlet Macaws that deprived him of sleep, parroting Harold and Gerald's effeminate chatter.

And he hated the Château Du Roy.

A political defeat by Rudy Castro might be an unintended favor. Then he could live anywhere besides the fifties taupe-colored brick fortress with steel doors, aluminum windows, and the most garish wrought iron west of New Orleans.

He suspected the Mafia owned the apartments. Even speculated a couple of missing teamsters might be buried beneath the freshly paved asphalt around back. But the rent was right and it allowed him to live smack-dab in the middle of his precinct, so it didn't matter if he stayed in a shit-sty with matted shag carpet left over from the sixties, as long as he kept his job. And if that sorry treasurer, Skeeter Clinkscale, didn't move from dead center and raise some money for his reelection campaign, the location of his digs might be a moot point.

Shooting pains held target practice behind his eyeballs. Neck muscles stretched tighter than a banjo string, and the Tex-Mex blue plate he had scarfed down at Betty's Café was doing the flamenco in his gut.

With the patrol car idling, he waited for the sting to pass.

Sitting behind the wheel gave him time to reflect on the day.

He'd taken leave of his senses, letting that horse-faced broad from the sheriff's department con him into buying her another meal. And he knew better than to order the roadkill special, especially since the discomfort radiating from his kidneys had worsened the past few days. He'd had enough surgery to last a lifetime, and with any luck, the stone would pass without a hitch. But this morning when he eked out a pathetic trickle, he swore he had a grassburr lodged up his dick.

He killed the motor, but not the twinge of guilt nagging his conscience.

Thoughts zeroed in on Raven.

He never should've let her talk him into making space for a few toiletries. It started with a pink razor. Then she hung a couple of skirts in his closet, and commandeered a drawer for lingerie. Now that she had her own key to the place, she showed up at inopportune times, overheard snippets of early morning phone calls, and worst of all—after three years, hinted for a ring.

But if she caught wind of what happened at lunch, she'd fly right out of his life.

He grabbed his briefcase and locked the vehicle. Strolled the length of the parking lot, and turned at the sidewalk.

She never did say what made her late. It wasn't like her, not phoning in, torpedoing the schedule, knowing he'd have to fight tooth and toenail for Dell's and Mickey's overtime pay.

Unless she got wind of his lunch with Horse-Face.

Which he could explain away as totally innocent.

Except for the dessert part.

If Raven stopped in and saw those stray pubic hairs before he took the hand vac to her side of the bed, he'd have problems. But she usually didn't drop in without a warning, and unless Air One was hovering outside with a video camera and a directional mike aimed at his bedroom window, only two people knew for sure.

A Comanche scream shattered the steamy memory.

"Stop, thief."

The cross-dressing Munsch brothers, decked out in evening gowns hiked up to the hip, were making a mad dash for the TransAm. The fags-in-drag were running from Glen Lee Spence, the only person Jinx knew with half-a-sex-change operation. The twins split off, forcing Glen Lee to choose between the flaming redhead, or the—what the hell color was that, anyway? Turquoise?

Jinx shouted, "Glen Lee, what's going on?"

The Château's token transsexual stalked over.

Jesus H. It turned his stomach to see Glen Lee these days. The guy stood six-feet-two with anchor tattoos on each beefy forearm, and a slicked back strawberry blond ponytail—which, at the moment, happened to be wrapped with a cut-up piece of panty hose and knotted at the top to accommodate a wig. Even though Glen Lee's muttonchops had disappeared, thanks to massive estrogen doses and some serious electrolysis, the perky tits jutting through his flimsy pink robe still boggled the mind.

The Munsches—a pair of virtual guiding lights—doubled back and flanked Jinx. Even after five years, he couldn't tell them apart.

One of the brothers shadow-boxed on the lawn.

With the petulance of an ingenue, Glen Lee lodged a

66

grievance. "Gerald took my blue sequin."

"Did not."

"Did, too, Bitch." One of Glen Lee's false eyelashes brushed against a tweezed brow; the other dangled above his cheek by an invisible thread, like a hairy tarantula. His robe flapped in the breeze, exposing a bulge trying to work its way out of a pair of fuchsia lace bikinis. "I was going to wear it 'til he stole it."

"Liar." Gerald coiled a coppery tress around a matching neon talon.

The transsexual pointed the finger. "Harold swiped my pearls."

Harold batted his Liza Minelli lashes and pursed his frosted lips. "Last year, Glen Lee said we could borrow them anytime we wanted."

"Not tonight." Glen Lee, out of control. "It's Ritz Night at Club Toucan, and you knew this was supposed to be my night."

Gerald fussed with a glitzy sash. "I'm wearing it and there's nothing you can do."

Glen Lee reverted to the basic temperament of an ex-con. He drew back an arm and bare-knuckled Gerald across the lip gloss. Harold crumpled at the sight of blood. Jinx glanced down at pindots of red staining the new shirt Raven had bought him and thought, HIV.

"Make him give back my blue sequin dress. I cannot be in the fashion show without it, and I do not have anything else to wear." Glen Lee hauled off and kicked Gerald in the jewels. "I am not a bitch."

Proned-out on a patch of dead grass, Harold came to and propped himself up on one elbow. While Glen Lee tried to peel Gerald's dress off, Harold rallied to his brother's defense.

"Him thinks him's such a big man, just because him's trying to be a woman," he taunted in pidgin-queer, baby talk. "Well, you'll never be a real woman, Glen Lee." Harold beamed, triumphant. "You're just too . . . *big.*"

Glen Lee unhanded the dress. He let out a shriek and doubled over, hiding his grief in his hands. While Gerald readjusted a dislodged falsie, Glen Lee's thick, muscular shoulders shook under the great emotional weight.

Jinx felt his gorge rise. He needed to head for the bathroom.

The geezer with Alzheimer's from apartment 210 strolled past with his oxygen canister, and a yippy Chihuahua on a leash.

This time, the old coot had on a tattered REGIS PHILBIN RULZ T and a pair of ratty house slippers. Nothing else. Something shriveled and gray poked out from beneath the hem of the shirt.

Jinx felt his eyes cross. He needed to call a halt before he found himself looking at two limp dicks, two transsexuals, and four drag queens. If he wasn't so bushed, he'd call the Mental Unit. Have them run the old boy in for observation and maybe some meds. But not tonight. He needed sleep. Or to slam down a few drinks. An activity he swore off twenty years ago last November.

He called out. "Did you forget something, Old-Timer?"

"Got it right here." The man waved the oxygen canister in his wrinkled hand, and his shirt rose up enough for everyone to get a good look at his Slinky. "Will you be flying your kite tonight, Mr. Franklin?"

Jinx forced a smile. He almost wished he was Ben Franklin; then he could deposit himself into his own zero balance reelection campaign fund. Castro was operating on the budget of a Greek shipping magnate. And less than a month before the primary, Jinx finally discovered the identity of the fiend subsidizing him.

Denver Steeple.

Glen Lee prissed up to the white-haired man and steered him back into the courtyard. He called out to the Munsch brothers in the operatic moan of a diva on opening night, "I'm not finished with you, Gerald. You either, Harold. I'll be back for my ballgown if I have to stalk you to Club Toucan and claw it off during the fashion show."

"Bite me." Queers in stereo.

They hitched their evening dresses high enough to shimmy into the TransAm's bucket seats. With a waggle of fingers and a cheery "Toodles," they made their getaway with Jinx choking in their dust.

Pain knifed through his lower back, zigzagging up his side. Damned stone must be rocking around again. He stood rigid and held his breath. The agony subsided. With only three weeks until the primary, he couldn't afford time off for a hospital stay. Even if he *did* have to check in and the doctor filleted his penis, then what? Piss like a sprinkler head?

He noted the time on his watch.

Any minute, Raven might show up. When the catch in his side abated, and he could finally breathe without discomfort, he headed for the stairs.

The Siamese waited in the window with his chin quivering in a silent meow. One thing about Siamese—and Caesar was no different—they never had anything good to say when they tuned up yowling. The seal point lodged complaints daily, and after five years, Jinx still couldn't tell if the carping meant, "Pick me up" . . . "You're late" . . . "What about that bowl?" . . . or "What took you so long?" But this time, when he opened the door and tried to pat the kitty, Caesar telepathically suggested he should go screw himself, and took off down the hall.

In front of the bathroom mirror, Jinx studied his forehead with the dedication of a forensic pathologist. Still a little sunburned from walking the neighborhood, pounding on doors in the sweltering Fort Worth heat. A blistering reminder of the vacuous stares he encountered each time he shoved a pushcard into the reluctant hands of the woefully uninformed.

Hi, I'm Jinx Porter.

Who?

Your constable. Vote for me.

I always vote a straight Democratic ticket.

Morons, all of them.

Then he had to explain in a Mr. Rogers's Neighborhood voice, that, yes, voting a straight Democratic ticket was good; but there were two Democratic candidates for constable this time so they'd have to *choose.* Then convince them they should pick him. Making him even more cognizant that the only people stupider than the ones working for the county were the voters who elected the officials to run it.

He climbed into a tepid shower and cranked the hot water on all the way, spiritually resuscitated by the spray. The splash of H_2O on the old kisser filled him with a kind of narcotic euphoria. Let somebody else deal with the kooks, fags, transvestites, and transsexuals.

And that little kid from the writ.

He thought of Raven, trying to shame him.

Never should've gotten involved with a lady cop.

Come to think of it, getting intimate with females made them feel they had the God-given right to control everything men did. Miss Stand-By-Your-Man had bat radar for barmaids. She'd missed her calling. The Feds ought to recruit her. Let her monitor their phone calls.

But in his mind, he couldn't erase the look of betrayal on her face.

She'd walked into the bathroom and stared with unblinking doe eyes. Gave him that Joan of Arc expression before dropping an anchor on the countertop. A man couldn't very well set up a sizzling rendezvous with Miss Wiretap velcroed to his side.

Pipes shuddered behind the tiles. Seconds later, bullets of icewater pelted down. Jinx let out a yelp, hurdled over the edge of the tub and body-bagged himself with the curtain liner.

Sprawled face-first across the bathmat gave him time to rethink his position.

Why settle for one woman?

Okay, so he was aware of his shortcomings. So what? Porking barmaids happened to be proof positive the plumbing still worked. A place to hang your star if turning fifty meant a once-sleek body needed an overhaul, you'd blown all your gaskets, and your hose needed replacing.

"Butt-pirate."

The unholy laugh of an ancient Macaw pierced the carpet, followed by a whistle with the shrillness of an incoming round. While wondering whether the bird's message carried the first omens of disaster, Jinx found it positively gratuitous to hear the squawky reply.

"Give up the goods, Butt-Munch."

Jinx's plan to spend the rest of the evening in front of the TV backfired.

In the same way he knew not to spit in the wind, he figured no good could come from answering the telephone. He beached in the recliner with a mindset to ignore it, but by the eighth ring, it had become a siren's song. When he gutted up and lifted the receiver, his mother's voice stung in his ear.

"How could you?" Kamille Porter, screaming like an incoming scud. "In thirty years, we've never canceled a bridge game."

"What're you talking about?"

"How dare you pretend? You humiliated me in front of my friends."

"You're not making sense."

"THE COUNTRY CLUB." Her voice went ultrasonic.

He jerked the phone away from his ear and winced.

"We were having dinner at River Crest and my friend Molly stopped by our table." She sucked in a breath. "What do you think she said?"

He wondered what took so long. Apparently the well-greased gossip pipeline of River Crest's aristocracy had clogged up.

"Eleanor Thornton's my childhood friend and my bridge partner."

"It's part of the job, Mother."

"Have you lost all sense of decency? Do you have any idea what this does to my Saturday afternoons, not to mention my social status?"

He set the phone on the arm of the recliner and walked to the kitchen. For the first time in twenty years, three months, and seventeen days, he broke the seal on a fifth of whiskey stashed beneath the sink. Before chug-a-lugging from the bottle, his thoughts turned to his ex-wife, Shiloh.

And to the reason he quit.

He upended the bottle. Listened to it glug. And emptied the contents down the drain.

When he returned to the lathered-up woman on the

other end of the phone, he did something he usually reserved for people he never intended to see again—

—hit the off-button and unplugged the cord from the
wall jack.

Raven arrived at the Château Du Roy in time for the ten
o'clock newscast. She flopped onto the leather sofa and
dropped the window motor at her feet. The Siamese
dropped down from the top of the bookcase and padded
close enough to eye her with contempt.

"You're still holding a grudge about the vet visit, aren't
you?"

He narrowed his slitted eyes and chattered in rebuke,
then stomped out of sight.

Jinx was still in the bathroom with the water running
when she noticed the phone unplugged.

It rang as soon as she reconnected it.

Startled, she answered.

A sultry female said, "I must have the wrong number."

Raven swallowed hard. Her heart thudded and her scalp
burned as if it had gasoline rubbed on it. "Maybe you
don't. Who were you calling?"

"Like I said, sweetie, wrong number."

The click of a dead connection hummed in her ear.

Jinx walked into the room with the inflatable donut
looped through his arm. "How come you were late?"

She didn't come in spoiling for a fight, but that wrong
number put her in the mood. "I tried to call."

"That doesn't answer my question."

"No? Well, maybe I've got a few questions of my own."

"What's that supposed to mean?"

"Who called here at two in the morning?"

"Get your shit and clear out."

Chapter Eight

By Monday morning, the temperature dropped forty-five degrees and hovered close to freezing.

In the county parking lot behind his office, Jinx fished for the keys to the patrol car. It bothered him the way Raven breezed into the office, swept by in the background, snatched up her briefcase, and left in a huff. Still flamed out about that phone call, he supposed. But she stored enough doodads at the apartment to give her a built-in excuse to return, and that created a natural opportunity to patch things up.

He checked his watch.

Skeeter Clinkscale should be at work, hawking used cars. With any luck, he'd drive out and catch the big galoot before the rush; maybe have a little Come-to-Jesus meeting with him about filing those campaign contribution reports on time.

His mind strayed from the election.

Anyway, it wasn't like Raven caught him red-handed. He'd dumped Toni, Terry—whatever the barfly's name was—months ago. Raven couldn't prove anything, and she wasn't the type to charge him with a sex crime without hard evidence to back it up. Good thing he got rid of those panties from that parking lot quickie before Raven found them stashed under the front floorboard.

Damned females. It was almost like Tori, Tammy—whatever—left her undies on purpose.

That was the trouble with hitting on crazy women—not knowing how they'd react when they learned you had a

74

steady . . . when you told them to get lost.

He slid behind the wheel and took in the lingering scent of Raven's perfume. Not that it mattered she preferred Dell's company to his today. Let the hulking German deal with her raging hormones. He could use his experience living with that hypochondriac wife of his, the one he was too noble to ditch now that the kids started families and Miz Dell had a colostomy.

The engine gasped, then caught. Jinx pulled into traffic.

In less than a mile, a series of Castro's yard signs sprang up in a vacant field near a railroad track. Reminiscent of an old Burma Shave serial ad, they were spaced about twenty feet apart in a row that ran parallel to the tracks, positioned along the easement, to be read from a speeding car.

RUDY
CASTRO
LIFELONG
DEMOCRAT
VOTE
FOR
CASTRO,
TRIM
THE
FAT!

"Well, isn't this a kick between the legs?" Jinx grumbled. The guy was what? Old enough to have voted in two elections? "Lifelong democrat, my ass."

A few blocks down, an entire neighborhood had hammered Castro signs into the landscape. Jinx sneered. It hardly seemed fair for a sixteen-year incumbent to have to operate on a beer budget while some stooge barely old enough to vote had the budget of an Arab Sheik.

Snotty pipsqueak.

Jinx needed damage control. Word had it the brass-balled upstart was actually going around mouthing off how Jinx Porter'd lost touch with his constituents. Fat chance. Nobody knew folks in the precinct better than Jinx Porter. Hell, since he first took office, he'd kicked in at least one door on every block.

Trouble was, advertising cost money. And if brains were heavy machinery, Skeeter Clinkscale couldn't clear his throat. The used car salesman, con artist, and occasional best friend apparently decided to sit this one out. Goofball hadn't bothered to solicit a crying dime for the Constable Jinx Porter campaign.

Jinx drove past the home of an area landlord. The man hammered down a yard sign the previous week, but feigned poverty when asked for a donation. Now Jinx's gut roiled. Although his sign was technically still in place, a pair of Rudy Castro signs sandwiched on either side obstructed it from view.

Well, hell. Do a guy a favor and evict people on Christmas Eve. . . .

Time to drop in on Ol' Skeeter. Stick a mirror under his nose and feel for a pulse. Zap him with the stun gun. Maybe ask if he thought a treasurer's job ought to include something innovative, like raising money. Get the bohunk's head screwed on straight.

Jinx gripped the steering wheel. "For Chrissakes."

Don Pedrito's displayed a Rudy Castro sign in the plate glass window next to the whitewashed two-ninety-five lunch special. So much for eating *migas* there once a week for sixteen years.

With purpose in his foot—the same foot he planned to kick butt with—he floored the accelerator. Up ahead, the huge sign for Harry Fine's Auto Mall swayed in the breeze.

Jinx wheeled the Chevy through the parking lot in time to see Skeeter through the smoke-colored glass, hoisting himself out of a chair, lumbering out to head him off at the pass.

"Pod'na." The treasurer's grin angled off to one side of his doughy face. Shocks of flaxen hair curled up from his forehead in cowlicks. "Good to see you. Been meanin' to call."

Lazy bastard had been dodging him for weeks.

"Wouldja look at this hunk o' tin?" Skeeter brushed a pudgy hand over the squad car's hood. "Piece o' crap's got more spots than a cheetah. Ought to let us buff these dents out."

Jinx popped the door open and swung out a leg. He had three words for the unenergetic, low-grade con man. "Contributions and Expenditures."

Skeeter stood slack-jawed. A calf-struck-in-head-with-sledgehammer expression settled over his face.

"You didn't finish them, did you?"

Skeeter's eyebrows arched.

Exasperated, Jinx slapped his thigh. "You're the one told me to pick them up today. You're the one said they'd be ready." He pounded the hood. "You trying to get me kicked off the ballot? It's the law, Skeet. We have to file that report."

Skeeter stared, raisin-eyed.

"You don't want to be my treasurer? Just say the word. I'll find somebody else."

Raven.

"It ain't so, Pod'na."

Seemingly unfazed, Skeeter jammed his fists into his pants pockets. Heat radiating out from the Chevy's hood made him look as if he were swaying. Unless he was swaying. Which presented a whole new problem. That after seven years of temperance, Skeeter was back to belting down boilermakers before work.

"Why ya bawlin' me out, Pod'na? I ain't done nothin'."

"Nobody knows that better than me, Lame Brain. Have you not figured out I'm in a fight to the political death?" Jinx was treated to a blank stare. "Did it ever occur to you I could use some money besides my own?"

Skeeter pleaded with his hands. "What'dja want me to do? Shake down the boss?"

"I don't give a tinker's damn who you extort money from. I've already spent two thousand dollars, and I can pat my own back for nineteen hundred of it."

An eyeblink.

Jinx took a couple of paces, then whipped around. "Did you get back together with that screwball you were living with?"

"She wasn't a screwball. Don't stick your finger down your throat like you're gagging. Okay, it's true, one time she pulled a gun on me—"

"You still live on Owl Ridge?"

"—and set fire to my stuff, but I still love her."

"Let me see if I can get through to you," Jinx said, the burn rising to his cheeks. "You miss so much as one deadline filling out these C&Es, I'm driving straight out to Owl Ridge and screw your girlfriend."

Whaddayaknow.

A blip on Skeeter's radar screen.

While Dell waited in the drive of Sonny's Auto Hospital with the patrol car idling, Raven trotted the window motor past the charred Lincoln up to the only bay with feet protruding out from underneath a chrome bumper.

"I'd know those white socks anywhere," she said.

A tool clinked to the concrete floor and Sonny slid away from a jalopy in terminal stages of disrepair. He sat up and combed a grimy hand through sweat-soaked silver hair.

"Go away."

"Here's the motor for my window."

"Toss it over yonder."

"I'll just leave it here," she said, placing it on top of the tool-box. Maybe he'd feel guilty each time he walked past. "When can I get my BMW?"

"Now, if you don't want it fixed."

"I need it."

"Lotta people walk. Get a rental. Take the bus."

"I need that car."

"And I need that one." Using a wrench as a pointer, he gestured at the Lincoln's blackened shell.

"I'm confident once the investigation's completed, I'll be vindicated."

"Whatever in the hell that s'posed to mean."

They locked gazes. Finally, Sonny let her off the hook.

"Get your car keys out of the office, and bring the sardine can back in the morning. I'll put the motor in, first thing, and you can pick it up after noon."

"Deal." She disappeared into a small portable building, then danced out to the BMW and hollered at Dell.

"Meet me for lunch."

He saluted her, then pulled away from the curb.

She slid behind the wheel, patted the dash and inhaled the scent of leather religiously rubbed with balm. "Hello, gorgeous. Tomorrow we're getting a new window motor." She cranked the ignition, backed the Beemer out into the street, and zipped off.

It wasn't until she beat the yellow light that she glanced

into her rearview mirror and noticed the shiny chrome grill-work of an old Packard caught at the signal.

A shock of white hair barely crested the steering wheel. And as he shrank with each roll forward, she swore she saw the frenzied shake of an upraised fist.

Jinx made sure he left Skeeter inhaling large quantities of dust when he peeled out of Harry Fine's Auto Mall.

Thoughts turned to Raven as he radioed the base station to let Georgia know he was back in service.

Maybe Raven heard his transmission. He envisioned her sticking close to the office, planning to accidentally run into him. Females thought men were too dumb to figure out their scheming ways. Not him.

Then dread overtook confidence.

When Raven made a promise, she stuck to it like barnacle glue. That's how come, when everybody strolled out of Ann-Jeanette Rice's bedroom all smiles and tear-free, he knew the ball of paper crunched in the Rice woman's fist had Raven's lawyer-friend's number on it. That attorney who drove a silver Jaguar with personalized plates.

NT GLTY.

He remembered one other time she'd been this pissed. The night she left a barful of people slackjawed and a steroid-ingesting bouncer knock-kneed. She never had second thoughts about taking on a redhead twice her size. Made a big stink, just because the old heifer rubbed her tits against his chest on the dance floor. Whole embarrassing shitstorm damned near made him swear off honky tonks for good.

Then it hit him.

He couldn't recall ever feeling pangs of jealousy over her, until she made friends with that dickweed attorney. Who needed the aggravation? Why not just plug in a radio and take it into the shower? It'd be just as exciting and cause less damage.

Grim reality set in.

He needed her.

Raven's strength lay in the invisible tentacles she spread throughout the professional community. If she ever got it in for him, she had enough power to rip him to political shreds.

Chapter Nine

With her police handheld blaring in the BMW's passenger seat, Raven plotted Jinx's radio communication like a chess move. He probably figured she'd find some excuse to loiter around the office so they could bump into each other.

Fancy seeing you here. By the way, I'm over it now. Why don't I swing by and do your laundry so you'll have clean clothes to strip off in front of your new lover?

Well, from here on out, Jinx Porter's laundry wasn't the only thing he could do by hand.

She darted into the office and almost flattened Dempsey, the janitor, against the door. He was emptying Georgia's wastebasket, and his mouth split into a wide grin.

The big black man spoke to her, childlike. "Gilbert be doing magic tricks again."

"No kidding." She gave Jinx's chief deputy a wink. "You keep an eye on Gil Fuentes. He's pretty slick."

Gil straightened the deck of cards and tucked them back in the drawer. "Come here, Dempsey. Let's see if you've got any quarters in your ear."

Georgia turned her head from the computer monitor and gave a little wave. Her bright blue dress brought out the pink in her cheeks, and she wore a bow pinned near the part in her big Texas hair. "Hi, Honey. How was your weekend?"

"Lovely." Raven carefully modulated her voice to conceal her anger. "Any messages?"

"Just one." Georgia handed it over.

DIE.

"How nice. No name?"

Georgia shook her head. "It didn't sound like the same fellow who called the other day, though. You don't suppose two people are after you, do you? You know, Honey, you ought to tell Jinx."

"You tell him for me. Where's Ivy?"

"At the doctor's."

Raven sidestepped the janitor to get to Ivy's in-basket. She snatched out a stack of papers, scrawled a note to Dell, and placed it prominently on his blotter where Jinx could see. In a chair adjacent to Mickey's desk, a man sat wearing nothing but his 'Looms. She wondered if Mickey'd told him the office motto.

You run, you hide, you don't answer the door, you come as you are.

Dempsey let out a delighted squeal.

"You found that in my ear? Check the other one."

Gil reached up and removed a coin from Dempsey's other ear.

"Now I got enough for a sody-pop."

Gil closed his fist.

Georgia said, "Give it to him," and looked to Raven for support.

"You heard her."

"If you want a sody-pop, too, Gilbert, I'll let you pull some more quarters out of my head."

Grudgingly, Gil rolled his eyes and handed over the money.

Raven took her cue and skedaddled. On the road, she found herself lost in thought. An X-rated visual of Jinx thrashing between the sheets with the competition started a burning sensation behind the bridge of her nose that worked its way up to both eyes.

She stared out the window, past the Trinity River's olive water snaking along the banks, to a distant cliff dotted with million dollar homes.

Her eyes welled and she scrunched them closed.

For three years, she'd been his best friend, his lover, his constant—well, almost—companion.

Screw him.

She opened her lids. The last thing that registered in her conscious mind before glass shattered and the lights went out was the chrome flashing off a monster truck swerving to get out of her path.

The clang of the cowbell above the office door heralded Jinx's arrival. Beads of sweat popped out across his forehead. He sauntered past the tropical plants Georgia-the-Jungle brought in to camouflage cheap paneling, and angled over to the nearest desk.

"Top o' the morning, Georgia."

Instead of a smile, he got a smirk stronger than garlic. He suspected her desk drawer contained a pile of losing lottery scratch-offs. With a curt nod, he slung his briefcase on Dell's blotter, tossed the inflatable donut onto the chair cushion and navigated his haunches into the chair. Phone lines lit up simultaneously. He answered one while Georgia took her sweet time reaching for the other.

"Is my mama there?" Ivy's surly eleven-year-old.

"I don't see her, Amos."

"Liar."

"Wait just a minute. It works a lot better if you ask nicely."

"Put my mama on the phone, you bastard."

"Feel free to hold—"

"I cannot be put on hold."

"Betcha can." With the touch of a button, Jinx sent Ivy's little degenerate orbiting through the galaxy of county phone lines.

Across the room, Georgia hung up the phone and tugged at the polyester knit binding her ample midriff. "The computers don't work. Guess who let herself into the office over the weekend? And guess who else dropped in?"

He knew the tone of fiendish delight. Georgia jumped on the chance to demonize Ivy. He drew a bead on the queen of "I-told-you-so" and waited for her to tattle.

"Amos." She whispered the name like a four-letter word. "She let him tag along. Said he knows computers."

Jinx's gaze flickered to the blinking extension. The red glow extinguished itself before he could get Amos back on the line.

He glanced over at Ivy's desk. At the photos of Amos, pinned to a cork message board. Like Ted Bundy's baby snapshots, John Gacy's wedding pictures, and Richard Ramirez's family reunion photos, the chronological photo spread would someday net Ivy a big haul when the tabloids ran a feature on serial killers. People in grocery lines all over the globe could see little Amos with chipmunk cheeks and a gap-tooth grin; Amos with a wan smile; and a beady-eyed Amos with a sinister smirk plastered across that fat, moon-pie face.

Jinx could say he knew him when.

Georgia's hefty chuckle upended the imaginary shoot-out playing out in his head—the one where lawmen stumbled over carnage to click on the cuffs, followed by Ivy's plaintive wails of, "He's a good boy, don't hurt him."

The secretary presided over her desk, arms folded across her bosom and her laughter muted like an Uzi with a silencer. "Computer's locked up tighter than Dick's hatband.

I told you not to let her bring him here."

Jinx turned his attention to the computer. A couple of keystrokes later, Georgia's grin evaporated. Amos's message popped up on the screen, oozing radioactive green waste.

"SHITSHITSHITSHITSHIT" scrolled across the width of the monitor to form a horizontal loop.

The cowbell clanged and Jinx shifted his gaze. Ivy dragged in balancing a plateful of watermelon slices, her shoulder weighted down by a saddle bag she tried to pass off as a purse, humming the low-downest, wallet-stealin'-est, car breakin' down-est tune he'd ever heard.

"We need to talk, Jinx." Ignoring Georgia, she tossed her head in a way that made her wheat-colored bob fall back from her face. "Your office."

While Georgia muttered cryptic insults about a certain deputy who had the personality of a bloated cow, Ivy placed the dish on Mickey's copy of the morning paper and they adjourned to the back room.

In the generous broom closet some sadistic SOB in the commissioners' office thought should pass for a workspace, Jinx eased into his chair. Near the corner of his desk, surrounded by a volcanic flow of paperwork, Raven's framed image fixed him with her omnipotent stare. He snatched the picture and tossed it into the bottom drawer, where it would stay until she realized what a great deal she had.

The door snapped shut behind him. He swiveled his chair around to face Ivy in her neon purple pantsuit, sitting two feet away. It was plain to see from her oatmeal complexion that her extended warranty had run out about ten thousand miles ago and she needed a complete overhaul.

At first, only her chin quivered. Then her shoulders quaked. Followed by wracking sobs. "It's Amos."

He knew he shouldn't come down too hard—it wasn't

Ivy's nature to come unhinged—but the killer instinct got the better of him.

"Been telling you for years to get that little recidivist under control. The time to correct him is before he turns into a homicidal maniac, not after he's behind bars. Corporal punishment. I got a whippin' every day until I was ten, and look how I turned out."

She gave him a bovine stare. Dragged the back of her hand across the underside of her nose.

"Amos and me had a rough weekend." She swiped her baked potato nose again, repositioning her nostrils until they took on a porcine quality. "First, there was that call from the police station. The dispatcher said they had a bomb threat." Jinx narrowed his eyes. Ivy avoided his gaze. "Okay, she said she recognized Amos's voice."

Jinx reared back in the chair and mentally gnashed his teeth.

"Oh, all right." She rose and paced the length of the room. "Amos did it. Little stinker called one in to the Five-and-Dime, too. I ended up having to sponsor him down at Juvenile Hall. The whole thing's enough to give me the heebie-jeebies."

Jinx cyphered in his head. With a good agent, he might be able to sell the book rights for, oh, say, half-a-mill. Then there was the possibility of screenplay and movie rights. Look at *Dead Man Walking*.

"I came down hard on him, I really did." Ivy went through a multitude of linguistic contortions. "He lit out for that kid Stevie's place, down at the trailer park. But I caught him before he slipped out the gate. He was screamin' bloody murder, 'Don't worry, Mama, I disguised my voice.' "

"That's rich. A real humdinger." Jinx sensed the tale was only half through.

"He was twistin' like a washing-machine agitator, and me all the time fixing to clobber him." Finally, she wound down. "He didn't mean anything by it, though."

Jinx rolled his eyes heavenward. If brains were dynamite with a match tossed in, there wouldn't be enough of an explosion to fluff Ivy's outdated hairdo.

"Later, we were sitting on the couch. He looked up at me and said, 'Don't worry, Mama; I'm not.' "

Jinx stood up. He'd heard enough. It was time for Ivy to hit the street, harass some quacks in the hospital district. Maybe catch that Lebanese butcher who'd been ducking service on that malpractice suit. The signal to leave apparently flew right over her.

She said, "I need time off. A week at most."

"Do you people think I work here merely as an advisor? Have you forgotten the announcement I made last month? That nobody takes time off until after the election?"

"I don't have a choice. I have to go into the hospital."

Jinx heaved an exasperated sigh and wondered what imagined illness Ivy conjured up out of the medical books this time. Looney broad wouldn't be content with the common cold—no, Ivy sought out bizarre, trendy, or downright mythical illnesses like *Ethiopian Speckled Swine Flu*, then tailored the symptoms to fit.

No wonder her little Unabomber was screwed up.

He rested his wrist on his gun butt and narrowed his gaze. "How much do you know about the management style of Stalin?"

Ivy would've been liquidated the first day.

"Huh?"

"Stalin." The woman had a room temperature IQ. "Russian leader? Never took a day off?" Ivy gave him a blank stare. "Calling in sick was considered treason. People ended up in the gulag, or dead."

Ivy continued her petrified wood imitation.

"Khrushchev was on vacation when he was defeated. Gorbachev was on vacation when the coup occurred. On the other hand, Stalin never slept. Kept his light on in the Kremlin twenty-four hours a day."

"Last I heard, this was America."

"I can't afford to have people out the last two weeks in the campaign."

"It's female problems," she said archly. "You wouldn't understand."

"If Rudy Castro wins, you'll have all the time you need." He waited for that complex thought to register. If brains were computers, Ivy's hard drive was so small she could store everything she knew on a floppy disk.

"I need an operation."

Two words: Munchausen Syndrome. The woman carried elective surgery to a new zenith.

Jinx simmered. Those corpulent do-nothings in the DA's civil section wouldn't represent him in a fair labor standards lawsuit if Ivy turned sour. Although Georgia would consider Ivy's absence manna from Heaven. "All right. Do what you have to."

The deputy dried her tears. "There's more. Amos is on three months' probation. Except for school, he's under house arrest."

Uh-oh. Something's dead up the creek.

Ivy shrank in her seat. "There's nobody to watch him while I'm gone."

Even the vilest objections were too mild. Jinx's RPMs revved into the hot zone. His blood pressure soared.

"I'D RATHER GOUGE OUT AN EYE."

Ivy let out a yelp. "He needs guidance. A firm hand."

"He needs electroshock and a muzzle. Why not just give me a gift certificate for a six-month proctology exam?"

"THERE'S . . . NO . . . ONE . . . ELSE."

What started out as bellyaching disintegrated into a dying swan act. The shrillness in her voice climbed a range of tones and hung in an eerie pitch only a Malamute could hear.

Jinx frothed at the mouth. "Ever wonder why I never contribute to the United Way? Because, outside of this office, you're virtually unemployable. I consider you my personal charity. Get Juvenile Hall to clamp an ankle monitor on him."

"He could help you pass out pushcards."

"Have you lost your mind? I'm trying to win."

Ivy bawled harder.

His head swarmed with ideas, mostly bad. Left alone, the welfare office would take Amos—or worse. Maybe Skeeter could help. After all, didn't he say Rudy Castro had some greasy Cuban on the payroll—a pachuco rumored to be one of the Mariel boat lift criminals Fidel Castro pawned off during Jimmy Carter's administration? The scuzzy dipshit with tattoos in the webs of his fingers went door to door handing out Castro's cards, scaring the shit out of old folks.

Maybe Skeeter could use Amos to pass out pushcards. Force-feed the kid cheeseburgers, maybe rent some Freddy Krueger flicks. By then, Raven would come back. Let her manage him.

Jinx laid down the law. "If he doesn't behave, I have permission to break both arms and a leg."

"You have my permission to discipline him."

"I wasn't talking about him."

Ivy brightened. "Amos is a good boy. I told him to remember he's a guest. One more thing." She took a deep breath. "You'll need to drive him to school for a few days. He got kicked off the bus again. But it wasn't his fault. That girl shouldn't poke fun at him."

They migrated back into the main office. Mickey and Dell had settled in, dabbing paper towels against the watermelon juice trickling down their chins. Across the room with the phone grafted to his ear, Gil—looking swarthy in his black suit—listened intently. His eyes bulged in their sockets.

"Ivy." He waved the receiver.

To the others, he opened his palms and shrugged. "I was just playing with him, you know, telling him, 'What does your mama look like? Does she have two arms, two legs?' He said, 'Put my mama on the phone, Cocksucker.' "

Jinx couldn't help himself. He mimicked Ivy's irritating alto and fluttered his hands the way she did when she worked herself into a tizzy. "Amos is a good boy. He doesn't even know what that means. Probably picked it up from that kid, Stevie, down at the trailer park."

While the others polished off melon, Ivy got in a few good telephonic licks. When she hung up the phone, Dell caused a cease-fire on chatter by favoring everyone with one of his rare speaking engagements.

"Thanks for breakfast."

"I was saving it for the weekend, but Amos sneaked it into bed and cut a hole in it. I guess he couldn't wait."

Stuffed faces melted into revulsion. Deputies stampeded the bathroom.

So much for the Unabomber.

"Jinx!" Across the room, Georgia, color drained from her face, held the phone aloft. "It's the police. Raven's been in an accident."

Chapter Ten

Raven rallied at the touch of an icy metal disk pressed against her flesh, vaguely aware she had the muscular control of a ragdoll. The distorted face of a paramedic came into focus.

"Welcome back." He squatted beside her. "From the looks of your car, we figured you were a goner. Know where you are?"

The sun beat down on her face like a giant magnifying glass. Over body aches and knifelike pain, she became aware of the gnawing rebellion from a fire ant bed.

The emergency medical technician held up his hand. "How many fingers do you see?"

"Hundreds," she said hoarsely. "Ants."

"Pardon?"

"Crawling in my hair." She clutched at his shoulder in an effort to pull herself upright.

"Lie still."

Didn't he see the red devils dotting her hands? She flailed her arms but the tech held her down. Clamping onto the stethoscope, she cleared the dust from her throat. In a carefully metered voice, she told him just how the rabbit ate the carrot. "Let go, or you'll be taking pulses rectally."

An accident reconstruction investigator appeared at her side. He flipped through the pages of a small notebook. "How's she doing?"

"She'll bounce back."

"Any other witnesses?"

They talked over her, as if she were invisible. But the

next question brought her to life.

"What about those little guys watching from the corner?"

"What guys?"

"Those runts. Think they can add anything to what happened?"

By the time Jinx arrived at Seventh and University, west of Downtown, the sun had heated the temperature to eighty degrees. He found Raven sitting on the curb, slumped over, resting her head in her palms. Several yards away, three angry Mexicans with arms folded across their chests tried to bore holes in her with drill-bit stares. Crumpled lawnmowers lay strewn across the road; a flatbed trailer displayed a jumble of mangled metal, like modern art on a parade float. Miraculously, the truck appeared only marginally skinned up. In the distance, a wrecker disappeared around the corner with chunks of smashed BMW arcing sparks against the blacktop.

Jinx sat beside her. "You all right?"

"I think I need my head examined," she answered without looking up.

"Want the ambulance attendants to take another look?"

"That's not what I meant." She lifted her head and gave him a flat stare. "What're you doing here?"

He tried to suppress a smirk. Did she really think if she badged the police to worm out of a ticket, they wouldn't call the office to say she got hurt? "Georgia told me."

"Did she also tell you I phoned the number Marina's so-called daddy gave us?"

Amazing how Raven tried, sentenced, and executed him with a high-voltage glare. So much for due process. He knew by the way her eyes sparked that the phone number was either disconnected or bogus.

He scanned the perimeter for a brother officer. The uniformed troop sealed inside the air-conditioned patrol car had yet to glance up from his clipboard. Jinx smoothed away sweat beading up on his bald spot. A few more minutes of blazing sun and those migrant workers Raven T-boned might try to pluck the vine-ripened tomato growing out of his shirt collar.

He took another stab at conversation. "How'd it happen?"

"I just picked up the phone, punched in the number, and a recording came on saying—"

"I'm referring to this mess."

She scrunched up her face. Chewed her bottom lip. "I was westbound on Seventh, when I suddenly wondered how my car might look imbedded in the side of a truckful of Mexicans."

"Sarcasm doesn't become you."

"Caustic humor always makes me feel better." She drew up her knees, folded her arms, and sank her head against them.

"Certainly, you're not blaming me for this."

"Certainly."

He cut his gaze to the lawn crew. At the moment, they appeared to be in fine form. But a few coins dropped down the chute of any pay phone to the right lawyer, and they'd be wearing cervical collars, screaming the only English they knew in a thick Spanish accent—Weep-lash. He glanced over at Raven. Burned oil hung heavy in the air, but she scarcely seemed to breathe.

"Anything I can do?"

"Loan me your POV for a few days." Her eyes thinned into slits. "Why does that surprise you, me asking to borrow your personal vehicle? You have the patrol car."

"Fine." A lie, since he couldn't remember if he cleaned out all the incriminating evidence from the night he slipped off to *Lickety-Split's*, after Raven left for night class.

Jinx swallowed hard. Most females carried purses with lipstick. But it wouldn't surprise him to learn his woman carried around a little crime scene kit. Probably used surgical gloves and tweezers to collect hairs, or smeared crusty scrapings from the rear seat onto slides for later comparison and analysis. And even if she didn't, she had this funny way of looking right through him that made him squirm like she'd been there watching the whole time he banged those two withered old hides trying to pass themselves off as sisters.

Fort Worth's Finest ambled over to return Raven's license. While the officer helped her to her feet, Jinx shoved a pushcard at him. *The Blue* mumbled something unintelligible and strolled back to the sanctuary of the patrol car.

Jinx jingled the keys. "Need a ride to the apartment?"

Her eyes glowed with an unfamiliar intensity. "I already called someone."

That ass-wipe attorney friend, he'd bet Ivy's paycheck.

Raven dusted off her rump and took the keys, the full weight of despair apparently lifted. "So you'll have a heads-up, I want you to know Marina's daddy just became my personal project."

"You can't be sure he won't show up at the hearing. There's still time."

She jammed her fists against her hips. "You just don't get it, do you?"

She strutted across the street toward a restaurant, with her hips swaying hard enough to knock down a wall. She had to know every gaze at the intersection locked on her svelte body.

It wasn't until she disappeared through the glass door that it hit him. From the time she lifted her head until she turned her back and slinked off, she never lost the disappointment in her eyes.

Worse, she didn't even blink.

Not even when a couple of greasy Lilliputians down the street jumped up and down, shaking their fists.

Chapter Eleven

In the sixties, a highly placed official in local government nicknamed Gladiola Brooks the *Mayor of Meacham* because of her uppity ways. But Gladiola presided over the only completely black enclave in Jinx's precinct, and after decades of untiring community service, the moniker stuck.

Jinx considered the octogenarian more than a close friend. Gladiola Brooks just might be the only female he actually revered. Not to mention, having an old black lady with skin the color of dried corn for a pal provided a double bonus. Merely envisioning his association with Gladiola Brooks sent his mother scurrying for the vapors.

As precinct chairperson, she'd saved his bacon four years before. The Mexicans made a run at him, and Gladiola, "Ola" to her friends, registered every live person of voting age. Her detractors speculated she'd even signed up a few dead ones, too. After the absentee votes were counted, only a handful of people didn't vote a Jinx Porter ticket. Better yet, Gladiola Brooks knew who the traitors were. Those she couldn't urge back onto the road to righteousness, she ran out of the neighborhood.

Jinx had personally overheard her phoning the old folks about the absentee votes, heard her say in that syrupy plantation dialect, "That's okay, Baby, you don't have to fill in nothin'. Just sign your name, and I'll swing by and pick it up."

She won the election for him before, and she planned to again. Trouble was, Gladiola, the daughter of an East Texas sharecropper, recently celebrated her eightieth birthday. Although her memory had a glitch, it still combined with sudden bursts of clarity.

The moment Georgia routed Jinx the call, Ola launched into a diatribe.

"Jinx, I need you to come by the house." She hollered loud enough for him to pull the phone from his ear. "Cupid done stole my pills."

Cupid.

Rhymed with stupid.

Which is what he'd be if he let Ola suck him into thinking an arthritic, seventy-five-year-old beautician broke into her house and mucked around with her stuff.

"Are you sure you didn't misplace them?"

"Would I be botherin' such a busy man if that's all it was? I'm telling you, Cupid broke in while I was at church and stole my pills." He waited for Ola to run out of steam. She knew her lines by heart, and seemed hell-bent on speaking every last one of them. "My eyedrops moved, too. I think she put poison in 'em, and now I'm gonna need another subscription."

"You don't need a new prescription, Ola. We'll find them."

He'd have to drop by, of course. Search the house until he found where Ola mislaid them. She'd practically thrown him out last time it happened. Almost as if she didn't want things to turn up, just check in with her and pay her some attention.

Damned women.

As always, he played along. The windows on Ola's pitiful lean-to were reinforced with burglar bars; the front door had three deadbolts, each requiring a different key. When the police chief finally tired of her calls, he played along, too—temporarily installed a couple of pin cameras and surveillance equipment from the Narcotics Unit. The only way an intruder could get into that rickety shack would be to parachute through the ceiling.

He said, "How would Cupid get in?"

"Through the roof."

Which meant she expected him to climb on top of the house and check for holes. Jesus H. Poor feeble old Cupid, bearing the brunt of the nefarious activity. Cupid couldn't even navigate her way around her own house without the aid of a walker, much less shuffle up the street to play cat burglar.

This called for Voodoo.

They'd done it before—he, two cops, a prominent medical malpractice attorney and a Congressman—choreographed an exorcism with the aid of a visiting Nigerian medicine man. Actually, the shaman hailed from Stop Six, a few miles east of the freeway, but Ola didn't have to know. Jinx felt foolish, clasping hands with a bunch of men, while the fake priest hopped around on one foot and chanted shit that sounded hauntingly like a Beatles record played backward. The ruse worked, but only for a while. Once the attention slacked off, the break-ins increased.

"What you need, Ola, is a cat."

She rejected the notion flat out.

"But people full of the Devil are scared of cats. If you had a nice cat, maybe Cupid would be afraid to come over."

"You'd be trying to pawn Cecil off on me—"

"His name's Caesar."

"—and I seen Cecil's pictures—"

"Caesar."

"—That's what I said. I seen his picture. Raven showed me a long time ago. Cecil's got a evil face, so, no thank you. Come check the roof, that's all I'm askin'." She punctuated the demand with a "Humph," and slammed the phone in his ear.

Jinx grabbed his coat and positioned two sets of hand-cuffs so they rode comfortably over his belt and settled in the small of his back. He made a beeline past Georgia's desk.

"Going out again?" She glanced pointedly at the clock.

"I'll be back in time for you to go to lunch." As if watching a Richard Simmons videotape instead of eating a bacon-double-cheeseburger might kill her.

At the traffic signal adjacent to Our Lady of Mercy Hospital, Jinx slowed for a careening ambulance. Getting caught at the light gave him a chance to study the crimson yard sign—the one that read REELECT CONSTABLE JINX PORTER—staked at the south curbline. With Castro's thugs swiping his signs right and left, he considered it a miracle they overlooked this one.

He allowed his thoughts to free associate. A handful of nurses gathered at the corner, and he gave their attributes an appreciative once-over. The python stirred in his pants. He couldn't remember when he'd felt so energized.

Night before last.

When the barfly called.

Which left Raven grinding her teeth.

He tried to force another intrusive image from his memory. Raven, wearing a similar childlike scowl after the bouncer from that nightclub hoisted her up on tiptoes, steered her to the door, lifted her by her beltloops, and tossed her out of the honky tonk—a place where they remained unwelcome this very day.

The nurses crossed against the light, and he watched a big blonde jiggle across the street in her tight uniform skirt. For several surreal seconds he imagined how great it would be to possess the stamina of a mechanical bull.

The fantasy wilted quicker than a hothouse orchid.

Impossible.

Directly across the street, pulsing against the bright blue sky like a neon abscess, stood a Rudy Castro billboard.

"What the hell?" He enunciated each word, his face as tight as a fist.

To the rear, a horn sounded. One glance in the mirror and an upraised fist came into view.

"Sonofabitch, I'm moving." He hoped the guy could lip read.

Jinx floored the accelerator. The car lurched forward, and stalled in front of the bleached blonde. She shot him the finger, rippled to the opposite curbline, and joined her friends. Fat slut.

He'd see about this sign bullshit. Two could play the game. The engine gave an infantile *wa-wa-wa-wa-wa-wa* but didn't catch. Over blaring horns, he pumped the gas. The traffic signal flashed to amber. The ignition fired, but the light turned red. Jinx shot through the intersection, right up the tailpipe of a carload of Orientals. The impact mashed an anguished face against the window, more gruesome than any clip taken from newsreel documentaries on the Rape of Nanking.

The Chevy's airbags deployed. Once the powder settled, they dangled from the steering wheel and hung over the glove compartment like the Jolly Green Giant's used condoms. Jinx curbed the vehicle and flung open the door in frustration.

Jesus H.

Between him and Raven, people might suspect his office had developed an immigration policy harsher than anything the INS could concoct. He stepped out onto the street.

Little yellow people spilled from a fishbowl car—a Pacer held together with Bond-o—and surrounded him with sing-song chatter. Munchkins straight out of Oz. With slanted eyes and flat faces.

"Hold your horses." He dug out his operator's license, making sure the driver caught sight of the badge clipped to his belt. Let him mull over that, in case he didn't carry insurance, or had an outstanding arrest warrant. See if the Asian wouldn't let him pay the damage out of his own pocket.

Angry staccato voices softened into a buzz. Jinx scanned the area.

Across the street, a bus bench advertisement for an unwed mothers' home snared his attention. He studied the possibilities with keen, if not downright unhealthy interest, and strolled away from the melee. A tingle began behind his ears, raced up his head, and centered in his brain. The out-of-body experience blurred his surroundings.

Bus benches.

That's what he needed, a shitslew of bus benches. Maybe even a parade of busses to advertise his campaign. Big ugly busses that dominated the roads and mowed people down if they got in the way. Castro wouldn't know what hit him 'til he found himself steamrolled into the asphalt, staring at a REELECT CONSTABLE JINX PORTER sign racing off to the next stop.

He keyed up the handheld radio. Georgia took her sweet time answering.

"Get my ad man on the horn. Number's on my blotter. Tell him to print up some bus bench signs. And one big enough to fit on the side of a bus. Pattern them after those red and white bumper stickers he did for me. And tell him no later than tomorrow."

"What if he can't do it that quick?"

"If you tell him I'll pay out the wazoo, he'll get them."

Confidence restored, Jinx whipped around in time to see a carful of Chinamen roaring off in the distance.

After Dell dropped her off at the Château, Raven let herself into a gunmetal gray clone of Jinx's patrol car, complete with police radio, siren, and a couple of Kojak lights he kept on the passenger floorboard.

The man was eaten up with law enforcement.

She nestled her shoulderblades against the velour upholstery and tugged on the sun visor. A computer-generated list of Jinx's personal phone numbers drifted into her lap. She ran a finger down the alphabetical order of names.

Shiloh Wilette.

Jinx's ex-wife could fill in the blanks.

In a gutsy move, Raven took her chances and dialed.

Jinx arrived at Gladiola's clapboard shanty with a film of gray powder from the deployed airbags coating his head. He stood outside with the sun beating down on his scalp, waiting for Ola to patter to the door before the powder formed a paste. A trellis of roses caught his eye, and he marveled at Ola's ability to bring beauty to what would otherwise constitute an embarrassment.

The snap of deadbolts brought him to attention. The door jerked open and Ola started finger-wagging.

"Cupid left toothpicks, too. All over the house. Put 'em in the shape of 'X's. You comin' in, or not?"

Jinx stepped inside the living room and immediately felt the heat. Ola kept the temperature at a sweltering ninety degrees year around. While she rambled about Cupid, his eyes drifted over the walls to the familiar faces of autographed photos.

Bill Clinton and Ola. *Ola—Wish I was twenty years older.*

The Governor and Ola. *To Ola—the real Yellow Rose of Texas.*

Kofi Annan and Ola. *Gladiola—Many thanks for all your sound advice.*

Queen Elizabeth and Ola. *Gladiola Brooks, you are a Princess.*

And a new one.

Raven and Ola. Wearing straw sunhats at the July Fourth celebration, with arms slung around each other's shoulders. *To Ola—Women rock.*

Gladiola whirled around and took off down the dark hallway. "Old fool, tryin' to kill me off."

"I don't think—"

"Is. You comin'? Lookie here. Evil witch busted through the ceiling."

Jinx's gaze flickered to the trap door. Gladiola jammed a fist against her hip and fixed him with a shrewd eye. Surely, she didn't expect him to crawl around in that attic. Be like trampling on cardboard. One false move, he'd sink right out of sight.

"And she stepped on this, comin' down." Ola pointed to a circa-fifties dinette chair covered in marbled plastic, part of a set matching a red formica table. An interested fly buzzed a hacked-up chicken ready for frying.

"Get on up and see what she bugged my house with."

"Why on earth would Cupid—"

"I done told ya and told ya, she finds out when I leave so she can steal my things."

"What things?"

Ola scowled. "My new dress. The one the Congressman gimme for my birthday."

"Why would Cupid want your dress? Y'all aren't even

the same size." He'd almost slipped up. Nearly said Cupid was a beanpole, that the dress would've hung on her like a gunnysack.

"Use your noggin. She want it so I don't have it."

"You've got more clothes than Raven. Are you sure you didn't hang it in the closet? I can't believe Cupid would steal."

"Did." That put a period to it. Ola set her jaw and fixed him with a harsh glare. "Quit dawdling and find the bug."

He let out a disgusted sigh. While Rudy Castro was out politicking, the incumbent was chasing phantoms for Gladiola Brooks.

A virtual Don Quixote.

He dragged over a chair and tugged the cord. The door gaped open like a hungry mouth. Shards of sunlight sliced through the rafters. Slivers of gold, filtering in from unmitred corners, divided the area into geometric shapes. As he hoisted himself up for a look, the skittering of rat feet clicked across bare wood.

He rifled through his pockets. His breath grew shallow with the smell of fetid air.

"Find anything, Jinx?"

"Believe I did."

"Did?" Ola sounded shocked.

He eased back down the opening. Held out a fist. Relaxed it enough for Gladiola to glimpse a wad-cutter left over from the last firearms qualification practice.

"What that?"

"Bug."

"Lemme see."

"No. We don't want to damage it. I'm taking it straight to the lab."

A mass of kinky white hair drooped over her forehead

and she pushed it aside. Her cataract-coated eyes and suspicious expression warned it might take up to thirty minutes, convincing her.

Never in his life did he think he'd be relieved to hear one of his deputies screaming for help over the police handheld. He bolted to the car and activated the emergency lights and siren, leaving Ola standing in her house dress with her hands pressed against her ears.

Ivy's Code-Three vehicle chase ended at the airport. When she contacted Jinx by radio to let him know the doctor avoiding a malpractice lawsuit had been served his papers, he sent Gil to mend fences with five police agencies caught up in the hot pursuit.

Leaving himself free to scrounge for campaign donations.

Chapter Twelve

In Rivercrest, one of Fort Worth's ritziest residential neigh-borhoods, Jinx chugged the patrol car to the curb, engine knocking, and killed the motor. The curtains inside the two-story rock-and-brick Tudor had been pulled to filter out the setting sun.

Best he could tell, the homeowners were inside.

Rampant griffins perched atop brick columns on either side of a wrought iron gate, prepared to do battle with in-truders. Or persons such as himself, blackballed by the Country Club. Jinx clenched his teeth, punched in the secu-rity code, then stepped inside and lifted a brass gremlin door-knocker. A carved door with stained glass inserts swung open.

"Mother."

He bent over and gave the petite dynamo a stiff hug. Her black silk blouse made her seem more formidable, even with a pearl choker clasped around her neck. Satiny skin, virtually ageless and powdered white, brushed against his cheek. She inflicted a dry kiss on him before jerking away.

"Hello, Jinx. You just missed Mimzy."

He wanted to inject sarcasm into the conversation. Say, "Hurt me," or maybe ask what flavor of the month his sis-ter's hair was. Or inquire as to whether she could still stand to shed twenty pounds, and if the latest trend in Mimzy's social circle called for a bout with anorexia, bulemia, anemia, or a trendier malaise?

Pity he had an agenda.

He planned to ask for a campaign donation.

A big one.

"I need a favor." He hoped she wouldn't invite him inside. For good measure, he "X"ed his fingers behind his back, the way he'd done as a kid.

"Come in. You're letting out the cold air."

He looked at his watch for effect. "I don't have much time."

"You never do."

His shoulders sagged and he felt a familiar wrenching in his gut. He stepped inside the palatial foyer, heard the lock snap, and immediately felt the pangs of claustrophobia. Their visits always started the same. The criticism. The negative slant. He could count on one hand the times he'd been near her without feeling a diarrhea attack coming on. At seventy-five, Kamille Porter still knew which buttons launched nuclear missiles, and she didn't mind pushing them.

"I don't understand why you refuse to spend more than two seconds here. We never see you. Naturally, I'd be content to visit at your place, but you never ask."

He wanted to tell her she'd need a bulletproof vest to enter his part of town—the seedy part—the part she used to shield him from, growing up. His friends opted for the filling station down the street rather than subject themselves to his bathroom, and the landlord threatened to call HAZMAT after the maintenance guy demanded a Level Four bio-hazard containment suit to repair the toilet. Making it quite impossible for Kamille to visit, since it was legend she'd sooner swap spit with the dog than use public restrooms. The woman had a bladder the size of Greater Miami when the need arose.

"You wouldn't like my apartment. It's not what you'd call clean. People often remark on it."

"I might not be averse to loaning our maid for the after-

108

noon, but you never ask."

Jinx shrugged off the offer. "I got used to it being filthy. It's healthier, you know. I haven't been sick since I stopped picking up after myself."

In the winter of her years, Kamille could still chill him with her disapproval. Besides, no good deed came without a hefty pricetag. Why sell his soul to the Devil when he could come here? Jinx planted his feet firmly against the marble floor, mentally insulating himself for the lambasting.

"I suppose it's just as well Paloma won't have to clean your place. I'd hate her to think you were raised with swine. I did, after all, try to teach you to keep your affairs orderly."

"You did a bang-up job, Mother."

She waved a hand in front of her face, making him wonder if he smelled. "I must have taken leave of my senses. We don't need Paloma taking sick. Do you still own that horrible cat?"

"He's better behaved than a lot of Country Clubbers. And Caesar's cleaner than most surgeons."

Kamille wrinkled her nose. "I seriously doubt that. No wonder you don't have nice furniture."

"Says who?"

"You couldn't possibly. Not with animals parading in and out."

He winced, wondering whether the Bobby Fischer of cerebral chess had pulled one of her double entendres. Surely she didn't expect him to live like a Trappist Monk?

"The cat keeps me warm at night."

"You let it crawl in bed with you? Good Heavenly Days." His mother touched a delicate hand to her bosom and grimaced—an old Country Club fetch-the-smelling-salts attention-grabber the immediate family had learned to put up with.

He started to smart off. Tell her a lot of hairy heat had worked its way under those sheets. That Caesar wasn't the first pussy, or the worst pussy, for that matter. But there was something no-nonsense about the way she smoothed the pleats of a gabardine skirt as platinum as her hair that dulled the tendency to spar.

"I came to ask you to let me hammer down a yard sign." Forget begging a contribution. He'd sooner take the hammer and knock out a molar.

"You never come around unless you want something."

"I dropped by last week and didn't ask for a thing."

"I'm sure it has nothing to do with the fact we weren't home. Besides, what good will a yard sign do? We don't even live in your precinct." The tiny lines around her eyes relaxed and she smiled.

"People who can vote for me may drive by and notice—"

"I rather doubt it. Unless you're referring to the hired help."

"—and tell their friends." Jinx fumed. May as well explain it to a tire iron. "Of course I mean the maids and gardeners. Why can't you do this without giving me a ration of—"

Kamille's icy stare froze the S-word in his throat.

"How long would we have to leave it up?" Her gaze flickered in the direction of the next door neighbors'.

"Never mind. We wouldn't want anybody to know your son's the law. Let them think I'm an entrepreneur, like Dad."

With an aristocratic sniff, she fluttered her perfectly manicured nails to her neck and grazed the pearls. "We tell them you're a department head. That's all they're entitled to know."

"I've gotta go."

He let himself out. Pausing at the cobblestone walk, he surveyed the surrounding estates. He decided not to tell the woman who had given him life that the old lady across the street agreed to put up a sign. Because if he did, Mrs. Scorekeeper might have a snippy retort—like how it was high time the favor got returned, since he used to mow the woman's grass after school and never came home with anything to show for it besides sweat. Then he might blow a fuse and tell her about the cash-or-couch arrangement he made with the very snooty Mrs. Selma Winston, the one who introduced him to his first set of store-bought tits. Information which might cause him to have to perform CPR on his own mother, a blueblood who couldn't even pucker up to kiss him hello without worrying over whether she had the proper inoculations.

Unexpectedly, Kamille brightened. "Don't run off. You'll want to hear all about Mimzy getting into the Junior League."

Jinx hurried out the gate before the lifestyle he'd grown to hate contaminated him.

Chapter Thirteen

Raven drove Jinx's car down Pennsylvania, then turned south on Eighth Avenue. Knee-deep in the Hospital District, she spotted Ivy, blocking in an unattended Porsche parked under a cloth awning behind a strip center of doctors' offices.

Hair hung in damp strands around Ivy's face. Her exposed neck gleamed with sweat, and her shoulders hung limper than Jinx's pecker after a hard night of hot sex.

"What's up?" Raven asked.

"This is Dr. Haik's car. His receptionist says he's not in, but I know in my gut he's seeing patients. When I asked to have a look-see, we got in a lively discussion and she said I couldn't go past the lobby."

Raven lusted after the Porsche, a lipstick red Carrera. She envisioned herself behind the wheel, purring out to the firearms range, looking like a Hollywood starlet in her shooter's glasses, wearing enough gold to weigh down Jimmy Hoffa.

A gust of wind flapped the awning and shattered her daydream. Raven took a deep breath. The air seemed as stale going in as it did coming out.

"It's awful hot out here, Ivy. You don't want to get heat stroke. He wouldn't come out to the foyer and get it?"

"Haik's been dodging service. Eventually, he'll go home. When he does, I'll pounce on him. 'Til then, I'm not budging."

"And you won't budge when he shows up, either, because you'll be stiffer than a cinder block when rigor mortis sets in."

Ivy threw a pen against the dash. Frustration played across her sun-blotched face.

"What else am I supposed to do? I'm down to my last petition. Jinx'll kill me if I don't get this paper served before I leave."

"You're leaving? Jinx said we can't take any time off."

Ivy brightened. "I'm having surgery. Fibroid tumors."

"Who's going to watch Amos?"

Besides the police?

"Jinx agreed to look after him a couple of days."

Raven let go a belly laugh. "Jinx? You're kidding."

But Ivy wasn't.

Imagine, Jinx holed up with the incorrigible Amos. Talk about a style cramper. Tears of mirth trickled out the corners of her eyes.

"You think it's funny?"

"No." Raven bit her lip. "I'm thinking about how many heads I could turn driving that car. You sure this is Haik's Porsche?"

Ivy nodded. "I ran a registration on it last week, when I first tried to serve him."

"What-say we give it another shot? I have an idea."

To prevent escape, they angled their cars behind the Porsche. Raven trailed Ivy through the glass doors to Haik's office.

The instant the receptionist spotted Ivy, the smile died on her lips. "Like I already told you, the doctor isn't in. Try back later."

"That's what you said before," Ivy reminded her.

"Why don't you let me sign for it?"

Ivy gave the woman a disdainful sniff. "Because Dr. Haik'll say he never got it."

Raven's head oscillated to keep pace. The interchange

took on all the qualities of Wimbledon tennis, heating up.

An elderly couple came through the door and Ivy stepped away from the glass partition to let them sign in.

The receptionist redirected her attention to Raven. She handed over a clipboard. "Fill this out."

"Actually, I'm with her. I'm just hanging out while the pharmacy fills my Ebola prescription."

Two women within earshot exchanged electrically charged glances. They dropped their magazines and left the room in one fluid movement. Raven slid into a warm seat and patted the one beside it. Ivy stayed put.

The door opened and an old man navigated his way inside with the assistance of an aluminum walker.

The receptionist interrupted with a bulletin. "Folks, Dr. Haik's not here. He's been delayed."

Raven and Ivy exchanged knowing glances.

Ivy said, "We'll wait."

"Suit yourselves." The woman juggled phone lines and purred saccharine greetings into the mouthpiece.

Raven scanned the standing-room-only crowd. A nurse holding a chart appeared at a side door and called out a name. A teenager toting an infant seat gathered up baby trappings and wedged past. Across the room, a woman with a portable oxygen tank wheezed through a plastic nose shield.

Raven nudged Ivy.

"Let me understand this," she said in a low voice. "The doc's not here, yet they're calling people back?"

"Appears so."

A middle-aged man on crutches limped out the same door, churning out crop circles and digging up divots on his way to the counter to settle his bill.

"This is bullshit. Gimme the paper." Raven jerked hard

enough to give Ivy a paper cut. She cleared her throat with a loud, "Ahem."

Several patients looked up from their magazines. The woman with the oxygen tank peered past the fogged-up nose cup like an alligator peeking over a log.

With stern authority, Raven read from the lawsuit.

" 'Comes now, Reginald Joe Willie Latham, hereinafter known as Plaintiff . . . does hereby swear and affirm . . . ' "

The hint of stubbornness left the receptionist's eyes. She violently pushed back from the desk and rocketed to her feet. Patients lowered the latest copies of *Forbes* and *Good Housekeeping*.

" '. . . that on the fourteenth day of July the said Dr. Hakeem Haik, hereinafter the Defendant . . . ' "

The receptionist knocked over her chair. She flew out of sight, leaving the front counter unattended.

" '. . . did then and there commit acts of gross negligence and malpractice. Plaintiff further alleges Defendant did then and there perform a wrong-site surgical procedure, to wit: amputate the right leg . . . ' "

She paused to study the sea of faces. A blue-haired lady with her mouth agape snatched a pashmina and rose from her seat. A slightly younger version lunged for the woman's elbow and steered her to the exit. An elderly couple jockeyed for position, but a wiry old coot beat them by a nose. Somewhere to the rear of the building, shrieks echoed and doors slammed.

Raven faked distraction. "Where was I? Ah, yes. It states Dr. Haik, your doctor, '. . . did then and there amputate the Plaintiff's right leg . . . ' " She paused to ad-lib. "Which was actually the wrong leg. The left leg was the right leg. Or, I guess I should say, the correct leg." Beyond her view, a trayful of metal crashed to the floor. "Did I say that right?"

She directed her question to no one in particular. "This is so confusing. Not confusing enough to hack off the wrong leg, of course."

People left in droves. Determined, she continued.

"Anyway, it alleges Dr. Haik, '. . . in a state of intoxication and otherwise under the influence'—that means snockered, for those of you who still wish to keep your appointments—'removed the wrong leg.' Which was the right leg. When he was supposed to cut off the left leg. Which was actually the right leg. The correct leg."

She continued reading aloud.

The last patient made a beeline for the exit.

"Wait," Raven called out to the disappearing swatch of plaid. "I'm just getting to the good part."

A new victim entered the waiting room. Gripping a cane topped with a brass giraffe head, he navigated his way across the dense carpet. Beyond the glass partition, a fluttering white coat burst into view with a wild-eyed foreigner wrapped inside.

"Hi." Raven winked. "I was just about to start over."

The embroidered nametag identified the man behind the glass as Dr. Haik. He leaned close enough to steam up the window, seemingly unaware of his mass profusion of nose hairs.

"What is the meaning of this?" he demanded in a clipped, non-native tongue.

Raven favored him with a dimpled smile, and refolded the lawsuit into thirds. "Are you Dr. Hakeem Haik?"

"I am. And you are, how do you say? Disrupting the peace?"

"I have a court paper for you."

"I want you out of my office." A bronze finger sliced the air and pointed to the exit. "Immediately."

116

Raven scrunched her chin and pressed an index finger to her temple. "Let me understand this. You want me to leave because I'm scaring off business?"

The lawsuit found its way into the mitt of the rightful owner. The bug-eyed Dr. Haik frothed at the mouth. "Out."

Ivy's raisin-eyed stare broke. The corners of her eyes crinkled, and fine lines webbed her face. "Say, Raven, while I'm recuperating, could I maybe sic you on a couple more barnburners? I've got a stack of them out in the patrol car."

"Why not?" At the door, Raven glimpsed the stricken Dr. Haik, staring at the cover page. "I've had it with insufferable pricks."

But she was thinking—

—It'll give me another chance to run into Jinx.

He owes me an explanation and I'm, by God, gonna get it.

At the final turn to Jinx's apartment, Raven got caught at the traffic signal.

A late model Caddy with a crumpled front fender cruised up even with her. A stunted man whose unruly gray hair barely came even with the top of the steering wheel balled up a fist. His lips parted, forming an ugly gash in his face. He mouthed one word before flooring the accelerator, busting the red light and careening out of sight.

"Balogh."

Chapter Fourteen

Jinx arrived home, infuriated.

First, the pimply cashier at the grocery asked, loud enough for the stacked blonde standing in line to overhear, whether the twenty-four twelve-packs of toilet paper in the basket meant the stuff was on sale, or if he'd purchased tickets to Europe.

When the leggy twit snickered, he felt compelled to let the clerk in on the wisdom of a middle-aged man recuperating from hemorrhoid surgery: if he lived long enough, he'd use it all up; if he died with a stocked closet, big damned deal.

'Nuff sed.

But when Zit-Cheeks called for a price check over the intercom on the large jar of glycerine suppositories, the droop-titted slut with the urine-colored hair doubled over in a fit of laughter—thereby killing any chance of ever getting a date with him. By the time his bald spot felt as flambéed as his hemorrhoids, while everyone had a rollicking good time at his expense, the checker dared to scrutinize his face against his driver's license before insisting on a second ID. When the manager strolled over to make a check approval and called him by name in a tone that suggested he might be a baby raper, well, that put the ox in the ditch.

Thanks a bunch. See if I ever trade here again.

It didn't take poking his head through the door of a blast furnace for Jinx to know his life sucked and the Château's air conditioner had gone belly up again. He could tell by the way every door in the complex gaped open as he walked through the courtyard. Aromatic curiosities of cross-racial sweat and ethnic foods mingled with the cloying scent of honeysuckle. Even the Alzheimer's geezer took refuge on the balcony with his oxygen tank in one hand and the Chihuahua in the other.

Jinx tried to ignore Glen Lee Spence, draped across the couch like Norma Desmond, with a washcloth pressed against his forehead, but the transsexual called out with the petulance of a debutante on the eve of her presentation.

"I'm not putting up with this."

"A/C on the fritz?" Jinx's waistband captured the sweat trickling down his sides.

"Section Eight will not pay rent on an un-air-conditioned apartment." Glen Lee raved on, but Jinx kept an eye on the Siamese in his window, and walked without breaking stride. "I called the subsidized housing office today and they crawled up the owner's shorts. Told him they'd withhold the rent until—"

"Many people would consider themselves fortunate to live in a dwelling that's not provided by the State penal system." Maybe the rest of the complex had forgotten about that armed robbery charge, but to Jinx Porter, Glen Lee Spence would forever be the getaway driver in a foiled stick-up.

"Now, listen here, Jinx." The transsexual swatted a perturbed hand. "You know very well I did not rob that store detective. A ball-point pen is not a deadly weapon; that DA just did not like me. Anyway, I did my three years in the Windham Unit. My debt to society's paid.

"Besides," he added, "I did not shoplift, I don't care what they said. I merely wandered into Men's Furnishings with a tube of lipstick. . . . Why're you giving me that look?

Don't roll your eyes at me, Mister."

Glen Lee'd spent barely enough pen time to receive the appropriate estrogen dosages compliments of the State, not long enough to qualify for the entire sex change operation. Anybody who broached the subject could see, even after thirteen years, the ex-con was still bitter. At least he didn't have those muttonchop sideburns anymore. And he'd stopped wearing a pack of Luckys rolled up in the sleeve of his T-shirt. Once the testosterone dwindled and the tits ballooned, Glen Lee'd assumed his prissy role like a little girl takes to her first Barbie.

Out of the blue, Jinx wondered if the Rice kid had a Barbie. If not, she should.

Marina.

The name came back with a deluge of unwanted memories.

"We've certainly gotten off on the wrong track, haven't we?" Glen Lee dramatized his exasperation by swiping his forehead with the back of his hand. "I only mentioned the heat because I volunteer at the old folks' home on Tuesdays, and this unfortunate occurrence has sapped my strength. I cannot sleep when it's hot, and if I don't rest up, there won't be anyone to read to them tonight. C'mere, Pookie."

A furry flash of white zigzagged across the room and sprang to the sofa. With a set of blood-red lips, Glen Lee nuzzled the Pekingese, smooching "a-moo-moo-moo" against the silky fur.

Jinx grimaced. The pop-eyed hairball spotted him. It snarled and let out a string of frenzied yips.

"I saw a mess in the middle of the road last week that resembled *Poo-Poo;* I kinda hoped it might be your dog."

"Pookie does not care for you, Jinx. Do you, Pookie?

Pookie says, No. She does not care for the way you treat Raven. Dogs understand these things—don't you, Pookie? A-moo-moo-moo."

"When I need an interpreter, I'll get one."

"By the way," Glen Lee needled, "Raven was by earlier, boxing up some stuff. You ask me, she ditched you."

"Thanks for eyeballing the place. What'd you do? Ordain yourself the Neighborhood Watch block captain?" Jinx shifted his gaze upstairs, dreading the climb. God knew what he'd find.

Or worse—what he wouldn't.

With a toss of his strawberry blond mane, Glen Lee bounced up from the couch. He strutted across the carpet, his perky tits twirling like pinwheels beneath his T-shirt.

"You should treat people with respect, the way Raven does." He propped himself against the doorframe and planted a fist against where his hip would've been, if he'd had any to speak of. "She gave me her Hawaiian skirt before she left. And a lavender silk blouse I admired."

Jinx's eyes narrowed into slits. He looked past the sofa at what appeared to be the leg of a blow-up doll sticking out of the closet. "Been to Oklahoma lately? Because you bear a striking resemblance to a mug shot I saw on *America's Most Wanted*."

Glen Lee stared, bug-eyed. He quit wringing the washrag, and a chalk-white hand fluttered to his brow. "To think I was rounding up a group for a pajama party, to get the vote out for you." He slammed the door in a huff.

Disgusted, Jinx snorted. The gender-confused freak ought to spend less time dreaming up nocturnal shenanigans, and more time outdoors. Maybe get some vitamin D. Keep him from looking like Count Dracula. Besides, convicted felons lost their voting rights. Was Glen Lee's clientele any different?

Jinx rolled his eyes Heavenward and conducted a mental inventory. He'd signed on to babysit a ragamuffin who didn't have enough candlepower to converse with earthworms on their own level. The apartment was sizzling, and it didn't take Amos showing up to set fire to the place.

Which cheated him out of dropping the little thug off at Juvenile Hall until Ivy checked out of the hospital.

And meant he'd have to brat-proof the place.

Somewhere, he suspected Raven was yukking it up.

Worst of all—the very worst thing—was that haunting look on the Rice kid's face. In the middle of a race to the political death, he found himself wanting to get her a Barbie for Christmas, still nine months away.

A gift from Blue Santa, of course.

Because Jinx Porter wouldn't be caught dead buying a doll for some kid whose name he couldn't even remember.

Marina.

By the time Raven removed the last of her things from Jinx's apartment, drove them home, returned his car and hiked the two miles to Sonny's Garage in pumps, she'd worn blisters on her feet and rubbed holes in her pantyhose.

Shimmering in axle grease, Sonny peered out from behind the crunched Beemer's wheel rim.

"Go away."

Heat beat down on her aching shoulders. She hurt like a bad case of the flu, and wasn't in the mood to take lip off Sonny or anybody else.

"I want to know when my car'll be ready."

The mechanic unfolded his legs, and slid out from behind the wreckage. He struck a menacing pose. "Call a priest. Give it last rites."

"I'll pay extra. Just don't make me pick up any parts. So, when can I have it?"

He stared impassively into oblivion, as if channeling a message from the Great Beyond. "Whaddya reckon's the temperature?"

"Do I look like a thermometer?" A depressing idea flared through her head. She steeled herself for the worst. "Along with the rest of the damage, the A/C compressor's fried, isn't it?"

Sonny tuned in to the sky for more spiritual guidance. "How cold do ya think it has to be 'fore Hell freezes?"

The crumpled hood lay off to one side, separated from the body like a diseased limb.

She viewed the mechanic through slitted eyes. "Just fix it."

"Can't. Sum-bitch's been disintegratin' ever since it rolled off the conveyor belt. Might even be you own the model the U.S. gov'ment sued over. Surprises me it lasted this long."

The smell of tar bubbling around her feet tweaked her nose.

"She was a present. I've babied her my whole adult life. I cannot accept that she can't be repaired." She ignored his obnoxious facial contortions. "So, when?"

He screwed up his face in a way that gave off the impression he might actually be thinking of a solution, then strode to the rear of the Beemer and propped his grease-stained butt against the trunk. "Knock-knock."

"What is this? Mechanic humor?"

He sharpened his sweaty squint against the sun. "Knock-knock."

With grudging enthusiasm, "Who's there?"

"Lemon."

That ripped it. She clenched her fists. "Have your fun."

"Lemon know when you plan to stop throwin' money away on this piece of shit, and buy yourself a real car." He slapped his knee and let out a guffaw that disintegrated into a raspy wheeze.

This time, she conjured up a crazed expression that seemed to sober him. Not resorting to sarcasm took a Herculean effort. "When can you finish the bodywork?"

"Coup'la weeks. *If* I can round up the parts."

"I'll be needing a loaner."

He slammed the wrench down on the trunk lid. She winced, then craned her neck to see if he chipped the paint. He dug in a pocket, fished out a plastic fob and gestured to a low-rider parked on the lot.

She drew back defensively. "I'm begging you, don't make me drive that."

"Then getcha some comfortable shoes."

For several seconds, they eyed each other with contempt. Finally, she broke the sweltering silence. "About that loaner . . ."

"It's the Monte Carlo, or nothing. Live with it."

Revulsion stirred inside her. She took the keys and gritted her teeth.

"I'll be callin' later with a list of parts I need," he added wickedly. "Sooner you get 'em, the sooner you get your car back."

Depleted, Raven slunk over to a metallic purple low-rider with flame decals belching out from the hood. The ugly vinyl roof had hundreds of cat-ear triangles poking up—evidence of an ugly hailstorm that made it look like a scratching post for the snow leopards at the Fort Worth Zoo. She cranked up the engine and wondered what she had done to deserve this car. It backfired, shimmied a few times and did the Jerk all the way down the block, while the accordion strains of "Cielito Lindo" blared out of a radio missing an off-switch.

The Siamese glowered from the top shelf of a seven-foot bookcase. Jinx was about to offer him a morsel of meat from a fast-food taco joint when the phone rang. It trilled three times before he decided to answer.

After all, it could be Raven.

She'd say, I'm sorry; he'd say he hadn't eaten, then invite her over to cook his supper. In a chipper mood, he lifted the receiver.

A deep voice with a Hispanic accent spoke. "Are you registered to vote?"

"Who is this?"

"This is the Holy Father, Pope John Paul the Second. Bishop of Rome, Primate of Italy, Successor of Saint Peter, Sovereign of the Vatican City, Patriarch of the West."

"You've gotta be kidding." Oozing sarcasm.

"No, my son. God came to me in a vision. He wants you to help your people. Vote for Rudy Castro in the primary."

Jinx's mouth went dry. So this was the cheap ploy Castro was using to get out the vote. He'd heard about the elaborate phone banks, about Castro's volunteers mounting dinnertime invasions by working off lists of Democrats in the precinct who voted in previous elections. But he never thought Castro's people would be stupid enough to phone the incumbent.

He shouted into the mouthpiece. "Who the hell told you to call me? Do you have any idea who you're talking to?"

"I no speak-y English, Señor. I reading from paper."

"You don't speak English? Well, let me help you out. I know a little Spanish, *mendigo infeliz desgraciado.*" He severed the connection and went back to his taco.

The Siamese growled in rebuke as Jinx bit down. When he swallowed, a sharp edge caught in his throat. He abandoned his food in a coughing fit, and bolted to the kitchen for water.

The tortilla shell scratched, and left him teary-eyed. But he swiped his nose with a napkin and headed back to his easy chair—

—where Caesar cleaned the last of the taco off his dark brown mask.

Chapter Fifteen

The first pitch of the Ranger game coincided with the *ka-lunk* of a broken doorbell. Jinx peered out a gap in the cat-customized blinds, sighted the misshapen blob standing outside his door, and cursed through clenched teeth. At the turn of a knob, Ivy's pint-sized Ritalin-ingesting lummox stood before Jinx in sagging jeans, with a *Nine Inch Nails* T-shirt binding his oversized breasts.

"Come in," Jinx said dully. "I'll show you where to put your stuff."

Amos shuffled past, slinging a gym bag, with a copy of *Living Life on My Terms* tucked under one armpit. The strap caught the television and sent Raven's photo crashing to the floor. The Siamese took off and rappelled straight up the bookcase.

"I'm allergic to fur." Amos's malevolent tone eclipsed his menacing glance sideward. "You get the Playboy Channel?"

Jinx gave the Unabomber the once-over. "How old are you?"

"Eleven. You?"

"I'm asking the questions." He retrieved Raven's picture and repositioned it in the dusty outline.

Amos appraised the image of Raven in a string bikini against a backdrop of palm trees. Beady eyes glittered with approval. "Nice cheeches."

"Does your mama know you talk this way?"

"My mama don't keep pictures of big-titted women around."

Amos stretched out a grubby hand for a closer inspection, but Jinx snatched the frame out of reach. Shrugging, the boy pitched his belongings against the wall and slumped to the floor in front of the TV. The cat presided over the room from afar.

"Got any Freddy Krueger?" Amos reached for the remote control.

Jinx beat him to it. "No. You can watch Ranger baseball with me or stay in your room."

"You have to let me watch what I want. *I* am a guest. My mama said so."

Their eyes locked in a murderous bent.

"I don't think that's what your mother meant."

"What's for supper? I'm starving."

Somehow, Jinx didn't figure Child Protective Services would act on a failure-to-thrive complaint if he didn't feed Ivy's little heathen. An idea flashed into his mind. Maybe the Unabomber knew how to cook?

"Can you make tuna sandwiches?"

Amos screwed up his face. He eyed the refrigerator with unhealthy interest. "Women cook. Got any leftover pizza?"

"No."

"Baloney?"

"No."

"What about beer?"

Raven shielded her eyes from the glare of a tangerine sunset. She still couldn't believe Jinx's ex-wife agreed to speak with her. Or that she had driven thirty miles into the next county so they could meet.

"Walk with me." Shiloh Wilette bounded down a set of steps that ran off a wooden deck built flush against her double-wide. Thin lips, glossed in a berry-colored stain, tipped up in a smile, and Delft-blue eyes sparkled when she spoke. "Kenny and I—Ken's my husband—we raise rabbits. It's been real hot and we had a power outage yesterday. I have to check in on them more when the temperature goes up, so if you want to talk, follow me."

Lemminglike, Raven trailed her hostess down a path flanked with scrub oaks and stinging nettle. She found the need to make small talk with her hippie-throwback guide overwhelming.

"It's nice out here. Serene."

"Keep to the trail. We found a snake in the barn this morning. Kenny chopped off its head, but not before it ate some babies. He threw it out here somewhere. I plan to autopsy it later. See how many bunnies I lost."

Raven scurried up even with Jinx's ex, then fell into step with the rustle of her crisp overalls.

"We enjoy the country. It's beautiful out here. Away from the city lights, the night's as black as velvet and the stars sparkle like a million diamonds."

What's not to like? Raven thought. The grass needed mowing, pollen coated the trees in a golden dust, and the smell of fresh rabbit pellets drifted across a half acre of poison oak to tickle her nose. She sneezed.

"Potent, isn't it?" Shiloh stepped ahead, grabbed the handle of a weathered wooden gate hanging by a hinge, and gave her a backward glance.

They ended up inside a decrepit barn. Ceiling fans and evaporative coolers moved the air and lowered the temperature. Raven stood before dozens of rabbit cages, breathing in ammonia fumes, while Shiloh conducted the grand tour.

"These are show bunnies. Here's a Satin. Wanna feel?" Without waiting for an answer, she removed a bunny from the hutch and handed it over. "Kenny watches over the Rexes and Sables."

"Nice." Raven backed away.

Shiloh blew a soft breath across the fur until it separated into a cowlick. "See how the hairs are ringed with different colors? This little guy has five." She gave it a maternal smile, then returned the fluffy ball to its wire mesh suite. The latch snapped, and Shiloh's Earth-Mother persona took a drill sergeant approach. "Anything I say has to be confidential." The twinkle left her eyes. "Kenny didn't want me to let you come here. He said it would reopen old wounds."

"It wasn't my intention to intrude. I need to verify some things." Might as well cut to the chase. "Did Jinx ever cheat on you?"

"Before, during, or after our marriage?" Shiloh tossed a long strand of hair the color of rusty rebar over one shoulder.

Raven closed her eyes and blew out a resigned sigh. "Did he ever hit you?"

"You mean that time I caught him with a barmaid in the parking lot of the Hanky Panky Lounge? Or after I broke the news that I filed for divorce?"

Her gut sank.

"He whacked me across the ribs with the butt of a shotgun when I gave him the gate. Broke a couple, in fact." Reflexively, she rubbed her left side.

"He told me he never laid a hand on you. That he didn't chase women."

Shiloh let out an unamused chuckle. "I admit he was pretty likkered up—but he told you he wasn't slipping around, didn't he? So, we already know Jinx is a liar. Looks like he's still running the same scam from thirty years ago. I used to pretend it wasn't happening."

The devil on Raven's shoulder goaded her. She needed to hear it, wallow in it, experience the whole seedy past, before she could accept the notion that he'd do the same to her. Her stomach went hollow. "Start with the first time you knew your mind wasn't playing tricks on you."

"I followed him to his favorite beer joint. Sat down the block with binoculars. A patrolman rolled by, saw me scoping out the place, and rousted me. When I told them who I was and what I was doing he said to go home."

Fascinated, Raven moved closer. Shiloh opened another hutch, picked up a rabbit and cuddled it.

"I wouldn't leave. Like you, I had to know for certain. Wasn't long before some pockmarked bottle blonde staggered out and scooted into the passenger seat of our car. I left my Malibu, trotted into the parking lot, plopped down behind the wheel, and said, 'You don't belong here.' I'll never forget the look on her face. She said, 'I didn't know this was your Cutlass. He just told me to wait.' "

Raven could almost see the girl bolt and run. Shiloh's story summoned up an ugly memory. Brazen, she'd sashayed across the dance floor at *Stagecoach* and tapped Jinx's shoulder. Then in a ladylike voice asked a woman most men would be scared to meet in a dark alley if she'd still feel like giving Jinx a tit massage with a Justin boot pressed against her thorax.

But Shiloh was talking. Disclosing things she needed to hear. Tossing out a lifeline. Doing her damnedest to pull her out of the quicksand of denial.

"After we got home, I packed his bags. He was drunker'n Cooter Brown. Kenny Rogers was on the radio, singing, 'You Picked a Fine Time to Leave Me, Lucille'. First time I ever heard that song. I told him I wanted a divorce. The Mossberg was the last thing to go into the car, and that's when he picked it up by the barrel and swung it." Shiloh shook her head. "Oh, he was sorry. Said he'd give up drinkin' for good. But I'd reached my limit."

Raven didn't need to hear anymore. It should be enough. Jinx had a pattern.

"Our kid resents him. Mostly because of the first one, Bubbles. Bubbles was old when Central Park was a flower pot. She lasted the longest, but Jinx diddled a string of white trash before the marriage breathed the final death rattle. Don't ask me why, but he always went for older women."

"I won't bother you again."

With a feather touch, Shiloh brushed Raven's hand. "What are you looking for? He's mean-spirited, his dick's a divining rod looking for a wet spot, and he doesn't drink coffee. In short, he's an android."

Raven raked her fingers through a handful of limp tresses and hooked them behind her ears. Her energy level sank further with each breath of stifling air. "I used to want a ring. A three-carat diamond so clear a glass-eyed ape could see straight down to the bottom."

Shiloh's eyes widened. Raven knew the look. It said, You've got a screw loose.

Jinx's ex returned the speckled fluff to its cage. "There are easier ways to commit suicide. Faster, too. If you want to cut throats, slit his, not your own."

"I didn't expect him to marry me. I just wanted to wear it around." A gust of wind whipped up a dirt devil, carrying with it the citrusy scent of bois d'arc apples dropped from a nearby tree. "He wasn't always this way. He used to be so nice to me." Raven took a deep breath and held it. Her throat tightened.

"Listen, Sugar. Men are like banks. Would you tie your money up in one that didn't pay dividends?" Dry chuckle. "Your investment earns the lowest interest rate in town. And to top it off, you're not getting proper servicing because the sonofagun's making regular deposits to somebody else's account."

Raven felt the urge to shower. And not because of the humidity.

"What you need's a frontal lobotomy." Shiloh cast a hard glance. "I got out. No reason you can't."

Raven blinked. Pulled in another long breath. "Let me tell you a story about a remarkable man."

"Nothing you say's gonna make me change my mind about Jinx Porter. I know all about him finding those people in the nursing home a new place to live. Means nothing."

"It's not about Jinx." She leaned back against the cages, stared at a pyramid of rabbit pellets on the straw-covered floor, and found herself slipping into the Texas drawl of the country folk she'd grown up around. The same speech she'd left behind when she moved to the big city. She'd worked hard to become cosmopolitan. But this simple farm woman took her back to her roots, where a handshake deal meant more than a signature on a ten-page contract. Shiloh Wilette made her feel at home.

"There was this old lawdog. Folks called him the Coyote. Meanest son of a bitch that ever rode with the Texas Rangers. Once, there's talk how, in a jailbreak, a whole string of cons from a chain gang killed the head boss and escaped in the tar truck." Raven glanced up, feeling the gleam in her eyes. "This all happened before I was born. Might just be talk."

"Go on."

133

"The Coyote rode horseback into the rugged terrain of the Davis Mountains. Alone. He brought them all back, of course. Seven dead inmates, shot through and through with a .30-30, and that old Ranger dragging 'em behind his chestnut stallion like a stringer of dead fish. Bloodied up from the brush and the gravel road. Could have buried the whole lot in a cigar box." She kicked at a mud-dauber's nest that had fallen from an overhead beam.

"Wasn't another jailbreak that grisly until Fred Gomez Carrasco tried to bust out of Huntsville in the seventies, and ended up dead after an eleven-day seige." Raven gave Shiloh a sad smile. "Cons used to say, 'Mess with Texas law, get your ass chewed off by the Coyote.' But they said it with reverence. What's your opinion of a man capable of something like that?"

"Sounds like a hell of a wicked man. Though I reckon I don't mind that brand of justice being sprinkled around from time to time."

"Hell of a wicked man," Raven mused. "I suppose you'd have to be pretty wicked to do something like that. Suppose it'd be hard to love such a man?"

"What's your point?"

"The old fella, this Ranger, he liked to take a nip. And he was rough around the edges. I expect he ran off a wife or two in the early days." She stared off into the Wilettes' hay loft, searching a shadow for a memory. "But he had another side. When one of his wives took off, he raised their boy. And when that boy grew up, he joined law enforcement."

The cadence of crickets chirped loud in her ear. She wiped her damp brow and continued. "Some thugs who'd just pulled a gas station heist killed that son on a traffic stop. When his widow dumped a squalling laundry basket on the old tough's front porch, and walked off into the pasture to commit suicide, who do you think raised that baby? What do you think happened to that kid?"

Shiloh's eyes narrowed.

"I still smell plastic-tipped cigars and Jim Beam." Raven grazed her jaw with her fingertips. "His cheek always did give me whisker burn. Once when I was seven, he let me help him clean his Colt Peacemaker." She chuckled. "Everyone was afraid of him. Or hated him. In the end, most people thought he was deranged. To me, he was just ol' Pawpaw."

Shiloh seemed to be sizing her up. Her expression, though softer, said so. Raven fidgeted under her watchful gaze. Behind them, fans stirred the air with a soft whir. Jinx's ex linked arms and ushered her back out into the open air.

Shiloh stared into the distance. "I've got a cousin the spittin' image of Ted Bundy, before they sent a gazillion volts of electricity through him—doesn't make them the same. What you're telling me, Little Miss Raven, is you're still looking for Gramps. Well, Jinx smoked a pipe when I knew him, and he quit his love affair with Jack Daniels a long time ago. As for Gramps, he might've treated you fine but don't forget, he did louse up a couple of marriages." Shiloh grinned big. "That sounds like Jinx."

Raven smiled through tears. "Jinx has to have some good in him. You married him."

"That dream's nothing but a nightmare. You think I'd have picked him if he started out treating me rotten? He's got a good line of bull, he's not altogether unattractive, he's capable of making a living, and he's intelligent. But I'm telling you, the man's wicked. I realize the bad ones are attractive. But before you know it, you're sucked into the undertow, holding three fingers up."

Shiloh spouted high-voltage information, but the breakers in Raven's head were short-circuiting from the overload.

"I'm afraid—" Her voice dissolved to a whisper. "—I don't just love him . . . I'm *in love* with him, too."

They shared the miserable groan of kindred spirits. Shiloh grabbed her hand and pulled her back down the path. Gentle gusts lapped at Raven's soaked tendrils.

"What do I do, Shiloh? How do I get through this?"

"When somebody offers me free beer, I drink what they give me. When I buy my own, I get what I want."

Raven blinked.

Jinx's ex did some serious eye-rolling. "Do what I did. This time around, I snagged myself a dumb one." Pride bordered on preening. "Kenny knows how to open the refrigerator. He can operate the controls on the washing machine, and I never have to wonder where he's been. This time, I found a companion."

"But I want *him*. Jinx took the Coyote's place. That's the part I miss, when Jinx was kind, and fun, and listened." She didn't want to add that lately, she saw only occasional glimpses. After all, didn't the Coyote teach her the cardinal rule? How a body didn't have to tell everything they knew?

Inside the Wilettes' double-wide, Shiloh motioned Raven to a seat at the table. She poured two stems of merlot, slid one across the checkered vinyl cloth and raised her glass.

"The dinghy is leaking. It's taking on water faster than you can bail. Cut the rope. And next time you run across another Jinx—somebody who tries to charm your drawers off—remember: if he's not married, he's unattached because somebody somewhere didn't want him."

The words replayed in Raven's head.

After a dreadful silence, Shiloh asked a provocative question. "Now that you got the facts, what's your plan?"

Raven sighed. "Ride off into the sunset, I suppose."

"Sugar, if I were you, I'd be whipping that horse over and under."

Shortly after midnight, Jinx looked in on Amos in the spare bedroom. He studied the lump under the blanket with the intensity of the Warren Commission before deciding the body was, indeed, Amos's, and not plumped-up pillows left behind in a breakout. Satisfied, he retired to his room with a book. Several chapters into serial killer profiling, he snapped it closed and stared at the phone.

She hadn't called.

He could phone her.

Why should he? She was the one walked out.

By one o'clock, the tension left his jaw and he dozed off.

Raven held a deck of playing cards.

Did he want a hit?

No thanks, I'll hold.

She smiled—and he folded on four aces.

She reappeared in the white sands of Hawaii, frolicking in the surf with NT GLTY. He called out her name, but she didn't hear him.

Or maybe she did.

Jinx jolted awake, certain it was time to leave for work; the neon blue numbers on the clock pulsed two-thirty.

He reached for the phone, then hesitated.

No way. She'd think she'd broken him.

Bullshit. Once she recognized his voice, he'd hear more wailing than the Wall of Jerusalem.

He dialed.

Lofty anticipation took a nose-dive.

Several miles away, inside a jewel-box bungalow tucked into a residential area of million-dollar estates, Raven's phone went unanswered.

Chapter Sixteen

Tuesday morning a slow, rhythmic rain almost made Jinx late getting Amos to school. By the time he dragged into the office, he was treated to the invigorating aroma of fresh coffee—not that he'd drink it, but he did enjoy the smell—a box of warm donuts, and Georgia engaging Mickey in an animated conversation.

"Of course there's a Devil. I was raised on it." Georgia's plastic manger scene was still in place three months after Christmas, and she repositioned the wise men and a couple of crippled camels around the Baby Jesus. "If there's one thing I'm convinced of, there's a Devil."

Mickey taunted the secretary with logic. "Ever seen him? No? Then how do you know there's a Devil?"

She snatched up the Christ child and brandished it like a Saturday Night Special. "Because if there wasn't, my income taxes would look a heck of a lot different."

"What about angels?"

"Certainly there's angels. And Heaven. And Hell. And when the saints go marching in, I'll be sitting on Jesus's knee."

Dell lifted his lids to stare at her from across the room, then stuffed a donut in his mouth. Jinx imagined he and his men shared a simultaneous thought: that if Jesus had a knee, it would have to be pretty damned big to hold Georgia.

Jinx picked up a napkin and dusted the sugar from his chin. "What if there's no Devil?"

Georgia scowled. "There has to be. Otherwise, I've been good for nothing."

"Only simpleminded people, hillbillies, and Gladiola Brooks believe in the Devil."

"Are you calling me simpleminded?"

"There's no Devil," Jinx said. "Like there was no ark."

Georgia sucked air. "Of course there was an ark, or we wouldn't be here."

"Do you really think they got two elephants, two giraffes, two hippos, two rhinos—"

"I certainly do."

"—on a little boat? I guess there aren't any unicorns because the rabbits got to whooping it up, and knocked them overboard."

Georgia lifted her chin in defiance. She swiveled her chair around and inventoried her stash of saints. Gil and Mickey shrugged. Dell rolled his eyes and went back to the crossword puzzle.

After Georgia re-diapered the Baby Jesus, she whipped around and gave them the third degree. "I suppose you think when you're dead, you're dead?"

Jinx closed his eyes. Wished he'd never gotten into the whole life-death conversation, especially when he was in sudden death with Rudy Castro. After all, Castro might be flitting around the Southside, buttering up homeowners in exchange for a sign staked out in the yard. Or nuzzling up to the defense bar's deep pockets. Here he sat, trying to reason with screwballs.

Georgia locked him in her stare. "Well, Jinx?"

"Dead is dead."

Horror flashed in her eyes. She gripped the St. Christopher medal around her neck and hung on.

"And when I'm dead," Jinx continued, "I think I'll have my funeral in Dallas."

"Dallas?" Everyone, in quadraphonic stereo.

The deputies stared in disbelief. Revulsion registered on their faces, as if he'd said he wanted to be buried in a pair of fishnet pantyhose with a feather boa around his neck and a nose ring.

Jinx nodded. "Preferably somewhere off the North Central Expressway and 635. Mourners can play inchworm getting there."

Besides, he thought, if anyone bothered to show up, it would be to make sure he was really dead. Might as well devise a way to make the experience as unpleasant as possible.

Georgia pressed the religious medal to her lips and let it drop. Her hand flittered to her forehead; she made the sign of the cross.

Mickey's mouth split into an evil grin. "Get the barebones package. If it's summer, pay for the service in the un-air-conditioned chapel. If it's winter, have the funeral director put it in your contract to make people stand outside. What do you want on your tombstone?"

"You do understand I'm not planning to go anytime soon."

"Yeah, but when you do go, how do you want the epitaph to read?"

Jinx thought a few seconds. "Too old to cut the mustard, but he could still lick the jar."

Mickey laughed.

Georgia pressed her lips together until they turned blue.

Dell blinked. In another rare moment, he spoke. "I decided not to attend funerals. I drew a moratorium on them."

"No funerals?" Georgia gripped the necklace again and tightened the chain into a tourniquet. "Not even mine?"

"If you don't come to mine, I'm not going to yours. Fair's fair."

The cowbell clanged; silence fell over the room.

Dempsey push-broomed his way through the door. "Mornin' Mistah Portah. How're them hemorrhoids today?"

"Itching."

Dempsey grimaced. "Did I say I'm gonna get mine operated on?"

"No kidding?" Poor bastard. "Where're you having it done?"

"In my rectum."

Georgia turned a peculiar shade of scarlet and hoisted her bulk from the chair. "I'm going after the mail."

Jinx watched her storm out the door, then pulled up a chair and fanned out a handful of mug shots from the Governor's Most Watched list. The way he had it figured, any con bad enough to have the Governor on his ass made a body wonder why the parole board ever set the sorry hump free in the first place.

"What do you say we go beef up our stats?" He jutted his chin at Gil. "Pick a card, any card."

The chief deputy ambled over, nattily dressed in a tweed sportcoat. With a lupine grin, Gil made a blind selection, then studied the sinister eyes staring back at him.

"What kind of uniform do you want me in?" Gil wasn't talking about suiting up in the ugly black uniforms the other precinct constables made their deputies wear—Jinx's guys wore plainclothes. But Gil's brother owned a dry cleaners, and supplied him with undercover costumes. "I got a new one. A UPS uniform. A dude left it at my brother's shop."

Jinx narrowed his eyes.

"It's true. They don't pick their clothes up in thirty days, they forfeit."

His lips thinned into a grimace.

142

"No, really," Gil said with conviction. "It's on the ticket, fine print, same as a contract. We could put the warrant in a cardboard box and deliver it to the door."

"In the projects? You'd get mugged with a package."

"I could do a TV repairman."

"May not own a set. What about a plumber?" Gil frowned but Jinx advanced his theory. "When did you ever know anybody living in the projects didn't need a plumber?"

Forty-five minutes later, Gil returned in a dingy gray jumpsuit, carrying a plunger. An oval nametag stitched over the pocket had "Carl" embroidered in red thread.

Jinx said, "Where'd that come from?"

"Maybe we don't want to discuss that. Besides, I'll have it back before they show up to claim it."

Dempsey picked up his broom and shuffled to the exit.

Jinx called him back. "What about that bathroom?"

"Bathroom, Mistah Portah?" Fleshy lips split into a wide grin. "Aw, don't worry about me, I already been."

At the projects, Jinx and Gilbert parked one building over from the target apartment, and slipped around from the back. The red brick structure showed advanced signs of decay. Jinx sidestepped the peephole, flattened his back against crumbling mortar and pounded the door frame.

Knock-knock.

Sounds of shuffling inside, then a gruff reply. "Who is it?"

"Otis Wells?"

"Who wants to know?"

"Plumber." Gil held up the plunger like the Statue of Liberty's torch.

A chain slid along its track and three deadbolts snicked open.

Jinx and Gil exploded through the cavernous downstairs of an empty dwelling. The smell of urine and vomit filled the room. Cockroaches big enough to install bucket seats in and drive around skittered across the floors. They latched onto scrawny arms and practiced their Olympic speed-cuffing technique.

Gotcha.

On the drive over to Ann-Jeanette Rice's, Raven took a detour.

A bulbous gray car jumped the median in a mid-block U-turn and roared up behind her. Grillwork glinted in the rearview mirror like the teeth of a great chrome shark. She couldn't make out the driver's features—the tinted windows obscured her view—but she recognized the WWII vintage Packard. Her stomach clenched. The Balogh tribe was still running amok.

She wrestled the low-rider's steering wheel—a chain welded into a circumference the size of a luncheon plate—and forced it into the mall parking lot. Without warning, the tail car shot past. She parked the low-rider, hurried in-side, and disappeared into the crowd.

Well, hell, didn't she have a birthday coming up? She could kill some time, grab a bite to eat, and hide out until the gypsy lost interest. And if she was still with Jinx, she'd already have her gift picked out, and she'd say what she always said when he got around to asking what she wanted.

Jewelry.

Come Hell or high water, she'd get that ring. And if she and Jinx called it quits, she could always turn it into a pen-dant or melt it into scrap.

While she was window-shopping outside the jeweler's, the smell of warm chocolate wafted over and momentarily distracted her from an enchanting princess-cut solitaire. Wistful thoughts filled her head. Her eyes did a double take.

There he was.

A short man, reflected in the glass, seemed to be sizing her up. She whipped around for a better look, but he disappeared into a group of passersby.

In the food court, she found a bistro table and sank her teeth into a steaming gyro sandwich. She'd almost forgotten the odd little man in the dark suit until he reappeared in a swarm of people migrating in for lunch.

Their eyes met.

He spun off with whirlwind speed, as invisible as a gusty breeze through a wheat field.

She told herself to settle down. Lots of people were short. Didn't make them sinister or nefarious. Blame it on this whole Jinx thing. Stir in a few hormones and—voilà— paranoid cop syndrome.

She hogged down bits of lamb until she satisfied her hunger. In less than a half hour, she'd head for Ann-Jeanette Rice's house. Get the wispy lady to give her the rundown on Marina's daddy. With any luck, Raven would track down that no-account Ray Sparks with the vengeance of a Colombian cocaine cartel.

She tossed the last of her meal onto a plastic tray, relinquished her seat to a teenage couple with their hair sheared into matching pink mohawks, and emptied the scraps into the nearest wastecan. She hadn't even made it out of the public dining area when an unexpected dread oozed from her pores like sweat on a hot Cowtown day.

Someone was shadowing her.

She could almost feel the hot breath on her neck.

Raven whirled around, heart drumming. The same fellow she'd seen reflected in the window advanced. Her breath went shallow. Panic surged through her limbs.

Balogh's gypsy curse ricocheted in her head.

I curse my dead mother and my dead father if I don't succeed.

The man bulldozed his way through the crowd. Onyx eyes grew wide. A paper napkin tucked into his shirt collar flapped at the neck.

Fear jolted her body. Every hair stood on end.

Fight or flight.

Her legs refused to budge. With all her might, she balled up a fist and reared back.

Him or her.

Self-defense all the way.

She opened her mouth and let out a scream to peel back a hundred eyelids.

The staggering commotion drowned out the crunch of cartilage from the man's bloody snout. He lost his footing and flipped like a burger. With a nasty *splat,* the man crashed into an industrial wastecan. Cheese-soaked broccoli trees and chili-dog remnants blitzed out of the trash and slid across the floor in a ten-foot crescent. His head hit the tile with a split-melon *thump.* A couple of ketchup-drenched fries landed on the assassin's forehead, and a black olive covered one fluttering eyelid. Limpid, fathomless eyes rolled back in their sockets. Bystanders' mouths gaped open.

A man with a similar Mediterranean complexion and diminutive build bounded over the counter of a fast-food station. Wringing his hands dry against a chef's apron, he flew to the hit man's side and loosened his tie.

Curiosity junkies rushed over while aristocrats rubber-necked from the safety of boutiques. Whispers turned to mumbles, then rumblings.

Raven flexed her throbbing hand. A dark hair protruded from the insignia ring she wore on her pinkie.

The fry cook stared up at her through glossy black curls. "What have you done? You may have killed him."

She heard a scream in the crowd behind her. Footfalls echoed in the distance. Raven stared at the man's chest for signs of movement. His face had turned an eerie gray.

"It is you who caused this tragedy. You must give him CPR," the fry cook said. "Quickly, or he will surely die."

"Do I look like Florence Nightingale? This man's a contract killer."

More shrieks, and the thunder of stampeding feet.

"He is my cousin. You must save him."

"He was going to cancel my ticket." Gawkers recoiled. Her eyes sought comfort from those around her. "You don't understand. This guy's a hit man."

"He works at the mall. Store detective."

Uh-oh.

"He's an employee?"

Lawsuit city.

Raven's eyelids fluttered in astonishment. Her hand ached with a vengeance. This time, when she looked at the insignia ring, she noticed what appeared to be a piece of ground meat wedged into the "R"'s inner curve.

She stared in disbelief. "You're kidding."

"It is true. You must give him CPR before he dies. He may already be dead." Haunting black marbles, similar to those rolling around in the little dwarf's head, bored into her soul.

She dropped to her knees. Shucked off her shoulder bag

and hoped that was ketchup on his lip, not blood. She shuddered under the weight of a bewildered crowd.

"Ohmygod, ohmygodohmygod. I K-O'd an innocent man. I'm so sorry. So very, very sorry." She ripped the tie from her victim's neck, opened the top two buttons on his shirt, and leaned down to listen for the miracle of breath.

Nothing.

"Somebody call nine one one," she cried.

Nobody moved.

Remorseful and determined, she tore open the rest of his shirt buttons, and pressed her head to the hairless, clammy chest, checking for a heartbeat.

Strong.

Thank God. Poor wimpy guy, and she'd cold-cocked him. What in God's name was the matter with her? Damned Jinx and his two-bit election—the guy was making her batshit crazy.

She flicked away the fries, tilted the man's head back and pinched his nose shut with her fingers. The olive rolled off and his mouth gaped open. Staring into a cavern dotted with neglected teeth, Raven felt her gorge rise. Repulsed, she pulled away.

The short-order cook urged her on. "Miss, you must."

You barf, you die.

She bent over, close enough to whiff the putrid mixture of rotten food dotting the little suit. In a flash, the dwarf bolted upright. Stumpy fingers twined around her neck. He delivered a message reeking in halitosis.

"Balogh."

Raven let out a blood-clotting shriek.

The crowd ran for cover, leaving her to whip the shit out of him all by herself. The cook jumped into the fray, all five feet of him, and pummeled her from behind. A fist crashed against her skull and the knot started to throb.

They screamed in stereo. "I curse my dead mother and dead father if I don't succeed."

She straddled the suited dwarf, grabbed hold of the cousin's collar and delivered a left hook. Trampling boots rounded the corner. The assassins spoke in tongues. The only word she understood tumbled out as a warning.

"Cops."

A couple of security guards pried her off the troll. The cook disappeared into the reassembled crowd. Before she could explain, the dwarf rolled over, hoisted himself up, and disappeared into the swarm.

"You're under arrest, Lady."

She sucked in a fresh intake of air. The taller of the officers stood over six feet, making her fairly sure his surname wasn't Balogh.

"Me? Are you nuts?" She got up on shaky legs. "Those guys tried to kill me."

The rent-a-cop she could look at eyeball-to-eyeball said, "Who tried to kill you? That little bitty guy over there?"

The exit banged open and a swatch of dark cloth disappeared.

She stood there a good half hour, exchanging names, swapping stories and talking herself out of jail. Worse, the manager of the hot dog stand never heard of the fry cook. Not to mention when she went for her badge case to produce ID, she realized the little pickpocket snatched her wallet.

Which contained her driver's license.

The Balogh tribe had her home address.

Jinx was in the office file room running a teletype and arguing with the chief of police when three phone lines lit up simultaneously. Out of the corner of his eye, he saw Dell and Mickey each grab one; the other fell to Georgia.

In a sugary drawl, she said, "Good afternoon, Constable Porter's office." Short pause. "He's not available, Amos."

Jinx's ears pricked up. The chief put him on hold, so he dragged the telephone closer to the door. Classical music blared in his ear. Out in the foyer, Georgia was stirred up.

"Well, I never. Don't call me a liar, you little scamp. Hold."

Jinx set his jaw. Georgia knew not to interrupt him, especially when he had to get to the bottom of this auto-pedestrian accident involving the only bus with a REELECT CONSTABLE JINX PORTER sign riveted to the side of it. He agreed the cops had the right to seize the bus since the driver mowed over a pedestrian. The disagreement hatched when the crime scene detective refused to release the sign so the company could mount it on another bus. The way Jinx had it figured, unless there were chunks of flesh hanging off it, the police should return it.

Georgia glanced around wistfully. "I often remind myself he's just a lonely little boy." She stabbed the hold button and launched Amos into another dimension. "But then, somebody named Glenny-Something called up yammering awhile ago. Seems Amos timed his spit to drop over the balcony with deadly accuracy."

Dell spoke. "Ritalin."

"He's already on it, Honey. Lithium, too. Lord only knows how Ivy talks those quacks on her HMO plan into prescribing that stuff."

Glassy-eyed, Mickey stared at the winking red dot. "What's he want?"

"To talk to Jinx." She furrowed her brow. "Wonder why he'd be interested in turpentine?"

"Did he say that?"

Jinx stuck his head out the door. "What's going on?"

Dell and Mickey exchanged electrically charged glances. They sat up in their chairs and grew steel rods for spines.

"You don't reckon . . . ?" Mickey asked.

In the same breath, Dell made another rare but ominous contribution. "Jinx loves that cat."

The chief came back on the line.

Georgia cried out. "Oh Good Lord, surely you're not fixing to—" Her jaw went slack and her eyes bulged.

In a stage whisper, Jinx covered the mouthpiece and said, "What is it?"

Across the room, Dell gave his head the kind of shake generally associated with freshly bathed dogs. "Turpentine, my ass."

"Not *your* ass. The cat's ass." Mickey.

They gave Georgia pointed looks.

She said, "Amos, Jinx cannot be disturbed. What's the problem? Maybe I can help." Shrugging, she looked to Dell and Mickey for support. Mickey played charades, noosing his own neck. Dell slit his carotid artery with a finger.

"No, Honey, I don't have any idea where Jinx keeps his razor."

Jinx hung up on the chief. He stepped into the foyer and braced his hands across his chest.

"Hold." Georgia pressed the button. "Isn't that boy just eleven? He's not old enough to shave."

The four swapped quizzical looks.

Then Mickey made a tenuous suggestion. "You don't suppose—"

"He's gonna shave the cat." Dell, finishing the thought.

Jinx sprinted across the room to Gilbert's desk.

Georgia retrieved the connection. "Amos, don't hang up."

By the time Jinx reached the phone, his secretary turned a new shade of white.

Click.

The buzz of a dead connection hummed in his ear.

"What did he say?" Jinx shouted.

Georgia dropped the receiver. She ransacked her purse, pulled out a prescription bottle, and struggled to wrangle the top off. "He said he called to ask if you thought the cat would still land on its paws if he dropped it over the balcony with its feet duct-taped together."

Raven spent the remainder of the afternoon guesstimating the number of inches of butt-crack peeking over the locksmith's saggy jeans. By the time he finished changing out each deadbolt for a higher quality lock, only a few hours of sunlight remained. After paying the man for his work, she headed across town for Ann-Jeanette Rice's house, secure in the feeling a crash of rhinos couldn't penetrate that door.

Marina's mother cooperated completely. She provided a sketchy background of Ray Sparks, but made up for it by supplying current photos of her daughter.

On the way back to her house, Raven's conscience nagged her. She should call her lawyer friend, Ben Jennings. Should tell him to invite someone else to the candidate's debate. But Jinx would be there, and it wouldn't hurt him to see her accessorizing the arm of the most gorgeous man in Fort Worth. Finally, she talked herself out of scuttling the evening.

The way she saw it, the chance of Jinx discovering Ben's true sexual preference carried about the same odds as a meteor dropping on her ex-mother-in-law.

Chapter Seventeen

Even Jinx knew he'd become borderline maniacal when he roared up to Harry Fine's Auto Mall. Amos wasn't at school. He wasn't at the apartment, either. And the sight of Skeeter, glued to his seat with his snout in a comic book and a meaty hand darting inside an open bag of potato chips, invoked homicidal thoughts.

He ground the gearshift into park, alighted from the patrol car and took the steps in twos. The automatic glass doors slid back, and Jinx flung himself through the opening.

Used car salesmen in partitioned cubicles appraised him with bored glances, dividing their attention between the sports page and wary customers. They didn't seem to care that he'd skidded to a stop on the rubber welcome mat, nor were they bothered by the jerky rhythm of the door mechanism, hung somewhere in the purgatory between open and closed.

Skeeter glanced up. With his mouth rounding into an "O" and a half-chewed glob of chips resting on his tongue, he dropped his copy of *Spider-Man* and motioned Jinx inside.

Jinx leaned across the desk. Shouted, "Where's the C&E?"

"I toldja I'd have it done by four o'clock, Pod'na."

Heat raged up Jinx's cheeks. He caught sight of his reflection in the floor-to-ceiling plate glass, and it pained him to see his sparse comb-over sticking up like the crest on a cockatiel.

He flattened his hair. Stared out the window. Fleetingly wondered if Skeeter would leave much of an outline once he curled his fingers into the man's shirt collar and pitched him through it.

"IT'S THREE-FIFTY-EIGHT, LAME BRAIN."

"I'm not deaf, Pod'na. You don't have to yell. People 'round here'll be thinking I'm hanging out with dements."

Jinx narrowed his eyes into slits. "How's your girlfriend?"

"Pulled a knife on me." Skeeter looked down at the knit shirt stretched to capacity and slashed a finger across his belly for effect.

The man was a kook.

"Have you always taken an interest in abnormal psychology, or is this a relatively new phenomenon? It's hard to admit, but you've gotten even more screwed up since you started porking Norma Bates."

Skeeter wrinkled his brow. "She ain't abnormal. Abnormal is when you do something that ain't normal. What she does is normal for her." A silly grin angled up one side of his fat face.

Jinx stuck the thumb of his gun hand into his beltloop. Pressure built in his head. He didn't trust himself. "You're the most fucked up person I know."

"Least I got a girlfriend."

"What?"

"Yours was here, checking out cars with some fella."

NT GLTY.

"Guy 'bout a foot shorter than a redwood? Custom-made suit? Driving a Jaguar?"

Skeeter frowned. "No. Cowboy linebacker type in a pickup. With blond hair and a pissed-off look like I just ate the last spare rib."

Jinx heaved a sigh of relief. He steered the conversation back on collision course.

"I need advertising. The Jinx Porter bus is out of commission. As gatekeeper of the funds, would you care to know why?"

Skeeter blinked.

Jinx told the sad, sorry story. "I've been on the phone all afternoon with the police chief, and they're holding the entire bus as evidence. Fucker's quarantined until the lab techs get through."

Skeeter brightened. "Think of all the free advertisement you'll get when the jury sees the photos."

"That'll take years, Numbskull. Did it ever occur to you I could use some money for a TV spot?"

That extinguished the sparkle in Skeeter's eyes. "Well, Pod'na, I'm not the one toldja to spend money on a bus."

"No, that's true. I have to admit you haven't contributed a single, cotton-pickin' idea."

"If you want somebody else to be your treasurer, Pod'na—"

"I don't have enough money to get eight hundred signs reprinted with a different treasurer's name." The muscles in his jaw stretched tight enough to play a tune on. "You don't get the C&Es ready on time, you don't raise money, you don't get your asshole buddies at the Fort Worth Police Department to endorse me through the Police Association, you don't even ask your pals to hammer a few yard signs in their flower beds."

Skeeter scratched his head. "I got a friend down at Fort Hood in Killeen that's got access to an Army tank. Maybe he could just pull a Dukakis and drive through the Northside, maybe ask 'em, Didja want a yard sign? And if they say No thanks, just eke the turret around, point it at the house like an anteater snout. Sombitches'll probably ask for two."

Jinx made a self-diagnosis.

Sleep deprivation.

It finally hit him he'd been running on fumes the instant he decided Skeeter had come up with an idea he could use.

The whole mystique surrounding the great BMW part search filled Raven with déjà vu. In trying to avoid Aardvark Al's, she ended up phoning the same fifty salvage yards from the sanctuary of Sonny's loaner. When it came down to the nut-cutting, she and Ali were unavoidably stuck to each other like corroded battery cables.

Prepared to do some blue ribbon crow-eating, she dialed the cell phone, then held her breath in anticipation.

" 'Mornin', Al's Four-A Aardvark."

An American. And a redneck at that.

"I need some parts." Her eyes flickered to the rearview mirror. Good. No strange cars trying to climb up her tail-pipe. By the time she glanced back at the stretch of road, she had to jerk the low-rider's steering wheel to keep from clipping a motorcycle cop on a traffic stop. Fuzzy dice rocked against each other, knocking a pine scented deodorizer cockeyed. She sucked in a breath, hoped the motor-jock didn't come after her on a loud muffler violation, and got down to business.

"Who am I talking to?" she asked.

"Chuck. Who's this?"

"Madonna. Look here, Chuck, I'm in the market for some BMW parts. For an eighty-three 318i. I need a windshield, a hood, both front fenders, a radiator, rack and pinion, engine and transmission. I have money."

Computer keys clicked in the background. He let out a slow breath and delivered the news.

"Got 'em."

"Really?" An orgasmic tingle exploded through her. She started to laugh uncontrollably and tried to think of something sad.

"Yep."

"All of them?"

"Yep. If you'da asked for a trunk and a rear windshield, I'd hafta to tell you we're fresh-out."

Thank God.

"It'll cost a pretty penny," he warned.

"Doesn't matter." She pinched the bridge of her nose to keep tears of joy from tracking both cheeks. "You deliver?"

Please, please, please. Say yes.

"You bet your boots."

She adored him. Not enough to donate a kidney, but the guy had something nobody else in a hundred mile radius had, and she was prepared to let him fill in the zeros on the check.

"Take the parts to Sonny's Auto Hospital on Seventh."

"Know it well." More clicking on the keyboard.

"I'll leave a check with Sonny."

"Lemme get your name."

"R-A-V-E-N."

"Thought you said you was Madonna." The hayseed baritone oozed disappointment.

"Just kidding. Although, prior to this unfortunate accident, people often confused us."

"Uh-oh." Paper crackled on his end of the line.

"Uh-oh what?"

"Uh-oh-you're-the-gal-caused-all-that-trouble-last-week."

Her intestines twisted into slipknots. Silence stretched between them.

"It's you, ain't it?"

She decided from the smacking he must be chewing

gum. "I don't know what you're talking about."

"Yes, you do. You're her."

"What if I am? I can still pay. Just deliver the parts and I won't ever come near the shop again."

Long pause.

"Ali left a message. He said if you ever needed anything, we're out. He said tell you Allah wills it."

Georgia answered the phone with the usual molasses, the way she always did just before she tried to pawn some sap off on him, but the extra injection of syrup was enough to put a diabetic into a coma.

"Yes, Honey, he's sitting right here. That's right, I'm looking at him."

Jinx didn't care for her expression. Wickedly amused.

She pulled the receiver from her ear and slipped a hand over the mouthpiece. "You want it in your office?"

He reared back in Mickey's chair and took it right there. *Up the wazoo.*

Like a zip down the Autobahn, Kamille's irritating ramblings on Mimzy's induction into the Junior League went in one ear and out the other. He placed the phone on the desk, and let her pipe her message into thin air—to be intercepted by alien life forms, FBI agents with directional mikes, or anybody within earshot who might give a rat. After thirty or so seconds, he picked up the receiver and took a pulse.

Still about Mimzy. Down it went.

He flipped through a stack of Blue Warrants, arrest papers ordering any peace officer to recapture paroled convicts, and entered several more bad-asses into the computer. The buzz on the other end of the line fell silent. He snatched up the phone.

"How's Dad?"

"I just told you. He's the one who asked me to call."

"Why're you doing his dirty work?"

"You know how busy your father is."

Busy supporting Mimzy. Jinx snorted. Not too many forty-five-year-old women were still on parental welfare. Poor old man, pushing eighty, and still kept an office.

"I was about to tell you, Mimzy picked out a new car. Pink. Can you believe? Your daddy tried to tell her the re-sale value's practically nil."

Jinx felt the blue-plate special he had for lunch reversing its direction. "How much will that set y'all back?"

"Stop being so disgruntled," Kamille snapped. "You should show compassion for Mimzy. After all. . . ."

Jinx dropped the phone atop the Kathmandu of paperwork peaking on Mickey's desk. He had no interest in hearing the story again. About how Mimzy's husband went to the drugstore to buy the giant-sized bottle of Pepto Bismol and never came back. Unlike the rest of the relatives, Jinx saw no point in advancing the kidnapping theory when the airport police found his roadster at the Delta terminal. Especially when the secretary turned up missing the same day. A month after Mimzy hired Evan Rainey to pick Romeo's bones clean, she received a card postmarked "Dublin" written in hasty script: *The weather is here. Wish you were nice.*

Besides, he could testify under oath, Mimzy wasn't exactly a sheer delight to live with. He'd been trying to get rid of her from day one, when his parents returned home from the hospital with a sister, instead of the collie he wanted.

Across the room, Georgia fiddled with a cactus while Rome burned. She glanced over and sniggered.

He picked up the receiver and covered the mouthpiece

with his hand. "What're you looking at? I know you think it's a hoot, but you don't know these people."

"I think your family's nice."

"My sister uses the word dysfunctional to describe us. I like to think we're just plain fucked up. But don't feel bad. My parents don't know it, and my sister thinks it's trendy."

Georgia cocked her head, pensive. Like a woman about to get too big for her britches.

"They seem well-adjusted, Honey. Maybe it's you. While you've got your mother on the phone, why don't you see if you're adopted?"

"And while you're leaving for the day, why don't you pick up a copy of the classifieds and glance over the Help Wanted section?"

"And maybe stumble onto an employer who'd appreciate me? You're pulling my leg. I wouldn't know how to act. But in this dump—" Her hand sliced the air. "—I know exactly what to do."

He put the phone to his ear. Kamille seemed to be winding down.

". . . your daddy thought he might work in some tax write-offs so we were wondering if you needed money for your campaign."

Jinx's heart jump-started itself. "How much we talking about?"

"It's not polite to ask people about their finances, Jinx. Anyhow, it's a gift so be grateful. But since we do for Mimzy, maybe somewhere between five and ten."

Five to ten thousand.

Not as much as Mimzy's new car, but cash just the same. He nestled his haunches deeper into the rubber donut.

"We'll put a check in the mail. Unless you'd care to stop

160

by. You never visit anymore." Her voice trailed.

"Post office'll work fine."

He hung up, elated, then telephoned the ad man to let him know he'd drop by later to pay for the bus bench signs. That meant the immediate worry was whether Raven would show up for the Democratic Party's candidate debate at the Medical Center in a couple of hours, and help put Rudy Castro on the hotseat.

Raven stalked into Al's Aardvark with the confidence of Napoleon standing at the peak of a mist-covered valley. A dusty-haired fellow in his late thirties wearing a black T-shirt and a red Peterbilt ballcap glanced up from the computer.

"Didja need some help?"

She knew who she was dealing with as soon as he spoke in fluent Elizabethan tongue. "Hi, Chuck. Where's Ali?"

"Out back." He cocked his head and frowned, then shoved a finger under the gimme-cap for a quick scratch. "Did we sleep together?"

"Not yet. Start pulling the parts for an '83 BMW 318i. I need a hood, both front fenders, an engine—"

"Uh-oh."

She tried to intimidate him with her cool stare.

"Can't do it." Chuck squirmed on the stool. "Ali's orders."

"Get him."

The stringbean assistant disappeared into the back. Ali could be heard speaking in tongues, long before his coal black eyes bored through the glass portal of the swinging door.

"I'm here to buy those parts."

"We are—how do you say?—fresh out."

"I have cash." She parted her wallet and gave him a peek.

Ptui. A spit-hocker hit the floor.

"I do not want your money. You are sent from Satan to test me, yes?"

She opened her palms in the universal gesture of harmlessness. "Look, Buddy, I just want my parts."

"You do not have parts. I have parts."

"Sell them to me."

"I shall see them in the dumpster first."

"Why?"

"Allah wills it."

Raven shook her head, confident in the American way. "You're a corporation. You have to sell to me. Otherwise, it's discrimination. You can end up in court."

The news took the raghead aback. He turned to Chuck.

"That is so?"

Chuck gave him a one-shoulder shrug.

"I might even end up owning this place."

"Let me see." The foreigner touched a thought-provoking digit to his temple. "You need radiator?"

Raven sighed in relief. "Yes."

"Anything else?"

"An engine. Transmission, rack and pinion, two front fenders, a front windshield, and a hood. That about covers it."

Ali issued the edict. "Pull the parts."

"How long'll it take?"

"Fifteen, perhaps twenty minutes."

Ali trailed Chuck out the exit, leaving her to blow the dust off a five-year-old magazine in the waiting area. Fifteen minutes later, a ghoulish reenactment of the wreck of the Edmund Fitzgerald brought her to her feet.

Raven rushed to the window. Next to the dumpster, a BMW fender teetered precariously over one edge. Chuck dusted off his hands and made way for a pit crew of Mexicans, line-dancing to the Macarena, each lugging a piece of BMW to feed the huge metal mouth. One by one, Beemer guts sailed over the gaping lip. She watched, spellbound, as the only 318i parts in the Metroplex disappeared from sight. She didn't even notice Ali slip up behind her until she felt his curry-breath searing her neck.

"I am sorry to report I am mistaken. We do not have parts for your car."

She gasped. "You just shitcanned a fortune. What's wrong with you?"

"Allah does not fear discrimination. Allah wills it."

Allah again. She wondered what kind of bartering she'd have to do to get Allah to switch sides. And then, the solution hit her.

Gil.

After all, didn't Allah help those who helped themselves?

Chapter Eighteen

Jinx studied Amos with misgivings. He hated putting poten-
tially explosive situations on autopilot. Might as well give
the incorrigible a rifle with a scope as leave him unattended,
even for a few hours. Heaven only knew what mischief that
kid could get into. But it was six o'clock, and if he missed
this opportunity to speak at the Medical Center, the voters
wouldn't see the cavernous differences between himself and
Castro.

And Castro would take pot-shots.

"Don't be touching anything while I'm gone."

Amos smiled, but the cold depths of his thick-lashed
eyes could freeze salt water.

"And keep your mitts off the computer. I don't want you
within a ten-foot radius of it. Don't even look at it."

Amos shifted his gaze, lazily, to the PC.

"I mean it." He could almost feel fireballs shooting out
as he worked up his most fearsome glare. "You so much as
breathe on the sonofabitch, I'll duct-tape your ankles together and toss your ass over the balcony, see if you land on
your feet."

Flat affect.

Jinx stalked over, unplugged the monitor cable and
stuffed it into his pocket. He tightened his jaw, smug in his
victory.

"And don't answer my phone." He gave Ivy's delinquent
a visual once-over. Frayed shoestrings drooped over the
sides of worn sneakers. The faded T-shirt seemed to make
reference to a *Twelve Foot Jesus,* but he couldn't be sure

with the kid's freckled arms folded across his chest. "Don't light the stove. And don't be ordering any movies from the cable channel."

Amos's lips thinned. Beady eyes narrowed.

"And don't call out for pizza unless you've got money to pay for it." Jinx's stomach tightened. A dreadful feeling he'd omitted something nagged him. "Don't be using my stuff."

He visualized Amos, lathered in shaving cream, slitting his big fat jugular with the razor.

Amos stared through obsidian eyes. "Does that about cover it? Reckon it'd be all right to get a drink while you're gone?"

"Feel free. This ain't Alcatraz." Jinx stepped out onto the balcony. "And don't open the door for anybody. So, 'X' what I said earlier about pizza. You cannot order take-out, even if you pay for it. Matter of fact, don't fuck with my phone at all."

The door snapped shut behind him. He bolted the lock, dropped his keys in his pants pocket, took a step and froze. His service revolver fit snug against his side. The sense of foreboding that snaked through his entrails during the laundry list of Do Nots constricted his chest and revealed itself. He'd left a .38 snub-nose out on the dresser.

He tapped on the door, intending to set things straight.

Inside, the television clicked on and the volume zoomed up.

He pressed the doorbell. *Ka-lunk.*

The recliner banged against the wall.

He hammered the door with his fist.

Decibels soared. Amos channel-surfed through snippets of commercials before eventually settling on a cop show Jinx recognized from its drumming intro. Through the door, Amos hummed along with enthusiasm.

Jinx dug for the keys. Fumbled with the deadbolt. Flung the door open hard enough to force the knob through the sheetrock. Amos, cradled in the recliner, clutching the remote, flipped through the TV schedule.

Jinx blew a fuse. "Didn't you hear me knocking?"

"Yep." The little thug studied the text with interest.

"Why didn't you let me in?"

"You said don't open the door."

"I meant for anybody but me."

"That's not what you said."

Jinx's blood boiled. The uninvited joker siphoned out the energy stored up for the forum. He hoped Raven would show. That she'd be a sweetheart and put some heat on Castro. God knew he didn't have enough spark to start a Santa Ana forest fire on a July noon.

He remembered why he came back inside, and stormed into the bedroom to stuff the stainless steel .38 backup down his boot. A rush of unsavory thoughts tumbled out. "When I said you could get a drink, I meant water. Or soda pop. No alcohol. And leave my cat alone. Are you listening?"

"Yep."

"Have I left anything out?" Their gazes locked in a contest of wills. "Don't leave the apartment for any reason."

"What if it catches fire?"

"You can leave if you didn't set it. Which reminds me. Don't be striking matches. And don't put anything metal in the microwave. I knew a girl who stuck a hand inside, and the beams arced into her wristwatch. That arm's still cooking like a pot roast."

"Aren't you supposed to be somewhere?" Amos looked away, as if bored. He clicked up the volume and riveted unblinking eyes on his program.

Jinx checked the ancient Timex, a prized possession inherited from his grandfather. An inner voice told him not to go. He thought of Glen Lee Spence downstairs. Of the paroled wife-killer in 208. And the new guy across the patio. The greasy haired Mafioso-looking hump that wore silk suits and tooled around in a dark-tinted Lincoln Town Car; a creep he suspected the Marshal's Office hid out under the witness protection program. And how could he forget Loose-Wheel Lucille, the hopeless alcoholic prostituting out of the corner apartment?

Time ticking, Jinx reassured himself. With Amos locked inside, they'd all be safe.

Rain fell harder than a cow peeing on a flat rock. A cattle trailer bound for the stockyards jacknifed on the West Freeway near the Downtown off-ramp, filling the streets with steers and the air with body. According to the news leadoff, cattle ran amok down Commerce Street. By the end of the broadcast, word circulated around the Medical Center how a couple of longhorns even nudged their way inside Fort Worth's toniest hotel, sidled up to the table, strapped on bibs and ordered a couple of Chicken Cordon Bleus.

A bunch of bull, Raven knew, but nothing close to what she was likely to hear tonight.

Inside the auditorium doors, she spotted Jinx trading handshakes and swapping yarns with the sheriff candidates. She tracked him with her eyes, watching him work the room like a pro. In short spurts, no one would suspect the man didn't have the stomach to be a social butterfly. But over the long haul, the irascible temper and abrasive nature that made Jinx a straight-shooter set him apart from the rest of the backslapping slicksters.

He narrowed the gap between them. She sidled up to Ben Jennings and linked arms.

Let Jinx see.

No way would she utter the first howdy. She'd only put in a cameo appearance because of a promise she made over a month ago. And in the cutthroat world of Cowtown politics, promises were as sacred as cows in India.

Jinx saw red.

Raven made an entrance worthy of a princess and she'd brought NT GLTY, just to piss him off.

She looked good, too, all dolled up in that skimpy black dress, wearing the gold chain he'd given her Christmas. He wanted to strangle NT GLTY with the lawyer's own cartoon silk tie, the way the man stood towering over her, scoping out the equipment.

Maybe he'd put them both on the spot.

Size up the competition.

He sauntered over and extended his hand.

"Jinx Porter." Fake grin. "Constable."

He clamped NT GLTY's hand in a vise grip and pumped, only to have the favor returned with equal enthusiasm.

"Ben Jennings. Counselor at law."

"Outlaw, did you say? Most attorneys I know don't admit to being outlaws." Jinx turned his attention to Raven. "Deputies aren't supposed to be fraternizing with outlaws."

Raven's cheeks flushed. "It's not a problem if there aren't any in-laws."

Well, la-di-da.

Their verbal fencing left Jennings' eyebrows twisting into question marks. The attorney said, "This must be a private joke."

The guy had snap. Probably make a good treasurer.

Jinx decided she wore too much mascara. Her eyelids must have to bench-press ten pounds to hold all that glob. He eyed the necklace and wondered who gave her the sapphire drop.

Raven's dress didn't have enough material in the front to keep her breasts in lock-down. Since they seemed to be mounting a frontal assault, he hoped Jennings' citrusy after-shave didn't tweak a good sneeze. The woman knew how to put on the ritz, all right. Not like Loose-Wheel Lucille— with her tattered bathrobe, false teeth, rancid breath, and pickled liver—who probably didn't even remember who stopped by for a hummer that same morning.

He locked gazes. "How's it going?"

"Lovely." She switched on the thousand-watt smile that made her the darling of the courthouse.

Jinx torqued his jaw. She could be infuriatingly well-bred. His eyes shifted back to the sapphire drop.

Whup. Caught him looking.

"Nice."

"Thanks. And the pendant's not bad, either." Slick red lips made her lusty grin positively wicked.

Jennings nearly split a seam laughing. He brushed her hair back from her shoulders and eyed her with a look of adoration. She didn't seem to notice, just took it as routine.

Jinx's anger flared. They acted way too chummy.

"By the way," she said, grazing a hand against his sleeve, "I promised Ivy I'd serve her papers while she's off. So I'll be in and out of the office this week."

"That'd be fine." He hoped he sounded unimpressed. In truth, he wanted to spring up and click his heels together.

"So, how've you been?"

He seized an opportunity. Raven was a sucker for the

169

underdog and the infirm. "Feeling poorly. My stitches itch, and those kidney stones're acting up again. Passing these boulders is like trying to cram a forty-five round into a twenty-two cylinder. Made me acquire a new respect for childbirth." Raven raised an eyebrow. He continued to milk the role of ailing patient. "The pain flared up so bad this morning I could hardly move. Had to crawl on my stomach to the bathroom. Reminded me of guys in the bush over in Nam."

She frowned, definitely worried. He gave it three days, tops, before she returned with a makeup bag full of girly stuff and hung a change of clothes in the closet.

Candidates for county offices forged their way through the crowd to reserved front-row seating. Jinx tried to buy a few more seconds. Create a sense of urgency so she'd get her ass back home where it belonged. What the hell? Maybe this time, he'd spring for that ring.

Not a marriage proposal, but let her think what she wanted.

She took Jennings by the elbow and pulled him away. He pressed a kiss into her hair and they shared a smile.

Playing the part with the passion of a Shakespearian tragedy, Jinx called out. "I had a bad reaction to some medicine. For a while, it was touch and go." She kept walking so he cupped his hands to his mouth. "At one point, I thought it was all over when I looked up and saw Jesus standing in the doorway."

"Honey, I've got bad news," she said over her shoulder, *"that wasn't Jesus."*

Smart-ass left him standing like a leper with his dick dropped in the dirt.

Damned Raven, making him think they might patch up this misunderstanding. And him not exactly sure why she'd

170

gone nuts in the first place.

Jinx took his seat and stewed through the introductions. Castro stood out like a sore pecker. White polo shirt, white slacks, white shoes and socks. And that porcupine hair, sticking straight up in a buzz cut—if the pipsqueak won, the first order of business should center around arresting his barber.

They drew lots, and Castro went first. Listening to his canned speech about wanting to give something back to the community carried all the allure of stepping on gum. When the goofball finished, the MC opened the forum up to questions. Jinx's heart thudded in his chest. After an eternal silence it appeared the kid would slip off the meathook.

The MC pointed. "I see a hand."

Jinx resisted the urge to look.

"You're what? Twenty-four years old, Mr. Castro?"

Yes! She came through.

He relaxed against the chair back.

"Let me understand this," Raven kept her tone even and measured. "You have no law enforcement experience. No credentials whatsoever. You've never done street patrol. You've never even held a job, and you believe you're qualified to run what amounts to a law enforcement agency?"

Jinx twisted in his chair. She had every eye in the place on her. Or on that skimpy dress.

"Let me understand this. From a management perspective, do you think it's fair to expect the taxpayers of Tarrant County to foot your bill while you take time off to go through a police academy?"

"I have two years to get my certification." Smooth-talking Rudy Castro developed a warble in his voice.

"I guess I'm not clear on who'll run that office while you're off at rookie school. Will you shut the office down until you learn how to do your job?"

Tiny beads of sweat popped up on Castro's forehead, glistening under the fluorescent lights like a hundred fiery opals.

"And there's a rumor circulating that you've threatened to fire the people who work for the incumbent," she added with the practiced look of innocence. "Is it your intention to replace good folks who've dedicated their entire adult lives to law enforcement with people such as yourself? People who have no real police experience?"

Ben Jennings supported her with an enthusiastic nod.

Before Castro could formulate a defense, she rattled off a question in Spanish. *"¿Es verdad que usted es de Arkansas, y que vive con sus padres?"*

Jinx's heart skipped. The honchos running the Democratic party knew Castro didn't live in the precinct but nobody had the cods to call him on it.

Until now.

Castro stood in stricken silence. At the rear exit, a frantic Hispanic male about Castro's age punched numbers on a cellular phone, drilled a finger in his ear to cut the noise, then disappeared from the room.

Raven's smile would make a gambler fold on four of a kind. Every eye in the place, women included, ogled her.

"I guess that's not fair," she said, seemingly guileless. "You see, Mr. Castro doesn't speak Spanish; yet most of the constituents are Hispanic." For the benefit of those who didn't understand, she interpreted. "I asked if it's really true that he's from Arkansas, and that he lives with his parents outside this precinct."

The auditorium sucked air like a wind turbine. Jinx mentally kissed the ground.

The information was true, of course, but it really didn't

matter. Politics worked like the Dow Jones. Even false rumors sent stocks snowballing south. Look at Black Friday.

The next candidate, a fossil straight out of Dickens, running for the Board of Education with no chin and no chance, rose to speak.

"I'm an old school teacher from way back," he rasped, "and I know we've been sitting a long time without a break. Why don't we stand and stretch our legs?"

Everyone did. Stretched them longer than a clot of Old Maine Trotters, buggy-whipped to the finish line, turning the exits into swinging saloon doors.

In the parking lot, a fine mist fell past the sodium vapor lamps. Topaz droplets glittered to the asphalt and glazed the blacktop with a golden sheen. Raven keyed the lowrider's ignition. Instead of starting, the old bomb ticked like a giant Timex. She banged a fist against the dash and made a choice.

Except for Jinx's car and a few she didn't recognize, the entire lot had thinned out. She'd rather perform open heart surgery on herself with a fingernail clipper than ask Jinx for a ride home, but an empty lot filled with ghoulish shadows gave her the creeps.

Which left her two choices: either head back through the drizzle to the pay phones inside the foyer, or thumb a ride.

When she was halfway to the front steps, a sleek Jaguar purred up beside her. She thought it was Ben Jennings until the window slid down to reveal the pasty face of the most hated lawyer in the Panther City.

Sporting his trademark leer, Denver Steeple gave her an appreciative wink. "Everything copacetic?"

"Mr. Steeple." She gave him a little finger wave and kept walking.

"Going my way?"

"I kind of doubt it." Snake.

He cocked his head toward the passenger seat. "I'd love to give you a lift."

"Thanks anyway." She sensed a double entendre and picked up her stride.

"Climb in."

"No, thanks."

"Your dress'll shrink before you make it up the steps."

A dim beacon from a one-eyed Rolls Royce swept across the parking lot, catching her in its eerie glow. She didn't like the way it cut across the striped spaces, aimed in her direction.

Steeple braked long enough for her to scamper to the passenger side and slide into the leather seat. She warmed her chilled hands against the dash vents, feeling Steeple's hot gaze fixed on her chilled nipples.

The Jag bounced out the exit and onto the street before he broke the vacuum of silence. "What's it take to be on the same side?"

"What do you mean?"

"The constable race. What'll it take?"

"You could write the constable a check, or start hammering Jinx Porter signs."

Steeple grinned. His gray-blue eyes looked white in the odd light of the parking lot.

"I live about five blocks from here." She gave directions, then glanced into the side mirror. Old "one-eye" had fallen into formation ten car lengths behind.

"You were pretty hard on my man tonight."

Raven's jaw went slack.

So Jinx's nemesis was Steeple.

Which made him her enemy, too.

After all, if it weren't for Steeple, Jinx wouldn't have an opponent. Wouldn't be acting so neurotic. Wouldn't be putting everybody through the wringer.

Undaunted, he massaged the steering wheel. "If Castro wins, I'd be in a position to make it worth your while." He swiveled his head. Steely beads bored deep into her cleavage. "You'd look good in our camp. And I'd look good on you."

"Know how you'd look best?" Sarcastic. "Headed east on Interstate Thirty at seventy miles per hour with the wind in your toupée. Pull over. I want out."

"Simmer down, Babe."

"Stop the car."

A block from the bungalow, Steeple lifted his haunches off the seat enough to dig out his wallet. He flashed a fistful of cash. "Would this change your mind?"

"You don't have enough money to buy me. Let me out. I mean it." She reached for the door handle and popped the latch.

Steeple curbed the Jag. "No need to get huffy, Babe."

"Jinx and I, we're not for sale." She swung open the car door. Stepped out and gave it a good slam. Steeple powered down the tinted window. Capped teeth glinted in the glow of the dome light.

"Everybody's for sale. We just haven't negotiated a price."

"Negotiate this." She flipped him the universal gesture of the terminally annoyed, pivoted on her heel, and power-walked toward home. The attorney floored the Jag, speeding off with a vengeance.

Dr. Kervorkian would probably do Denver Steeple for free.

The roar of a car accelerated behind her.

Old One-eye.

The Rolls bore down, closing the gap. In a gut-cramping moment, Raven jumped for the curb. Her heel hung in a crack and she pitched face-first onto the neighbors' sidewalk. She lifted herself up and made a frantic scramble toward the neighbors' gate. The Rolls hit a watery pothole and sped off into the abyss, leaving her soaked to the bone from the spray.

She never got a look at the driver because there wasn't one.

Crazy, but the car seemed to be operating on auto pilot.

A hideous scream jarred Raven from a sound sleep. As she sat bolt upright, her technicolor dreams vaporized. With a chill in her heart, she scrambled from the covers, grabbed her terry-cloth robe, wrangled into the sleeves, and rushed to the front of her house. Outside, a high-pitched note sounded other-worldly. She parted the curtains a sliver, and peer out into the yard.

The street was still bathed in a galvanized sheen.

She squinted enough to make out shadows in the dawn. A dump truck filled with rocks appeared between her house and the next-door neighbors'. The munchkin behind the wheel studied the two brick structures, held up a paper, scrutinized it, then scratched his head.

His cohort couldn't have been over five-feet-two in his stocking feet, but on top of the rock pile, he held more power in one fat little fist than a demi-god on Mount Olympus.

Especially once he commenced pelting the house next door.

Chapter Nineteen

A haze settled over the city, but it was only a matter of hours before the sun burned through. The county commissioners were coming on stronger than bad breath about carpooling on ozone days, so when Jinx heard the ozone alert announced on the public radio station, he began the day stewing about NAFTA. The government granted amnesty to Mexican nationals driving soot-spewing rattletraps through the Metroplex, yet demanded Americans be environmentally conscious. If Jinx did team up his men, he'd stick Raven with Mickey. People already noticed how Dell said more to her in the last two days than to anyone else the entire year. Let Dell and Gil serve papers together.

Ivy's frowsy-topped delinquent hadn't smarted off once this morning—just collected his books and backpack and ambled out of the spare bedroom wearing a cherubic smile.

It was enough to make a body check his hole card.

"Let's hustle. I've gotta stop by the office before I carry you to school." He dug a handful of change out of his pocket. "And since I don't know where I'll be this afternoon, here's money to take the city bus."

Amos took the money and fisted it into his pocket. He dragged his totebag along the carpet and out the door, letting it bounce off each stairstep on the walk to the car.

Bouncing the patrol car out of the Château's parking lot, Jinx glanced across the seat at Amos.

They rode in silence, which suited him fine. But when he wheeled the patrol car into the county parking lot, his eyes nearly bungee-jumped out of their sockets. Ahead, Raven slung a leg out of NT GLTY's Jag.

In a voice tight with controlled fury, he said, "Well, if this isn't a kick in the stones, I don't know what is."

Amos sat up and took notice. "Hey, that's the girl. The one in the picture." For a kid whose attention span had the shelf life of a bruised banana, the boy drank in the vision with enthusiasm. He eased a hand across his jeans and adjusted his crotch. "What's she doing here?"

"Working your mother's civil papers."

Raven blew the lawyer a kiss and Jennings sped away. Jinx knew she was in a hurry to pick up the keys to Ivy's patrol car and get started serving papers so she could knock off early. Probably had a date with that asswipe attorney.

Amos's voice was melodic and taunting. "She likes that guy, doesn't she? You think they kissed? Touched tongues?"

"No. She's doing this to get my goat."

"No way, man."

Jinx torqued his jaw. "See how she's pretending she doesn't see me?"

"She doesn't see you, Dude. She's totally not thinking about you."

"Put a lid on it."

"You got any naked pictures of her?" Amos lifted his backpack and positioned it over his groin.

"Mind your own business."

"Does she like him better'n you?"

"Of course not." Said with an edge.

The kid shrank in his seat, then bowed up and folded his arms across his chest. "You got license plates like that?"

"No." He had no use for vanity plates. If he did, he'd

have to figure out how to condense "Guilty As Sin" into six letters.

GLTY SN?

"Reckon if you drove wheels like that, she'd like you back?"

Jinx dismissed the idea. Based on his budget, for him to come up with a luxury car, he'd need asbestos gloves to touch the door handle and pot holders to steer it. He felt a tug on his sleeve.

Amos fixed him with an inquisitive glare. "Well? Would she?"

"Probably not."

"Is he rich?" Dollar signs ka-chinked in the Unabomber's eyes. His stare turned shrewd. "What's he do for a living?"

"The guy's a criminal lawyer."

"Can they prove it?"

Jinx forgot why he'd stopped by. He floored the accelerator, bounced onto the street, and blew the yellow light.

A few blocks from Amos's school, he said, "What're you doing about lunch?"

"My momma made me a sandwich."

"Did you refrigerate it?"

The boy shifted his eyes.

Jinx stiffened against the seat. "Let's have it."

Amos dug through the backpack and handed over a squishy wad wrapped in plastic. Jinx pulled over to the curb, opened the door, arced out a stream of tobacco spit and dumped it.

"Litterbug."

"Biodegradable."

"Huh?"

"Rotten. Like you."

Amos bowed up. "Hey, Dude, I don't like you, either. I got plenty of friends at school. I don't need you." He slouched down in the passenger seat. "Drop me off here. I don't want my friends to see you. Or this crappy car. It's embarrassing, all these ugly dents."

"Zip it." Jinx dug in his pocket, forked over lunch money, and kept driving.

"No. Drop me off." His voice skyrocketed. "DROP ME OFF."

"Clam up."

He pulled up in front of the elementary school and waited for Amos to climb out. Nearby, a boy in a cluster of hellions cupped his hands to his mouth.

"Strip my gears and call me shiftless, it's Porky. Hey, Porky, you got a pig bringing you to school?"

"Yeah, Dingleberry," another chimed in, "you under arrest?"

Amos launched out, slung his pack over one shoulder and slammed the door. As Jinx sped away, he could hear Ivy's brat matching taunts.

"Why don't you crawl in a darkroom and develop your brain, Shithook?"

Working Ivy's papers gave Raven a chance to put in her sixteen hours for the month, a necessity if she wanted to keep her police certification as one of Jinx's twelve reserve deputies. But what she really wanted was for him to hire her on permanent status once the funding came through. In the meantime, putting in extra hours allowed her to hunt for Marina and investigate the gypsies.

She entered the office with her mainspring wound tight. Georgia, spritzed in jasmine, glanced up from plucking leaves off a sickly potted plant.

The secretary measured her through theatrically made up eyes. "And to think I almost took a mental health day. This'll be entertaining, watching you and Jinx try to avoid each other."

"I need a criminal history. Complete." Raven forked over a scrap of paper with information on Ray Sparks. Sparks's rap sheet would show every charge by every arresting law enforcement agency, and this was important. Old police reports might provide leads to possible hideouts and known associates.

Georgia gazed at the page. "Honey, I can't. Our business with this case is over."

"Not as far as I'm concerned."

"Jinx checks every one of these. I can't just run rap sheets the way I used to. These days, you plug in an authorization code. And you need a good reason for pulling up the information, or they'll crucify you."

"They" meaning Jinx.

Raven's mind turned like a hamster wheel. She flopped into Dell's chair, spun around and faced off. "Let me understand this." She tapped a pen against the blotter. "Don't you have an authorization code?"

"Yes, Honey, I do, but—"

"Don't you take lunch?"

"Yes, Honey, but—"

"Don't you need somebody to cover the phones while Ivy's out?"

From Georgia's expression, she got the picture. She struck a no-nonsense pose behind her desk. "I will not do anything that's going to land me in trouble with Jinx, or get me prosecuted by the DA, and I suggest you follow my lead." Holier than Thou.

"Certainly." The heat of shame rose to Raven's neck. "I

would never ask you to do anything illegal or unethical—"

"However, if you relieve me while Jinx takes his three-hour lunch, everything you need to know if anybody phones—" She ticked the most common calls off on her fingers. "—amounts we charge to serve papers, who people should contact once we fill out the returns, telephone numbers and so on . . . everything's in this drawer." She flicked it with her finger. "This one right here. *Everything.*"

With a promise to return, Raven fumbled through Ivy's desk, unearthed the car keys and scrammed before Jinx showed up.

Jinx hovered near Georgia's desk while she played post office with the mail. When he sighted the familiar slant of Kamille's script, he snatched the envelope out of her hand with fiendish enthusiasm. Before he could pilfer a letter opener and feast his eyes on the zeros, the phone rang. Georgia answered and passed the receiver across the desk.

Anger blazed over the line.

Raven had treed the illusive Dr. Gessel, and her presence seemed to create an inferno to rival the last days of Hamburg.

A man identifying himself only as Gessel's office manager, Keith, ran down the problem in a strident tone.

"According to Dr. Gessel's housekeeper, that birddog you sent missed him by ten minutes."

Jinx said, "How come your boss doesn't just make it easy on himself? It's not a malpractice suit, just a subpoena."

"It's your employee's attitude I'm upset about. She scared the poor woman half to death. The maid said she pounded on Dr. Gessel's door for thirty minutes. I'd like to know how you do that without bloodying your knuckles?"

Knowing Raven, she used the heel of her shoe. Future

visitors to the Gessel compound would probably think a gang of woodpeckers did a fly-by on the doorjamb.

"This cleaning lady," he said, tapping the unopened letter against Georgia's blotter, "she doesn't happen to be in this country illegally, does she?" That shut the whiney bastard up. "Because if she's wet, maybe she mistook my deputy for *la migra*. You know, *Inmigración*. INS." Jinx tossed out an interesting tidbit. "Not that we can't enforce illegals, it's just that that's not her primary function today."

Put that in your anesthesia tank and sniff it.

Keith turned snippy. "My point is, Dr. Gessel's a very private person and your girl had the neighbors pressing their noses against the windows. She finally banged so hard the burglar alarm went off. Security showed up and she still refused to leave. She kept insisting Dr. Gessel was inside."

"Was he?"

"Of course not. He's performing surgery at Our Lady of Mercy. Now your deputy's here at the office, blocking the doctor's car in. We sent people out to ask her to stop, but she won't leave."

"Why should we believe Gessel's in surgery?" Jinx covered the mouthpiece and snared Georgia's attention. "Get Mickey on the radio," he hissed. "Tell him to meet Raven at her location."

Keith heaved an exasperated sigh. "Because he is in surgery. Some rich lady wants her pongs liposuctioned. Westside women're always having something tucked, plucked, or sucked. Dr. Gessel's their sculptor of choice."

Jinx thought of Selma Winston, pushing seventy. Anyone not legally blind could see the woman's face had been lifted more times than the pig iron down at Big Rollo's Hardbodies and Steroid Emporium. His mind produced an image of Selma, naked on the dining table, hair dyed an unnatural shade of red, skin glossed in suntan oil, and her legs sticking up like a Thanksgiving turkey. He was seventeen, and Selma, what? Thirty-seven, thirty-eight?

Keith's pitch turned whiney. "Your bloodhound managed to position herself right outside the window where Dr. Gessel's patients can see."

At the other end of the line, Jinx heard the crackle of blinds being separated.

"She's leaning against the police car, filing her nails. You'd think she just had the greatest sex of her life. It's quite upsetting."

Jinx stretched the telephone cord over to Mickey's desk, grabbed the chair, eased into the seat, and propped his size elevens up on the desk.

Keith huffed into the mouthpiece. "Oh, my stars. That *bitch*. She just blew me a kiss. Did you girls see that? Of all the cheek, I never."

"Hey—" Jinx vied for his attention. "—How long's this surgery deal supposed to last? Maybe I'll call her off, have her stop back by later." A lie. Ivy had made a number of unsuccessful tries to serve Gessel papers in the past, and now that his people were this close to snagging him, Jinx didn't want the doctor ducking out on them again.

"Hold on, I'll check." Canned music piped through the earpiece.

He flattened his palm against the mouthpiece and relayed the information to Georgia. "Get Raven on the radio. Tell her Gessel's supposed to be in surgery at Our Lady of Mercy. When Mickey shows up to relieve her, he can set up on the car while she bags Gessel at the hospital."

"Why don't you just send Mickey?"

"Because she's the one dogging him."

That ought to soften up his first mate. In all the time

he'd known Raven, only one guy'd ever gotten completely away. The way Jinx had it figured, even if he wasn't sleeping with her at the moment, he could still make sure she had an orgasm slapping papers on Gessel when he came out of OR.

"He'll finish up about two." Keith, back on the line.

"Mighty fine. I'll send her by."

By Our Lady of Mercy.

With a devilish chuckle, Jinx hung up. He focused on the envelope, slicing into it like a coroner at an autopsy. Out came the check. He blinked at the numbers.

Impossible.

Counted them again.

Must be a mistake.

Stared at the decimal point.

Sticking with tradition, Kamille stuck it to him again. The check was made out to the Jinx Porter Campaign in the generous sum of forty-nine dollars and ninety-nine cents. A penny more, and he would've had to furnish the name of the donor on the C&E forms Skeeter couldn't find time to draft.

God forbid anyone in Fort Worth might find out the Porters supported their own son.

After lunch, Jinx stopped by the apartment for a welfare check on the cat. He parked himself at the computer and decided to do the C&Es himself. Maybe even drive them over for Skeeter's signature; make the sloth sign on the dotted line. With the grace of an ice skater, Caesar made a figure-eight through his legs, flicked his tail and slunk out of sight.

When the machine didn't immediately engage, he re-membered removing the monitor cable. He retrieved it

Laurie Moore

from the jacket he wore to the political forum, reattached it, booted up the computer, and waited.

Without warning, a wave of *alt.sex* pages began to download.

Jinx reared back in his chair, dumbfounded.

How the hell did that happen?

A rap on the door shattered his thoughts. He glanced out the peephole, into the magnified eyeball of Glen Lee Spence. The bolt clicked back and he yanked open the door with enough force to rip it off the hinges.

"I'm busy."

Glen Lee, decked out in Raven's Hawaiian skirt, midriff top, and wooden clogs, cradled *Dog-Poop* in one arm, and planted a fist against his hip. "Well, aren't we the ingrate?"

"What do you want?"

The dog bared its fangs and wheezed through its glistening snout. "Quiet, Pookie." A-moo-moo-moo. "I want the monitor cable to my PC back, Jinx. The one your houseguest borrowed. Why're you looking at me that way?"

Mystery solved.

He felt the mercury rise.

It was all he could do to keep from belching a fireball.

"I'll have him bring it down when he gets home from school."

"See that you do, Jinx. I do not appreciate that I cannot play Mario Brothers." A low growl started in Pookie's throat, culminating in a barrage of neurotic yips.

Jinx watched Glen Lee and his sissified mongrel disappear behind the slamming door. The ex-con clomped off, uttering a string of colorful expletives, and a-moo-moo-moo.

He grabbed the telephone. Pressed the redial button and waited for Gladiola to pick up. Maybe she had inside information about the absentee ballots she'd be willing to pass along.

The voice at the other end turned out to be a real buttkicker. "Hello, Baby. I've been waiting."

"What?"

"Did you catch cold? Your voice sounds deeper."

"What the hell are you talking about?"

"Don't toy with me, Cranky Boy. If you're not naked and ready to spank, don't call back 'til you are."

"Who the hell is this?"

"I'll be anybody you want me to be. Are you down to your socks?"

Jinx's eyes darted around the room. "Listen here. I'm a peace officer—"

"Sure, Baby, be whatever you want."

"No, I really am."

"You can be Little Bo Peep if that's what whips your cream."

"Listen here. I'm the law."

"Whatever. Whip out your weapon, and let's see how many times you can fire it off today. Let Miss Vareesha help you turn that little twenty-two into a forty-five."

"Listen up—"

"Oooooo, yeah, Baby. Lay down the law. Strip off everything but your boots and gun."

"I'm the po-lice," Jinx yelled. "I don't know why my phone dialed your number."

"Baby, you've called at least a dozen times. You're logged in on Caller ID. Can't get enough of Miss Vareesha, can you?"

"Listen, Cocksucker, I made one friggin' phone call to this number three months ago and figured out you're a faggot—"

"Ten-four, whatever you say," Miss Vareesha said, his voice suddenly weary. "I thought we had a great session last night."

Amos.

He'd throttle him. Maybe choke him into unconsciousness for the rest of his stay. Give him back to Ivy on life support.

"Put your hand on that billy club and tell Miss Vareesha your deepest, darkest fantasy. You want to be in charge? Okay, go ahead. Dominate Miss Vareesha. Interrogate away."

"I really am a law enforcement officer, so you'd better start 'fessing up about these calls."

"Oh, Baby, make me confess. I'll do whatever you say, Mr. Po-lice-man. Gimme the rubber hose treatment."

"You're gonna get more than that, Asshole. You've been talking to a minor."

"A miner? You want to be a miner? Okay, be whatever you want. Take out your little pick and shine your light on *this* bad boy—"

Jinx slammed the phone down in Miss Vareesha's ear and stormed downstairs to the patrol car.

Still riding an adrenaline high, Raven called it a day.

It pleased her, not having to lie to Dr. Gessel; she never actually claimed to be a nurse when she entered the OR. Perhaps the hospital should keep better tabs on their scrubs.

And all that screaming he did when she served him during the final vacuuming of Lulabelle Hendrix's thighs, crazy talk about suing the county . . . well, that was all forgiven. Especially after she mentioned Lulabelle might not like having her privacy invaded while she was out cold with a sheet over her stomach, and her legs splayed. That she might see the intrusion of a peace officer as her plastic surgeon's fault, since he could have cooperated with law enforcement, and accepted the damned papers without acting like a Cream-of-Wheat-faced titty baby. That maybe his malpractice carrier might cancel his insurance if Lulabelle had to be paid off.

In the end, it was Dr. Gessel himself who pronounced them even-Steven.

With Sonny griping so much about having to send a tow truck to the Medical Center to haul the dead low-rider back to the shop, Raven didn't dare ask him to swing by the house and give her a lift. Instead, she got Ben Jennings to drop her off at the garage. She found the mechanic propped against a cinder block wall, puffing on a Camel. Judging by his demeanor, his level of tolerance was on "E."

"Go away."

"I need a car."

"Take the Lincoln."

"It's still smoking."

"My man Joe-Bob swapped out the guts and replaced the burnt hoses, and I tossed an old bedspread over the seat. Should be fine, long as you don't squirm. Otherwise you'll end up with a spring corkscrewed up your bo-honkey."

"The steering wheel's melted."

"That don't keep it from turning." He fished a set of keys out of his pocket.

"Pardon me for not wanting to smell like a brisket."

"Then walk."

"I'm not doing that, either." She planted her fists at her waist. "I want my car."

"You strike a hard bargain, Missy." Sonny scanned the

broken-down junkers waiting to have new life breathed into them. "Take Joe-Bob's. He won't be back 'til tomorrow."

She scowled. The VW Beetle, a sunflower yellow "cootie" with red and black lightning bolts shooting out of the headlights, had curb feelers on all four wheels and hubcaps that belonged on a gladiator's chariot.

"I'm not driving that."

"Runs great."

"You're not listening."

"There's always the Lincoln."

"Gimme the keys to the bug."

She watched Sonny shrink in the rearview mirror, but not so small she didn't catch the knee-slapping gesture when he thought he was beyond her view.

She turned the knob to the radio. The heavy metal station blasted through an intricate sound system, jury-rigged with mega speakers, in a volume loud enough to crack the glass. When she tried to lower the decibel levels to conform to the city's noise ordinance, the knob fell off and rolled under the floorboard.

Screw it.

At least it had A/C.

But where was the switch? She scanned the control panel while pulling onto Seventh Street into the five o'clock traffic. A red button on the dash looked interesting. She pressed.

The car rocked wildly. Son of a bitch installed low-rider shocks on it. Of all the stupid, imbecilic, low-class . . . This must be how it felt to ride the mechanical bull at Billy Bob's Texas.

A cell phone trilled a couple of stanzas of the William Tell Overture. Her eyes flickered to the dashboard, where Joe-Bob anchored the charger. She snatched it up, pressed the button and shouted into the mouthpiece.

"I forgot to tell you." Sonny. "There's a red button on the dash next to the radio and you don't want to push it."

No shit.

She yelled over the booming sound system. "How do you shut this thing off?"

Joe-Bob must've installed woofers under the seat. Might as well be sitting on a vibrator. Probably'd cause her to stick to the seat.

An older Bonneville with high gloss paint and a skull-and-crossbones decal on the passenger door skidded up even with her. A load of gangbangers moved around inside in a shadowed mass. The driver, unidentifiable through the illegally tinted glass, revved the engine. She stared at a bumper sticker slapped haphazardly across the window.

THEY CAN KILL YOU BUT THEY CAN'T EAT YOU.

Sonny said, "Turn the radio down. I can't hear."

"I can't. The damned car's having a grand mal seizure."

"Leisure? Well, I'm tickled pink somebody's able to take it easy. I've been workin' my ass off."

"Seizure. SEIZURE. It's epileptic."

"NEGLECTED?" His tone turned angry. "Now listen here, Missy, Joe-Bob pampers that car."

"Listen to me," she yelled. "How does it cut off?"

"You got a cough? See a doctor."

"OFF, DAMMIT, OFF. I'm talking about the switch to whatever's making this piece of shit bounce like a kangaroo."

"Oh, yeah? You're the one belongs in the zoo."

Raven pounded the steering wheel.

"LISTEN TO ME. I'M TRYING TO TELL YOU I PUSHED THE RED BUTTON."

"I wish you hadn't said that," Sonny answered mournfully. "Try shutting off the engine. Otherwise, I reckon you need to ask Joe-Bob."

"AND JUST HOW DO I DO THAT?"

She held out the phone. Behind her, a car horn blared.

She mashed her thumb against the off-button, and her eyes flickered to the rearview mirror. A troll driving a rusted-out Impala crawled up her tailpipe.

Or rather, Joe-Bob's.

The impact propelled her into the intersection. Cars with the green light honked. She popped open the door and got out to assess the damage.

The SOB parked on top of her.

She was pawing through her handbag for her driver's license when her eye caught a rush of movement in the side mirror. A little man rushed her with a baseball bat.

Unexpectedly, six gangsters bailed out of the Bonneville. They wielded tire tools, creating enough time for her to hop back inside the Beetle and clear the intersection. At the corner McDonald's, she flagged down one of Fort Worth's Finest. By the time they returned to the scene, there was nothing left at the intersection but chunks of shatterproof glass.

An hour later, a Fort Worth police detective called Raven at her residence. It seemed the county hospital had a man named Viktor Balogh, laid up in traction. Once Raven arrived at the PD and made positive ID on the Leaving the Scene charge, she caught herself humming the chorus to "Gypsies, Tramps, and Thieves" while she waited for the detective to take her statement.

Chapter Twenty

At six o'clock the following morning, a horn blared, relentless. It seemed to be coming from her backyard.

Raven dragged herself out of bed and trudged to the window. She lifted a slat, peered through the blinds, and sighted a vintage Rolls Royce with gangster-wall tires and faded burgundy paint rolling lazily down the alley behind her house. An undersized, balding old coot with an eagle-beak nose and sagging jowls slowed to a halt under the street light between her house and the next-door neighbors'.

The tinted window slid down.

A jaundiced elf behind the wheel leaned across the seat, and sharpened his gaze in a squint. The angry face contorted into a gruesome mask. He wielded his fist like a sledgehammer.

"Balogh," he screamed.

Before the Rolls lurched forward and died, Raven exploded out the rear door with a seventeen-round magazine loaded in her 9MM Glock, and ran barefoot across the lawn. The driver pulled away, farting exhaust in her face.

But not before she committed the tag number off the license plate to memory.

"I have trouble, Gil." Raven barged through the office door with her finger pressed onto the page of an open copy of the Texas Penal Code. She hauled herself up short. Dempsey loomed over the chief deputy's desk with his meaty hand outstretched and his eyes rimmed red.

"Give 'em back, Gilbert. They's my quarters, they come outta my ear."

"Yeah, but if it weren't for me pulling them out, they'd stay stuck, so they're mine. Finders keepers."

Dempsey's eyes misted. He turned the pockets on his dungarees inside out. A piece of blue lint drifted to the floor. "But Gilbert, my pants're empty and I need a sody-pop."

"Give him the damn quarters, Gil, so I don't have to hurt you. Besides—" Raven struck a no-nonsense pose. "—I could use some assistance."

Gil's bottom lip pouched out, but he forked over enough to cover the price of Dempsey's drink.

Dempsey grinned big. "Next time I come in, you pull out the quarters and I buy you a sody-pop."

After the janitor padded out the door, Gil screwed up his face.

"You helped him fleece me."

"Quit dicking with him." She shoved the annotated version of the penal code under his nose. "Read the case law. It says property's considered abandoned when it's put out for the trash collector."

"I dunno." Gil took the book and drew his fingertip across each line. He looked up, warily.

"Well? I need those parts."

"Technically, it's not stealing," he said. "But it has all the earmarks of stealing."

"It's not stealing."

"Crimes are best committed when they're done solo. And I'd need help with the lifting."

"I'll go. I'll scrunch my hair under a ball cap. And quit acting like we're thieves. Think of it more along the line of environmental cleanup—I know I do."

"You don't have enough upper body strength. I need a guy's help."

She cut her gaze to Dell, scribbling furiously at his desk—a cheap ploy he often used while pretending to ignore people. When she shifted her eyes back to Gil, she caught him studying the deputy with cold scrutiny.

He said, "My brother's got a jumpsuit that'll fit."

"I intend to pay for the parts, you know," she volunteered. "I'll send a check."

"He won't cash it. And it might even get him pissed off so much he'll try to file charges. Better figure out something else."

"A contribution, then. To his favorite charity."

Gil screwed up his lip. "And what might that be? Muslims-R-Us? No good."

"Cash shoved under the door."

That seemed to appease him.

It was almost seven o'clock that evening when two garbagemen arrived at Al's AAAA Aardvark in a pickup with a flatbed trailer. An old man out walking his dog probably thought it unusual the way they came a day early, in a strange truck. To top it off, they took only BMW parts and left the rest of the putrefying contents for the flies.

But the garbagemen assured him they'd be back at dawn the following morning, in a truck big enough to accommodate the whole load.

Jinx didn't intend to hide in the closet; he just happened to be there lifting the Siamese from his hiding place on the top shelf when Amos came in from school. Instead of announcing his presence, Jinx hung back and waited to see if the kid messed with the computer.

It took a few seconds before he realized Amos was on the telephone.

"It's me." Long pause. "Whatsa matter?" More silence. "I was worried when you didn't answer right away. I thought maybe something bad happened."

Another long pause. "Can we do it again?"

Probably talking to his mother.

"You flunked a test? Don't feel so bad, I flunked mine, too."

Must be a classmate.

Amos said, "Are you scared 'cause you flunked?" And then, "Nah, I'm not worried. You shouldn't be, either."

He started to step out and reveal his presence, but Amos's next words froze him in his footprints.

"Is an AIDS test multiple choice?"

Jinx's heart thudded. He took long, deep breaths and kept quiet.

"Are you gonna die, Miss Vareesha?"

Jinx pushed the closet door open a few more inches, and peered through the sliver. Amos sat on the carpet with an arm propped on his backback. He listened for a long time, then fisted one eye and wiped it on the leg of his blue jeans.

"Don't cry. If you cry, it'll make me cry."

Jinx realized he'd been holding his breath. Slowly, he let it out.

"But I don't want you to die." Amos swiped his hand across the back of his nose. Tears rolled down faster than his tongue could flick out and catch them. "If I gave you my blood, would it help?"

A few seconds later, Ivy's kid banged the cordless phone into its charger. He rose to his feet, hauled off and kicked the backpack.

"Everybody leaves me."

196

He hammered the front door, then slammed it so hard on his way out, the windows shook.

The clock struck seven when Amos returned, sullen and puffy-eyed.

Jinx hopped up from his place at the computer and braced his arms across his chest. "Sit down. We're coming to an understanding, here and now. You seem to think staying at my house gives you certain proprietary rights."

"Huh?"

He slapped the ad page of an alternative news rag called the Fort Worth Watchdog against Amos's ham hock of a leg. "What made you think you could just pick up my phone and dial this number?"

"I don't know what you're talking about."

"Bullshit. How many calls did you make?" Before Amos could answer, he said, "Don't think for a minute I don't intend to get back every crying dime, even if I have to put you in indentured servitude."

"Huh?" The kid's arms snaked defensively around his chest.

Practicing for that straightjacket, Jinx supposed.

"You're gonna pay for every stinkin' call, you little pervert. Any more one-nine hundred calls show up on my phone bill, I'll see to it you go to jail so fast they'll be airmailing your underwear." Amos narrowed his eyes. Clamped his jaw. "And fork over the *He-She's* monitor cable."

"Huh?"

Jinx moved in. "I'm gonna wring your neck."

The Unabomber bolted for the spare bedroom. He returned, grudgingly clutching the PC part. Jinx got his arm in a vise grip and trotted him down to Glen Lee's apartment on tiptoes.

Glen Lee answered the door. He stood there like a glittering Garbo, sewn into a turquoise sequin evening gown that accentuated his tits but failed to conceal his bulge, wearing elbow-length gloves and waving a cigarette holder. Amos stared, more fascinated by Mylar streamers hanging above a decorated cake than Glen Lee in drag.

Jinx gave the pudgy arm an elbow jab. "Cough it up."

The Unabomber handed over the connector.

"Well, thank you, Little Man."

Deep inside the apartment, a head moved, turtle-like, past the door molding and promptly retreated. Pookie streaked across the carpet and jitterbugged at Glen Lee's feet until his owner picked him up. A-moo-moo-moo.

Glen Lee inched over to the table with the tiny steps of a geisha girl. "That's very nice of you to keep your promise, Jinx. But if you haven't noticed, I've got company, so toodle-oo."

He didn't care if Glen Lee had a movie star and some gerbils waiting for him in the bedroom. He needed help.

"You volunteer at the nursing home, right?"

Glen Lee flipped his long mane off one shoulder and nodded.

He thumbed at Amos. "Think you could find him a job?"

"They have bingo every night. He could call out numbers."

Jinx gave Glen Lee the thumbs-up. "What do you want for taking him over there and setting it up?"

The transsexual waggled the cigarette holder. "Why, Jinx, I only want what I've always wanted. To live in peaceful co-existence."

He gritted his teeth, turned away, and motioned Amos to keep up. "He'll be over tomorrow at four." To Amos, he snarled, "I ought to tan your hide. But it's probably worse if you have to work it off."

Amos jutted his chin in defiance. "Why're ya bitchin' at me? I only called out of curiosity. *You're* the one who circled the ad."

Chapter Twenty-one

From the frontage road off the Interstate, Jinx had a clear view of Harry Fine's Auto Mall—specifically, of Skeeter's office. So he knew exactly when his campaign treasurer spotted him through the glass and knocked over his chair in a mad dash for the exit.

Skeeter flung himself out the rear door at the same time Jinx wielded the big Chevy around to intercept him. Sweat popped out on the salesman's forehead, and he grazed his leg against the front left fender hopping out of the way. Jinx slid down the tinted window to give the shiftless no-account a better look at unmitigated bitterness.

"Pod'na, I was just comin' to look for you. Whatcha doin' back here? Step on in."

"Do you have the C&E?"

"C&E? Why, sure. I got it on my desk."

Pinocchio.

"Let's find it." Through gritted teeth.

"Tonight, Pod'na. Tonight, for sure."

Jinx lifted a Fort Worth Mapsco, opened to a grid of Southside roads. Realization registered in Skeeter's eyes. His street, highlighted in neon yellow, had a big black "X" drawn across the block corresponding with his address.

"I'll be waiting at your house. With your girlfriend. You can bring the C&E home with you."

The corners of Skeeter's mouth took a hang-dog curve. "She ain't there no more, Pod'na. She put a screwdriver to my throat in my sleep. Damned shame, too. Best gal I ever had."

Idiot.

Jinx demanded a verbal accounting of funds. He didn't appreciate the vacuous, bovine expression settling over Skeeter's face.

"Well, Pod'na, I'd say we got two hundred dollars, three tops."

"Which is it? Two or three?"

With upturned palms, Skeeter shrugged.

Jinx cheerfully changed the subject. "You know a character named Bubba Johnson? Huge black guy? Gold front tooth with a cut-out star in the middle of it? Hands the size of construction scoops? Hangs out around the Glass Slipper while they do payroll?"

Skeeter shook his head.

"Good. I'm using that money to hire him to kill you."

"Something bothering you, Pod'na? I've been doin' stuff to help you, really I have. I mailed out a few letters here and there, and I thought a bouquet of flowers to an influential person might carry some weight."

"Flowers? What in the hell do flowers have to do with the constable race?"

"Ladies get all sentimental over 'em."

"If you're sending roses to Gladiola Brooks, fine."

Skeeter looked down and scuffed a boot tip against the gravel.

Jinx's pulse raced. Never again would he let a man who needed jumper cables to self-start manage his political campaign. "Just be watching for a large, black hump, recently got cut loose from the mental ward. Works best at night, you know. Harder to see, and all." He held out his hand. "Give me my money."

"Wait just a dang minute, Pod'na. I earmarked that money for T-shirts."

The news caught him off guard. "You ordered T-shirts

with my name on them?"

"No, with Castro's."

Jinx blew a gasket. "Imbecile. Who the hell are you working for when you go and buy T-shirts advertising Rudy Castro?"

Skeeter's eyes watered. "I work for you, Pod'na. I always work for you."

Jinx banged his head against the steering wheel. He clutched the two and ten o'clock positions in a death grip. "Why? Why would you spend my money to buy T-shirts for Castro?"

"Don'tcha know, Pod'na?"

He didn't. But the moron looked so pleased with himself, he decided to wait to have his aneurysm until he heard the reason.

"It says: RUDY CASTRO—A HARD MAN TO BEAT. With a picture of Castro sportin' that hyena grin a his. I gave 'em to prostitutes. Paid 'em twenty dollars apiece to wear 'em 'til election day. Come sundown, all the whores on Hemphill'll be struttin' their stuff in brand new Rudy Castro T-shirts. I already got a call in to Channel Eighteen."

Jinx slumped against the seat and wondered if the Hallelujah chorus in the background was real or imaginary.

"Besides, Pod'na, I gotcha five bus benches with your name on 'em."

Jinx managed a wobbly smile of hope. "You did?"

"Yeah. The one on Eighth Avenue's the best."

The news floored him. "The bus-bench guy told me I'd never get that location—that one of his regular clients bought that bench on a five-year contract, and the only reason he got it is because the guy who had it for ten years died." "Is this for real?"

"Yeah. So, does this mean my girlfriend's safe?"

Chapter Twenty-two

Around dawn, Raven awakened to the backup beep of a cement mixer, angling into the backyard with its snout pointed at her swimming pool. She threw on a terry-cloth robe, cinched the waist, and scampered out the back door clutching her Glock. A miniature male with a Fu Manchu mustache and a gold hoop dangling from one ear slid out of the cab and hit the ground.

She aimed the gun at his head. "Who are you, and what the hell do you think you're doing?"

"Ephram Balogh. I have come to reclaim my family's honor."

"You'll take a bullet if one speck of that shit hits the ground."

"I curse my dead mother and dead father if I don't succeed."

"No, gyppo, you'll join 'em." She racked the slide. Leveled the 9MM. Eyed the corpulent trunk of the ox-necked gyp through illuminated sights. "I mean it."

The gypsy unleashed a string of Romany curses. "May your children be born dead."

"Don't have any." She steadied her aim. "Get off my property."

"May your pets encounter a horrible end."

"No pets." She tightened her grip.

"You are our enemy and your friends are our enemies."

"I'm down to my last pal, Shithead. But he'll pick your pigskin ass up and punt it through those telephone poles straight down to the courthouse if you don't clear outta here."

The bullet should cut through the exact middle of the one continuous eyebrow that ran the width of Balogh's forehead.

The gypsy squared his hunched shoulders and pulled out all the stops.

"May you always drive cars such as that." He pointed to the yellow Beetle and fell into a diabolical fit of laughter.

"That rips it."

The first bullet zinged over his head and shattered the side mirror. Ephram Balogh's saucer eyes darted in their sockets like a couple of pinballs racking up points. He made a break for the truck. The second bullet ricocheted off the door molding above his head. He had barely slammed the door and fired up the engine when the third round cut a groove through the steering wheel. Balogh let out a crow-in-heat screech. He flailed his hands, groping for gears.

A noise that hung somewhere between a gurgle and a slurp rolled down the chute. The cement mixer bounced sluggishly down the alley and vibrated off down the street like a huge snail, dribbling a gray slime trail of fresh cement.

Raven needed a cup of coffee strong enough to lead a parade. She went back inside, dumped two scoops of fine grind into the filter, flopped into an overstuffed channel-back chair and waited for the coffeemaker to finish sputtering.

Distant sirens grew louder.

Two patrol cars screamed to a stop in front of her house. A fist on the door, and the Fort Worth Police arrived on a Shots Fired call.

She did exactly what she didn't want to do, given the fact she was running out of time and had a little kid who needed finding—spent the next two hours at Police HQ, explaining herself. When they finally turned her loose, she reached a cathartic conclusion.

Maybe it was time to pull some gypsy shit of her own.

She picked up Joe-Bob's cell phone and dialed Information. The operator found the number and rang her through. In a flash, a deathly calm voice answered with the standard bone-chilling greeting.

"Internal Revenue Service."

Jinx strode through the glass doors of the Constable's Office, batting his way past green pom-poms and doodads Georgia had strung up in anticipation of St. Patrick's Day. The woman's compulsion to decorate knew no boundaries.

He stopped short. A sable-haired beauty with her back to him flirted with Mickey. Her wavy curls fell past her perfect shoulders. She shifted in her seat, and the light from the overhead fluorescents rippled down each billowy lock.

The python stirred.

And keeled over dead.

If it wasn't Miriam Louise, there to induce a stroke.

Mimzy.

He surveyed his natural enemy with the attack instincts of the owl and crow. Mickey pushed back his chair from the desk, beyond their electrically charged force field.

Mimzy craned her neck. She rose and extended a manicured hand. "Hello, Jinx. May we speak?" Her gaze cut away to his private office.

He sensed the blood-sucking pull of familial obligation. Without a word, he sauntered past. When he glanced up from stowing his briefcase behind the desk, he saw she had chosen the seat closest to his, leaving him with the feeling of a cornered rat.

"Is there some reason why you're here?"

She let go a throaty laugh, the way she did when she knew she had the upper hand.

The way he tallied it up, he'd gotten his butt blistered every day of his life from the time they brought Mimzy home from the neo-natal unit till he reached the seasoned age of ten. Birthdays and Christmases excluded. His insides burned with a searing reminder. He hated the bitch. On the low end of the food chain, he'd mentally sandwich Mimzy somewhere between maggots and sadistic pedophiles.

"What do you want?"

"What do you want?" she asked, melodic and mocking.

"Besides you closing the door on your way out?"

"Don't be absurd. I'm here to assist."

Bullshit.

He sat rigid against the chair back. "Why?"

"Little known fact." She flipped her wrist with such force the gold bracelets clinked. "I dated Ben Jennings. He jilted me for Leslie. Don't worry about Raven. She'll be a victim, too, it's only a matter of time."

"That's it? That's what you came to say?" His eyes flickered to the door. Maybe she'd take a hint.

"You're worried, aren't you?" Smug grin. "Don't be. I know something you don't. Leslie's a man." She stood, and for a fleeting moment, he thought she would go. But she paused to rummage through her alligator handbag. "Here."

"What's this?"

He stared in disbelief. A thousand-dollar check, made out to his campaign. Signed by Mimzy's daughter, Gigi. His gut sank.

"Daddy says you don't have to declare the money on those election forms if it's from somebody under eighteen."

"You do. You have to list it as a contribution."

"Yeah, but Daddy says you don't have to say who gave

206

it," she said in that snotty tone he'd grown up with.

He counted the zeros until he convinced himself it wasn't a mirage. He almost felt remorse for setting fire to her crib forty-five years ago.

He locked her in his gaze. "Why're you doing this? Let's face it, we can't even get along."

"I blame you. I forgave you, years ago, for leaving me in the middle of our street. I was only six months old, but Momma says it happened and I believe her."

Jinx gulped. She'd crawled to safety—twice. There'd been no due process. No plea bargaining. Kamille convicted and punished him on the spot when she flew at him with the flat of her hand and repositioned his nose.

His sister gave him an icy stare. "Now, the bad Rottweiler I remember. Why'd you pen me in with the neighbor's dog? Did you think he'd take my head off?"

Mimzy had a way of seeing right through him.

"You had an accomplice that time," she said, going for the throat. "That freckle-faced kid down the block. I never did anything to you, Jinx. I never tried to hurt you. Never."

"Why're you doing this?"

"Bet you shit a telephone pole when Cujo licked my face." Blue eyes gleamed stubbornly. The pretense of forgiveness apparently lifted, she smoothed the front of her blazer and glided to the doorway.

"Why?" Ashamed, Jinx cut his gaze to his boot tips.

"Because I love Momma and Daddy." Mimzy's eyes rimmed red. "And it'll be so embarrassing to be linked with a loser. We won't be able to be seen at the Country Club for weeks."

Once again, he felt the urge to kill her.

Jinx radioed Georgia that he was taking an early lunch,

so Raven seized the opportunity to duck into the office long enough to run teletype messages. She was halfway through wiring the last law enforcement agency that handled Ray Sparks when the cowbell jingled over the door. From her place at the teletype she observed a trollop with no waist and small hips waltz inside in an agitated state, all gussied up in a pair of fire-engine red hot pants, and a silver lamé halter top with gold flames stitched on it. A marble-eyed fuzzball popped out of the shoulderbag.

Alarmed, Georgia dumped a handful of papers on the floor and backed away.

"*I* am Glen Lee Spence and this is Pookie. We're here to see Jinx."

"Do you have an appointment?"

Glen Lee scoffed. "Madame, I do not need an appointment. Jinx and I practically live together." Georgia arched her eyebrows. "I am here to speak with him about a juvenile delinquent."

"You mean Amos." She skirted the papers, took a professional pose behind the desk and gave Glen Lee the prerehearsed line, the one Jinx told them all to use when he wasn't in the office. "Jinx is on patrol. Making the streets safe."

"Then I will speak to Raven."

"Honey, she's busy."

Raven called out. "Back here, Glen. Be out in a jiffy."

While she typed fast, Glen Lee huffed out his complaint.

"I have a message and I do not appreciate having to leave it with someone I am not acquainted with. However, seeing as I have no choice in the matter, the message is this: Monster Boy got us both thrown out of the nursing home."

Georgia said, "Beg your pardon?"

"We have been banned."

Raven pressed the machine's Send button and stepped out into the foyer. Glen Lee fretted with a dainty gold cross flirting with his cleavage. With a degree of superstition, he kissed the catch on the chain and slid it back to the nape of his neck.

"Raven, Darling. Did you hear me tell Granny here that our enterprising little misfit cut a deal with some old coots to call out their bingo numbers in exchange for money? The little bastard even got a protection racket going—sneaking food out of the kitchen, taking them prune juice."

Georgia's eyes practically crossed, as if someone spiked her iced tea with an hallucinogen. She closed her eyelids, then snapped them open. Glen Lee was still there, nuzzling the furball.

"Anyway, the director discovered the little chiseler was racketeering and banished us. The old folks got the idea it's Jinx's fault and now they're not going to vote for him."

Raven reached up and patted him on the back. "If you want him to know that, you'll have to tell him yourself. The rest of us are walking on eggshells as it is."

Georgia seconded her.

"But what about me? What about my volunteer work? Those old people need me."

Georgia thumbed through her Rolodex, pulled out a business card for Ben Jennings and handed it over.

"Here, Honey. In the event you decide to kill Amos, this guy might can get you off premeditated murder."

Chapter Twenty-three

Castro retaliated.

Even before Jinx pulled up to the intersection at Eighth Avenue and Rosedale, he could see the untidy outline of a tramp sprawled across his bus bench. The sot had on an old trench coat, and his shoulder and hip obstructed the letters on the sign so that only RE ECT NX POR could be read from the Rosedale artery. Snot-slinging mad, he crammed the Chevy into park in the middle of the road and alighted from the vehicle. The light cycled to green and the cars behind him honked. With razorlike pain spearing his haunches, Jinx threaded himself through screeching traffic, yelling loud enough to burst a blood vessel.

"GET OFF MY BENCH."

The man didn't flinch. His fingers curled around a bottle-neck protruding from a brown paper bag. In the distance, the Tarantula, Cowtown's short-commute tourist train to the city's famous Stockyards, signaled its mournful approach.

Angry motorists blasted their horns.

Raised middle fingers in the timeworn salute of the impotently angry.

A few even shouted well chosen references to his parentage. He pulled his Smith & Wesson from its holster and pounded the gun butt against the sot's boot heel.

No response.

Across the street, a woman let out a Fay Wray scream. He turned in time to see her press a cell phone to her ear with one hand, and shoo stairstep brats back inside the medical plaza with the other. He refocused his attention on the wino.

"GET OFF MY BENCH."

He prodded the drunk's shoulder. Gave the old geezer a violent shake. The sack rolled off the bench and shattered against the sidewalk. A gust of wind whipped the alkie's trenchcoat open, exposing a buck-naked corpse, stiffer than a tundra drill bit.

Jinx blinked. In the distance, the wail of police sirens closed in.

Deader than a hammer.

The chariot swung low, and now, the man with the pickled liver obstructed his bus bench.

The scream of sirens abruptly stopped.

Tires screeched to a halt, spewing gravel and sand-blasting his freshly polished boots. The Blue bailed out with guns drawn.

He grabbed at the overcoat to cover the stiff's dick.

"POLICE. FREEZE. DROP YOUR GUN, YOU STINKING PERVERT."

He placed the .38 next to the dead man's knee. "I'm Jinx Porter, Constable." He eased back a flap of jacket to show them his badge.

"Why'dja kill him?"

Jinx shielded his eyes and squinted against the sun. The nametag on the uniform's shirt read B. G. TOWNSEND. Townsend's partner, D. S. DRISKOLL, executed orders with his eyes.

"I didn't kill him. I rolled up on a 'Man Down.' "

The Blue exchanged knowing glances. Facial expressions conveyed their sentiments better than words.

Sure you did.

So much for taking the rest of the afternoon off to knock

on doors and hand out pushcards.

The way a defendant knows his fate when the jury refuses to make eye contact; the way a parent senses bad news when a dependable offspring misses curfew, and a grim-faced State Trooper arrives at the door—Raven knew the instant she slipped the house key into Jinx's lock she should never have stopped by the Château for a bathroom break.

A faint rustle kept her from snapping the door shut. A low moan brought her within inches of Jinx's bedroom. The sound of a hog, slurping at the trough, gave her the mental push she needed to peek inside.

She spotted them first.

Her heart drummed.

Blood pounded behind both eyes.

Jinx either had a five-foot hard-on, or there was somebody else under the quilt she'd given him for Christmas. But it was the false teeth on the night stand that knocked her off the Richter Scale.

Jinx didn't have false teeth.

Start with the first time you knew your mind wasn't playing tricks on you.

The plea to Shiloh Wilette flashed in her head.

The spread shifted, then slid off the bed. Blue cotton sheets crested in waves. Raven watched, pulled in by the undertow. Like a drowning woman, she sank farther into the action with each undulation, powerless to run screaming from the apartment.

Her eyes flickered to the Smith & Wesson atop the dresser. An Aztec specter crept through her mortified soul. A murderous rage made her want to throw Jinx's pulsing heart onto the flaming altar.

They'd lock her up. Toss the key. She'd ruin her life. Or lose it to the State. Was a little hot pork injection worth lethal injection?

Her gaze lingered on the false teeth. She stood, transfixed, descending into icy numbness.

Waves rolled in with ferocity. She studied Jinx's face, eyes closed and devoid of emotion. The sheet moved in frenzied ripples. Then Jinx went rigid. He grabbed the rooting swine and stilled its head with a firm grasp. A calflike lowing filtered through the covers.

So, she'd been wrong about a hog slurping at the trough. She'd been replaced by a heifer.

Raven watched with morbid fascination.

Tension left Jinx's body like a rising spirit. He swung out a lazy arm and reached for the snuff can on the night table. The teeth clattered to the carpet.

His eyes popped open.

Color drained from his face.

"Raven."

He shoved wildly to keep the lump under the sheet, but she thrashed her way out before he could recover from the surprise.

A head with hair the color of a weathered picket fence, and chopped just as ragged, jerked up abruptly, then twisted around to face her.

Raven's jaw dropped open. Her world ground to a halt.

It couldn't be.

The lush from the corner apartment.

"Uh-oh, Dinks. I tink we dust got caught."

He pushed aside his toothless tryst, threw back the sheets, and slung his feet over the edge of the bed. He sat bolt-upright and aired out his alter-ego.

"Raven, it's not what you think."

Next, he'd be asking her to believe the old bag was just sub-

213

mitting to a breathalyzer to prove she wasn't publicly intox-
icated.

She cut her gaze to the dresser. Watched her arm go for
the gun.

"HONEY, NO."

He came at her, his face creased with horror.

Positioned himself between her pair of thirty-eights and
the one on the dresser.

She unsnapped her purse. What the hell? The Glock
would work better, anyway—more bullets.

Jinx's hand flew up. Gripped her shoulder.

She held tight to the shoulder bag.

He tried to ease her out of the room but she knocked his
hand away.

"Don't touch me."

Lucille.

Loose-Wheel Lucille, she'd heard him call her.

*"You Picked a Fine Time to Leave Me, Lucille" was playing
on the radio.*

The scrawny hag dropped one corner of the covers,
grabbed at a pile of clothes. Leathery skin, sunbaked and
creased, hung loose on her bones. It jiggled as she snatched
up her blouse. An unbridled breast flopped mercilessly
while she made several tries at stabbing an arm through the
sleeve.

"Raven, let's go." His lips grazed her ear, close enough
for her to sniff his musky breath. "I swear it'll never. . . ."

His voice faded.

Someone cemented her feet to the floor. She wondered if
she had the constitution to see the nightmare through
without violence. The idea of Jinx's women in the same
room had a kind of revolting magic to it. Lucille just finished her sword-swallowing act. For an encore, Raven

could pull the 9MM rabbit out of her purse.

Abracadaver. You're dead.

She pictured herself in jail blues and shackles. And Ben Jennings, defending her.

Crime of passion, Ladies and Gentlemen of the jury. Poor Raven watched them going at it and went nuts. Insanity. Would a sane person open her Coach bag, draw her piece and turn a body into a sprinkler? The prosecution'll try to make a big deal about her reloading. A lie. She didn't need to reload. That magazine had seventeen rounds in it.

The buzzing in her head disappeared.

Jinx pulled the purse from her grasp and pleaded in her ear. "Let her get dressed and take off. Then we'll talk."

Sagging breasts slipped in their skin. Lucille thrust a clumsy leg into a voile skirt. Unsteady on her feet, she wiggled until the gauzy fabric covered the unwelcome sight of wrinkled flesh pooling at the knees. Tits banged together like water balloons stuffed in support hose. Gelatinous buttocks jiggled, then disappeared from view.

Cruelly, Raven cut her gaze to Jinx's pride. It was as withered as Lucille's nipples.

"Dinks, I tink tee gonna be mad atchoo."

"Shut up. Raven—Honey, let me explain."

Grinding her molars, she wanted to empty both clips into his ice-cold, empty aorta. She refused to meet his gaze, afraid to alter the Old Master painted in her mind—an original of his placid face, just before. Fury died in her throat.

"You granny-fucking piece of shit," she hissed. "I hate your guts."

"Let's just—"

"Take your hands off me. I'm this far from destroying everything in this apartment." She measured an inch with her thumb and trigger finger, then shifted her gaze to the

Smith. Three feet, max. About the number of hours she'd spend trying to convince the grand jury she capped her lover and a gross old crone because she was in rat-fucking shock.

Lucille snatched up her dingy undergarments and wadded them into a ball.

Raven gulped in a breath.

Tried to reclaim some dignity.

She directed her attention to Loose-Wheel Lucille, keeping the fury in her voice tightly controlled. "How long's this been going on?"

"Long time, Sister. Dinks and me, we go back a long way."

"I see." She straightened her shoulders and ladled up some advice before walking out. "Don't forget your teeth."

"You did *what?*" Dell recoiled.

Raven stared at the floorboard of Dell's patrol car and relived the moment.

"Headed for the front door. When he opened it, I grabbed my Coach back and shoved him out on the balcony wearing nothing but a scowl. Then I threw the deadbolt."

Dell tensed his jaw.

"Far as I know, the rat-bastard's still out there looking for a fig leaf." Panic swelled in her chest.

"Gimme your hand."

She didn't have the strength.

Dell took it anyway. "It's ice cold. You're in shock."

"Shock? I'm frigging electrocuted. I watched that skanky barfly blow a Point-Four-O on Jinx's breathalyzer."

"Point-Four-O is the same as dead."

"Don't think the thought didn't occur to me."

"You've got bigger onions than me."

"No. Ballsy is when you strip your clothes off right there and say, Make room. I did what I had to."

Dell gave her a long stare. "I'm surprised you didn't dust 'em both."

For a split second, Raven smelled the remnants of Lucille on Jinx's breath, as if he were there.

She shuddered. "That's something I've never understood—why women want to nail the other woman. Seems to me if guys're the ones pulling these stunts, women ought to plug them."

She allowed Dell a few extra seconds to sort it out in his head. He nodded, so he must've gotten it.

"Anyway, she didn't do anything wrong. She's in love with him. He's the one who's defective. Lucille and I—that's her name, Lucille—we had a nice visit on the couch while Jinx pounded on the door, hollering for his clothes. You wouldn't believe it looking at Lucille, but in her heyday, she used to be a go-go dancer."

Raven stared off into the distance. A fiery tear slid over one cheek.

Bubbles.

He should've married the woman.

Could've spared four lives—five, counting the daughter who hated him.

She thought of Jinx skulking down to the manager's office for the master key. And when the manager didn't answer, to Glen Lee's apartment. Would've served him right if the zany transsexual loaned him the Hawaiian skirt and halter top. Not that she stuck around to see, nosiree. She am-scrayed, soon as Lucille disclosed she had terminal cancer and magnanimously offered up sloppy seconds—but only after her dearly departure.

Dell's hand warmed her shoulder.

"Don't go crying on me, Raven. I don't see you that way. If you start bawling, I don't think I can take it."

She lowered her window halfway. The sweet scent of rain hung in the air, and she focused her gaze on county employees, hustling to their cars in an effort to beat the first splatters. The hard-candy smell of blossoms from a nearby flower bed tweaked her nose.

"Thanks." She fought for control, then looked him in the eye so he'd know she'd be okay.

"Thanks for what?"

"For dropping all those hints."

His face flamed.

"Anyway," she said with a sigh, "I have a new respect for women who refuse to put up with men's bad behavior. I'm even thinking of forming a twelve-step program."

The humor fell on unappreciative ears.

Dell spoke. "Just don't go back to him."

"It's not easy to switch off your emotions once you've fallen head-over-heels in love with a person."

"Believe me, Raven—" He directed his thousand-yard stare out the window. "—Nobody knows that better than me."

Chapter Twenty-four

Reeking of stale cigarettes and Polident, Jinx made it back to the office in time to watch Raven slam down the phone and conjure up the fearsome glare she traditionally reserved for baby rapers. With all but Ivy present and accounted for, he knew she wouldn't make a stink. Like Kamille, dignity functioned as a major component for Raven. But that didn't stop him from feeling he'd walked into a shooting match with a giant target painted across his shirt.

His heart pounded. He detested having to walk to Ivy's desk where Raven had staked out her place, but it couldn't be helped. He had a job to do.

Unable to look her in the eye, he dropped three lawsuits on the blotter. "I wish there was some other way to do this."

The magnetic pull of her silence broke him. He cut his eyes and flinched under the weight of her glare.

Pewter irises penetrated his soul like lead slugs. But her words came out soft, with fake respect.

"You know I don't care how many papers I get." She snatched the suits and dropped them onto the pile.

"You might when you look at them."

Poor Raven, thinking the papers were for someone else.

He turned away and headed down the hallway to his office, half expecting a slew of curse words to catch up to him. They didn't.

He sat at his desk and entered the return information on the three personal injury and property damage lawsuits he just served—one from each of the Mexicans in the truck she ploughed into. When she didn't storm in and call him a shit-heel, he gravitated back to the front office. The staff's facial expressions conveyed their sentiments.

The boss was a sheep-killing dog.

Jinx broke the chilly silence. "Where'd she go?"

"Bathroom?" Gil, dressed in a Lone Star Gas uniform, shrugged.

Jinx looked over at Mickey.

"Beats me. She had a walleyed fit. Banged the receiver down so hard a piece of shrapnel went flying across the room and almost decapitated Georgia."

Dell's eyes narrowed into slits.

"You have anything to add to this Greek tragedy?"

Dell's jaw muscles flexed.

Georgia pushed her chair back from the desk, rose, and smoothed the front of her skirt. She walked to the door with her shoulders squared, stuck her head out and looked the length of the hallway. "She puffed up whiter than a marshmallow, and stomped outta here."

Jinx rallied to his own defense. "Somebody had to serve her. The office might as well get the fees and the credit."

Nothing but blank stares. They weren't buying it. Especially Dell.

Jinx wondered if his face looked as guilty as Thornton's maid, when she palmed the wad of bills Rainey gave her.

In a whirlwind of bad temper, Raven crashed through the door to the ladies' room and made a beeline for the rear stall. She threw the bolt, grabbed a paper seat cover, slapped it on the toilet and sat without hitching anything up or down.

Burying her face in her hands killed the smell of Pine-Sol, but not the swirling thoughts of the phone call she'd just taken from her personal physician.

The clap. Crotch rot. VD.

She sat in stricken silence, with one main thought spooling inside her head.

Get medicated, get drunk, get gone.

She pulled her hands away from her face. A limerick penned on the inside door in permanent marker caught her interest.

There once was a player named Jinx,
Who didn't know women could thinx.
Networking our thoughts,
Is what got him caughts,
And now we all thinx Jinx just stinx.

Signed, "Smarter."

Raven chuckled.

Miraculous how in an instant stars and planets aligned, clouds parted, the sun blazed through the cosmic magnifying glass and branded a decision in her wishy-washy head.

She got up, swept the paper into the commode and symbolically flushed Jinx Porter down the toilet. Checking her reflection in the mirror, she made an exodus with one consuming thought.

I'm gonna fix that SOB and I know just how to do it.

Jinx holed up in his office, awaiting Raven's return.

He dialed the phone.

Skeeter's answering machine kicked in on the third ring with a tailor-made message, and Jinx felt his blood pressure rise.

"If it's you, Pod'na, I took care of you. I called the drug rehab clinic and they're sending tons of information to Castro in care of Democratic Headquarters. As for the C&Es, I'll have 'em ready by four o'clock tomorrow. All others leave a number."

At the sound of a dulcet tone, Jinx left a cryptic message. It consisted of two words.

"Bubba Johnson."

Chapter Twenty-five

Jinx woke up at three in the morning, anticipating the alarm. By five, the newspaper carrier lobbed the morning's edition over the balcony, and it hit the door like a grenade. He climbed out of bed, made sure Amos was still asleep, and stepped out on the deck to retrieve the paper.

Caesar yowled in rebuke.

With the speed of a zombie, Jinx trudged to the closet for cat food, and refilled the Siamese's bowl. He returned to bed, switched on the lamp, and slipped on his wire rims.

When he pulled out the Metro section, his gut sank. Blood whooshed between his ears.

A photographer captured his picture at the intersection of Rosedale and Eighth Avenue, at an angle so unflattering that his face appeared to be in the dead wino's crotch. And while immunity to indignity was becoming a way of life for him, such an abomination could kill his parents. He dressed quickly and drove to Dan and Kamille's.

No newspaper on the lawn.

Jinx's father answered the door in his pajamas.

"Son." His eyes widened in surprise, but he grinned and stepped aside to let Jinx pass. "Want breakfast? Your mother's in the kitchen reading the paper."

Jesus.

Maybe he could still intercept the Metro section. Explain before they slipped into shock.

Kamille let out a shriek that sucked the air out of him.

"OH, GOOD GOD. DAN, COME QUICK. I CAN'T BREATHE."

Jinx winced.

Saucer-eyed, his bowlegged father tottered off. Jinx trailed him into the dining room. They found Kamille slumped against a chair in her silk kimono, with her face as colorless as her perfectly coiffed hair. She waved the page in a white flag surrender.

Dan said, "What is it, Honeybun? You sick?"

She pointed her talon. "You've always been trouble, Jinx. Even labor was a disaster."

"Mother, I can explain."

"Dan, we have to move. Preferably today."

"What on earth are you talking about?"

"I'm talking about not being able to show our faces again. Now everyone in Rivercrest will know our son isn't just a black sheep, he's a necrophiliac."

In an effort to bypass Jinx, Raven showed up to work thirty minutes early. Dempsey stood halfway up a ladder, changing a fluorescent tube, while Mickey dusted donut crumbs off his mustache.

"You should've been at the pub last night," he told Dell. "You'll never believe who I saw cryin' in his beer."

Dell's eyes narrowed.

"Rudy Castro. Channel Eighteen showed Jinx's bus bench on the six o'clock news, and Castro was fuming over the free publicity. By the time the ten o'clock news rolled around, he turned into a big titty-baby. I've got no use for whiners."

Raven retrieved her court papers from Ivy's in-box. Clearly, Jinx Porter led a charmed life. Rudy Castro did not.

"That dumb bastard got louder with every beer, pissing and moaning how it wasn't fair the way Denver Steeple paid winos to sprawl across Jinx's bus benches, and Jinx got the notoriety. You ask me, Castro's a glory hog."

Raven cocked her head. So, Steeple did Jinx an unintended favor. A minute of airtime translated into thousands of dollars worth of media coverage.

"By the time I suckered the last guy into a game of pool, Castro was plotting ways to find a fresh corpse. And a cherry picker, to drape the body over his own billboard— the one on the West Freeway Jinx said cost ten thousand dollars a month to rent."

Georgia sat in front of her computer screen, seemingly catatonic. But Raven suspected she was counting the fish swimming by on the new aquarium screen-saver Jinx gave her for Secretary's Day.

Raven strolled over to Mickey's desk. "Castro didn't notice you, did he?"

"Don't see how he could've. He was about two beers away from happiness when I got there."

"Do me a favor. Keep this to yourself for now. I have an address to check for Marina and I may need some help. I won't get any if Jinx has y'all out doing damage control."

One of Dell's eyebrows corkscrewed into a question mark.

"Don't ask," she said. "The less you know about what's going on, the better. I'll be back before lunch."

Georgia came out of her coma. "Before you go, Honey—" She wiggled a pink telephone message sheet. "—That police detective from New Iberia called. Says he has information about Ray Sparks. Does Jinx know you're doing this?"

Raven borrowed Mickey's phone and punched out the number. According to the Watch Captain, the detective was on a call. He took a message.

Dempsey got everybody's attention with a yelp. Electricity arced off his close-cropped hair, knocking him off the ladder.

"Sparks be flying," he cried. One overall strap dangled from the bib, unhinged by the jolt.

They'd be flying, all right.

But not the way the janitor meant.

Shortly before noon, Jinx was in the front office dressing down the newspaper's senior editor when the cowbell clattered, and Raven burst in with her hands fluttering like a hummingbird. She looked good in her Wranglers, but her eyes were fiery and swollen, and her face, the artistic envy of a mortician's cosmetologist.

She gasped for breath. "He's gone."

Jinx held up his hand and motioned her to wait.

He shouted into the phone. "What do you mean if I don't like it I can bring in my paper and you'll give me my fifty cents back? My lawyer'll be in touch, and I'll own the damned thing unless I get a retraction on page one. In seventy-two point headline." He crashed down the receiver with the fury of a wrecking ball, and reached for his tin of Copenhagen. Never mind the cease-and-desist-or-lose-your-jawbone verdict from the dentist. Right now, he needed the rush.

"Who's gone?"

"The writ guy, Ray Sparks. I drove by his last known address. It's a vacant lot. I told you we should've called the judge before we turned that girl over to that scummy bastard."

"We were acting pursuant to a court order." He eyed her warily, and stuffed a pinch of snuff between his upper lip and gums.

Gil and Dell watched the animated exchange. Mickey

and Georgia sat ostrich-headed, pretending to be fascinated with an eviction notice.

"We're protected," Jinx said.

"Protected?" Her voice grew strident. "You think this is about covering our asses? We've got a duty to find that kid."

"We did our jobs."

Raven flailed her arms. "Doesn't anybody give a tinker's damn what's happening here?"

Georgia and the deputies had no way of knowing the pistons firing inside that svelte body were about more than a missing kid, and Jinx hoped to keep it that way.

"What do you propose we do about it, Raven?"

"FIND HIM."

"Let the mother file on him. If we get the paperwork, we'll serve it."

"You don't remember how it is to be little." Words rushed out in shallow bursts. "Left with people you don't know." Red blotches spiked up her neck, leaving her pale complexion looking as if it had been licked by flames.

Jinx hit the ceiling. "I've got my own problems." He slid the Metro page across the desk. "This Castro nightmare isn't some brush fire I've got to put out, it's a forest fire."

"But she's scared." Raven's plea climbed to a feverish pitch.

"For all we know, she's having the time of her life. He's taking her on the log ride at Six Flags, and she's loving it."

"She's not. And I intend to find her."

Jinx snorted. He should've figured as much. Once Raven got focused, her dedication burned like a magnifying glass in the sun. He tried to rein her in. "You've got plenty to do. Ivy still has papers to serve."

"I'll use my own time." She took the new subpoenas

from the in-box, headed to the door and whipped around. "Is anybody coming with me?"

The place assumed the kind of salt freeze associated with Sodom and Gomorrah. She rolled her eyes in disgust and pushed her way out the door, leaving her colleagues shrouded in embarrassed silence.

Dell spoke. "What just happened?"

Mickey shrugged. "Beats me. When my wife gets like that, I open a can of beer."

Jinx felt the disapproval in their stares.

In an unusual twist, Dell pushed. "What's with Raven, Boss?"

Jinx snapped the locks on the briefcase shut and closed the topic to discussion. "She's just pissed because a house fell on her sister."

Dell caught up to Raven at Ivy's patrol car.

"Ride shotgun with me." He gave her sleeve a quick pinch.

She transferred her gear to Dell's unmarked Chevy, and they took the Jacksboro Highway away from the hubbub of Downtown. Silence worked like a narcotic.

She looked out the window with a newfound sense of determination. "Sometimes I hate this job." When she glanced over at her partner, his answer came in the form of a raised eyebrow. "Don't believe it?" She smoothed a maverick curl from her face. "I even have a *Buck-You-Fuddy* file on computer disk. It's got my resignation already typed out. One of these days when I get a gutful, all I have to do is call it up on-screen, and plug in the date."

Dell nodded. He didn't say where they were headed, and she didn't ask. A short spell later, tires crunched over the gravel parking lot for Dot's Café, and he wheeled the big car into a space near the entrance.

He took long strides, and caught the door for her.

Confused, Raven gave him the eye. In police work, chivalry was all but dead. Away from the office, Jinx never held the door open for her beyond the first date.

Dot covered the Formica tables with red checkered cloths. Norman Rockwell prints hung on the wall. Smells of freshly whipped potatoes, gravy, and chicken fried steak permeated the air, and homemade pies topped with meringue filled a lighted glass cooler.

"I love this place." Raven slid into the corner booth, opposite Dell. "I only wish you'd picked a time when I had an appetite. This Ray Sparks thing has my insides shredded."

He gave her a strained look. "Maybe it's not Sparks."

Dell pinned the tail on the donkey. He seemed to have a knack for figuring her out. He continued to stare.

"If you think I'm pining for Jinx, you're wrong."

"Maybe it's time somebody else had a shot. We could get a group together and go dancing."

She sighed. Well, hell, maybe he was right. "Jinx is color-blind. He can't two-step to save his skin. And he spends weeks—sometimes months—hunting down parole violators on Blue Warrants, but he can't spare a few extra seconds locating the G-spot."

"The what?"

"Never mind. I'm over it, okay?"

Raven ignored the menu. The blue plate specials listed on a dry-erase board were what brought in the customers. Dot's reputation for home cooking catapulted the small restaurant to the top of the food charts, but it was the chocolate pie she cooked from scratch, topped with real whipped cream and Belgian chocolate shavings, that made her more popular than talk of a Fleetwood Mac reunion.

Dell squinted at the menu board. "What do you want? Mickey says the meatloaf's good, but I'm ordering the corn soufflé and pot roast."

"Pass."

"You gotta eat. Besides, I'm buying, and Dot needs the money."

A young frizzy-haired blonde dressed like a Dogpatch character navigated her way over with a couple of waters and a ticket pad. She poised her pen to write.

"Pot roast special, for me, and whatever my partner says. And a chocolate pie, boxed to go."

"Chicken-fried steak."

She intended only to pick at it. But when it arrived, smothered in gravy and steaming, she all but licked the plate clean. After Dell polished off a wedge of coconut meringue pie and drained his glass, Raven dug into her shirt pocket for a twenty.

"What's your rush? Besides, I'm buying."

"I'm going out to find Marina."

He shook his head. "Not yet. Don't worry—I'll have you back within the hour."

She glanced around. Businessmen and regulars lined up at the cash register to settle their tabs. Dell, with his calculating stare, appeared to be taking it all in.

"I think I know where she is," Raven said with a hint of urgency. "But don't talk it up, because it's outside our jurisdiction."

"That so?" He seemed not to be listening.

"What are you gawking at?"

"Dot's packing in the business today." He crunched an ice cube and continued to watch some distant point. "How far out?"

"Outside the county line."

"We're supposed to let Jinx know if we take the cars out of our jurisdiction."

"Jinx is on a need-to-know basis." She twisted in her seat. More people got up to pay. "What's with you?"

She regarded Dell with interest. He didn't make small talk; a waste of time, he said. She'd be damned if she'd try to get him to do it now. She positioned her back to the wall and lounged in the booth. When the place emptied within a couple of customers, Dell raised his finger and summoned the waitress.

"We'll take that pie now."

When it arrived in a pastry box, Raven said, "Eating that all by yourself?"

"No. Let's go."

He wrangled with the table until he extricated himself from the booth and drew himself up to his full height. Pressing a clenched fist into his breastbone, he burped.

"Ate too much." Sheepish.

At the register, he handed Raven the box. "Put this in the car and come back inside."

She returned to find him counting his change. At a corner table, the last of the diners wiped their mouths and pushed back from their plates. Dell stayed put.

"Was there something else?" asked the cashier.

"Get Dot."

The girl frowned. "Was there a problem with the food?"

"No."

Dell never blinked. Under his cool gaze, she disappeared through a set of saloon doors leading to the kitchen. A slip of a woman came out, wiping her hands with a cuptowel.

"Hello, Dot. The meal was delicious." Dell pulled a paper from his hip pocket and handed it over.

Dot accepted it with enthusiasm. "Did you get enough

to eat? We have leftovers in back we can box up for you if you're still hungry." Her eyes drifted over the page. The cheer left her voice. "What's this?"

"A judgment."

Her joy faded. "Somebody took a judgment against me, Dell?"

"We're seizing the cash register." He lifted it off the counter with oak tree arms.

Dot's mouth gaped. Her eyes searched for help where there was none. "I don't understand."

"This ought to satisfy the bank for now. But you still owe money. Maybe if you called your creditors, you could work out a payment plan?"

Raven's pulse throbbed in her throat. She slunk out behind him and opened the car door. He set the cash register on the back seat, gave the door a powerful slam, then faced her with a question on his thin lips.

"What were you saying earlier about hating this job?"

Jinx nosed the patrol car around the back of Harry Fine's Auto Mall and purred up to the curb next to the plate glass window of the cuckolded Skeeter Clinkscale. The used car salesman hadn't spotted him; he was yammering on the phone. Skeeter swiveled his chair with his back to the glass.

Jinx cut the motor. He retrieved his handcuffs off the floormat, looped them between the small of his back and belt, and stalked past Skeeter's window. Inside the fishbowl, the receptionist's eyes grew wide. She flailed her arms in an unsuccessful try to warn the shiftless bohunk, but the stupid bastard waved back.

Jinx entered the office rattling a fistful of C&Es. His treasurer lowered the phone.

"Glad to seeya, Pod'na." He rustled a handful of papers. "Sorry I've got to run these over to Harry."

Jinx slapped the C&Es on the desk, braced his arms across his chest and loomed large. "You're on my list of people to kill if I'm ever diagnosed with a terminal illness. Right behind Denver Steeple."

"Oh, Pod'na, no."

"These are Rudy Castro's C&Es. I stopped by the clerk's office for copies. I'd like to call your attention to the lopsided contributions. And of course, you'll want to see how a real treasurer operates."

"Now, Pod'na, I know you been thinkin' I ain't done nothin', but lookie here." Skeeter pointed at two crates stacked in the corner.

"Enlighten me." Jinx held out his arm and flexed his fingers into a horseshoe big enough to snatch out a gullet. "Make the desire to put your neck right here go away."

"They're Castro's pushcards. Now, don't go frownin', Pod'na, I came by 'em honest. Went to the guy who printed 'em, and told him they was goin' like hotcakes. And don't be shakin' your head. I didn't have to pay one red cent. They must've got the impression I worked for Steeple, 'cause they tacked it onto his bill."

"You're a crook. I suppose I ought to find you a bondsman."

"Steeple ain't gonna do nothin', Pod'na. The guy's plate's full. It seems somebody identifyin' himself as the garbage collector telephoned the State Bar Association and told 'em he was concerned about all the empty whiskey bottles they were findin' in Steeple's trash every week."

"You're a screwball. Why am I putting up with this? We agreed to play fair. Now look what's happened. I put up a sign, he puts up ten. This has turned into a one-upmanship sideshow."

"Pod'na, no."

"I should've let you take that bullet back in '78 instead of knocking you out of the way."

"Why're ya sayin' stuff like that?"

"Maybe they'll throw in at least one count of mail fraud when they indict you. That'll be your chance to go to a Federal Correctional Facility instead of the State pen."

Jinx pointed to the boxes and condensed the confusion into one word. "Why?"

Skeeter lunged from the chair and gave him a good-natured whack on the back. "I hired a couple of street gangs to hand 'em out at the polling places on election day."

"You're insane. Are you asking for a drive-by, or did you think people wouldn't notice?"

Skeeter's face sagged. "I thought you'd be happy. You keep bitchin' about everything. Well, I just thought we could get the Bloods and the Crips to stand at the polling places and terrorize the Meskins; and the River Bottom Kings could pass 'em out at the white-folk boxes and scare the shit outta the liberals." A lopsided grin angled up his doughy face.

"I'm leaving."

"Wait, Pod'na, I haven't even told ya 'bout the juggler, the clown, and Marmaduke the Magician, flown in from Vegas to make Rudy Castro disappear."

Jinx kept walking.

"And I've been meanin' to talk to ya about this pussy chasin'. . . ."

"I've cut way back," Jinx snapped, staying on course.

"Yeah, Pod'na, and I'm 'fraid it's gonna hurt your credibility."

His head felt like someone inflated it to twenty PSI.

Skeeter called out. "And since you've been bellyaching ever since Raven flew the coop, I gotcha what you been missin' most. A piece o' ass."

Jinx felt the eyes of everyone in the room, boring into the back of his head. He grimaced.

"That's right, Pod'na, we got us a donkey. A miniature jenny about yea high. Her name's Jenny Lynn." His hand measured three feet from the floor. "Don'tcha like the idea?"

That was just it.

He did.

Chapter Twenty-six

Gray, gloomy skies fueled her foul mood, but Raven returned to the office, chin up. After she talked to the detective in New Iberia, endorphins fired through her body like pistons in a NASCAR racer.

She had a lead on Ray Sparks.

She opened the drawer to Ivy's desk and retrieved her pet rattlesnake and an extra clip. With the Glock on her hip and a .38 five-shot snug in her boot, that added up to forty fangs, counting the one in the chamber.

"Where you goin'?" The lines in Dell's face deepened.

"To right a wrong."

Gil, with a freshly starched oxford pinpoint draped over one arm and a FedEx shirt opened to expose a colored T, stared impassively from behind his desk.

Dell rocketed from his chair and grabbed his jacket. "I'm going along."

She strode to the door without so much as a backward glance. "Better you don't."

"I'm coming, too." Mickey reached for his spit cup.

She gave her colleagues a last once-over, imprinting their facial expressions into her memory. "Stay put. If it doesn't work, better it's my ass on the line, not y'all's. After all, I'm the one who picked this fight."

Georgia's eyes bulged. "Honey, whatever you're fixin' to do, you might ought to clear it with Jinx." She stared pointedly at Gil.

The chief deputy said, "Don't look at me. I'm not here; I'm still out delivering packages, remember?"

Raven gnawed her lip. Gil didn't owe her anything—didn't have to cut her any slack, and she knew it. She took one of Ben Jennings' business cards out of her wallet and handed it to Dell.

"Call this number. Tell him I'm being sued by three mad Mexicans because my insurance company won't pay their claim."

Balogh.

Lucky for the rapacious gyp, she'd have to settle the score with the Baloghs another time. She gathered the lawsuits and gave them to Dell.

"How 'bout being a sport and running the papers by so Ben can start filing an answer?" she asked, then focused her attention on Georgia. "Did Jinx send you flowers on Secretary's Day?"

Georgia shook her head, puzzled.

"When I come back, you're getting a dozen roses."

Georgia's eyes welled up, pleading. "Honey, what're you fixin' to do?"

Raven flashed a smile. "Bring a little kid home to her mama."

After reviewing Ray Sparks's criminal history, Raven figured she had called a dozen police agencies, read twice as many faxed reports, and culled through a shitslew of possible addresses of next-of-kin he listed on booking sheets, across the State and into Louisiana. But the best tip came from Detective Joe Petty in New Iberia. Since Sparks had served time in prison, Petty thought it might be a good idea to contact the Warden for names and addresses on Sparks's Visitor's List.

So, here she was, pulling surveillance not twenty miles from the office, with Ray Sparks practically right under her nose the whole time.

She watched the house through binoculars.

Gauzy curtains blew back from the front windows of the paint-chipped frame house. Beyond the filmy drapes, Marina watched television. The old rattle-trap Sparks hauled her off in sat rusting in the weed-covered drive.

Now . . . how to get the child out without creating a hostage situation?

She could do it if she overlooked that one minor element.

That fine detail, where there weren't any orders filed and not a leg to stand on if she did what she was planning to do.

Yeah, that one.

Dell stopped his patrol car fifty yards behind Ivy's, thankful Raven at least had the good sense to study the house before bailing out and rushing in. He shoved the gearshift into park, let the motor idle, and watched her get out. She left the car door ajar and glanced everywhere but behind her.

"We ought to let her know we're here for backup," Mickey said. "You listening, Dell?"

"No."

Raven bent over and picked up something off the street.

"I said—"

"I heard you. The answer's no."

"Why not?"

"Because we're not here."

Dell watched in silence. Mickey didn't say a word either, as if shattering the quiet would torpedo Raven's safety.

She crept to the door.

Flattened her back against the shiplap siding.

"Gimme the binoculars."

Mickey pulled them out from under the passenger seat. Dell focused the lenses. She tried the knob, and he knew by the way she winced it was locked.

Mickey squinted. "What's she doing?"

"Fixing to get herself killed."

Raven closed her eyes, offered up a silent prayer, then took a deep breath and a quick peek through the front window. Marina sat on the floor, her attention glued to cartoons.

Raven ducked out of sight and berated herself.

Any deputy with half a brain would've consulted Gil. The chief deputy was a master of deceit. He could run a con game with the best of the con men.

She eased back into the yard, stepping a good fifteen feet away from the house. What would Gil do? She gave the area a furtive once-over. Listened to the sound of her own rapid breathing. Thought hard.

Yes.

She picked up a rock and lobbed it over the shingles, listening as it tumbled end over end down the other side of the roofline. A faint *thunk* against the hard ground unleashed a dog's savage fury.

"Stop barkin' 'fore I knock you upside the head."

She recognized the chilling voice of Ray Sparks and lobbed another stone.

The dog went wild.

With her heart thundering, she crept back up the porch. A board creaked under her weight. She caught her breath and froze. Arm hairs stood on end. She could almost feel Sparks standing in the tiny living room, not ten feet away.

"Stay put. I'm goin' to check on somethin'."

"Can I have a drink?" Marina's cowed tone tore at her heart.

"I said to watch the fuckin' TV and shut up, unless you want another hidin'."

Marina whimpered.

Sparks shouted at the dog. "Quiet, Diablo."

Raven unsnapped her holster.

Son of a bitch had better not lay a finger on that baby. She eased to the window. Peered through the glass. Ray Sparks padded to the back of the house, barefoot, his pants dipping below his crack, to the quiet the hound of the Baskervilles.

Dell let out a string of German curses. "She's gonna get herself killed."

In a gutsy move, Mickey unholstered his .45 and grabbed the door handle.

"Don't." His heart hammered in his chest. He wanted to join her, too, but her plan didn't include them. He took another peek through the binoculars. "She's tapping the glass. Trying to get the kid's attention."

"I'm not blind, you know."

Dell knew, but Mickey couldn't see what he could see. That Marina spotted her. Jumped up excitedly. Made a beeline for the window.

Raven put a finger to her lip to shush her. She held her arms outstretched, then motioned the child outside.

She stepped away from the porch just as the door opened, pulled out the Glock 9MM and arced the last rock around the left side of the house.

The snarling dog went wild. Ray Sparks's epithets pierced the air.

"Oh, no." Chills raced across Dell's back. "He's on his

way back inside. We're gonna have a killing."

Raven chanted, "C'mon, Baby, c'mon, Baby."

As she waited for the door to open, a nauseating surge of adrenaline shot through her. She dropped to one knee to scoop Marina up. The door opened with a snap. A chain slid along its track and halted with a pop.

Raven's heart did the flamenco in her chest.

"Miss Police," Marina moaned, "where's Mommy?"

"Shhhhh." From the open sliver, she watched Ray Sparks. He picked up a branch and flogged a canine as big as a Volkswagon.

"Honey, listen," she said sharply. "You have to get a chair. Quiet. And make it fast."

An eerie howl carried on the breeze, eclipsed by Sparks' diabolical laugh.

Marina padded out of sight.

Shrouded in dread, Raven crouched at the foot of the door.

Hurry, hurry, hurry.

Chair legs whooshed against carpet.

"Hurry, Marina." She barely got the words out when the back door slammed and Sparks disappeared from view.

He resurfaced with a tire iron.

Ohgod. I may have to kill him.

Dell flung the field glasses on the floorboard and grappled for the door.

"Wait." Mickey grabbed his arm. "Look. Over there. Somebody's coming up the alley."

They both grabbed for the binoculars.

Mickey won. "Well I'll be a sonuvabitch—"

"WHAT? WHAT DO YOU SEE?"

"It's the gas man. No, it's—"

"Gimme those." Dell yanked them from Mickey's hand. "No, it isn't. It isn't Gil because Gil isn't here. Just like you're not here. I'm not here. She's not here. Oh, Jeez. The kid's on the chair."

"What about Gil?"

"You tell me. I'm watching them."

"He's in the backyard with Sparks. Know how Gil talks with his hands when he's excited? Well, I think he's approaching liftoff."

Dell gasped. "We've got trouble. I don't think the kiddo can reach the latch, even standing on the chair."

"Gil's pointing to the meter. Sparks dropped the tire iron on the ground. Now Gil's got Sparks flapping his hands."

Dell lowered the glasses. "It's a fucked-up deal." The dog rushed the fence, dragging its chain. He made a calamitous jump and unleashed a fury of rabid barks. "Time to bail her out."

"Wait," Mickey said. "Not unless Sparks starts for the house."

"It'll be too late."

"Give me the glasses. I wanna see Gil."

"No." Frantic, Dell watched the front porch. No way could he let anything happen to Raven. He wondered how to tell Nicole their marriage was over. That he'd fallen in love with someone else.

"Get out, get out, get out," he rooted.

The chair toppled over and the door opened wide, exposing a room like a gaping mouthful of abscessed teeth. The blast of fetid air was strong enough to knock a goat off the porch. Marina hurled herself through the opening.

242

Raven held out her arms. The child leaped off the deck as if she could fly.

"Hurry," Marina nestled a tear-bathed cheek tight against her neck.

She ran for the patrol car with the child's arms around her neck in a stranglehold. She yanked open the door and tossed Marina across the seat, then flung herself inside and snapped the electric door locks. Marina sat wide-eyed. With her sleeves ringed in sweat, Raven fired up the engine and tried to put the girl at ease.

"You did so good, Baby."

"I knew you'd come." Marina's thumb went straight to her mouth, and she hooked a finger over her nose.

With the yank of the gearshift, they squealed away in a belch of exhaust to freedom.

Dell lowered the field glasses. He relaxed against the seat, exhausted.

"It's kidnapping." Mickey punctuated his comment with a nod.

"No, it's tough." He flipped on the emergency lights.

Across the weed-ridden easement, the "gas man" glanced over with nonchalance.

Dell switched off the overheads. "Let's get outta here before the cow patty hits the turbo-prop."

"What about Gil?"

"Haven't seen him."

"What're you gonna say if they prosecute her? If they make us take the witness stand?"

"Same thing you're gonna say—we weren't here." Dell picked up the cell phone and dialed the number on Ben Jennings' card, then listened for a connecting purr.

Chapter Twenty-seven

With tires smoking against the red brick street in front of the old granite courthouse, Raven curbed the patrol car in a five-minute loading zone and bailed out. Without being told, Marina scrambled across the front seat and sprang into her arms.

Instead of entering the newer addition, with its *trompe l'oeil* exterior painted to resemble pink granite blocks and a couple of bas relief angels attached to the walls, they went in through the side with the clock in the bell tower and the coffin-turns hollowed out of the wall along the staircase. It was faster that way—the armed guards assigned to the basement level knew her on sight, and she wouldn't have to stand behind a long line of people trying to clear the metal detectors.

Schoolhouse fixtures on the high ceilings gave off a creamy light that faded before it hit the sheen of the chipped marble floor. She rushed down the hallway, hearing only the echo of her boot heels and Marina's steady breathing in her ear. Beyond massive wooden doors, they crossed into the add-on and took the elevator up to five.

Raven burst through the double doors to family court with her heart racing like an Evinrude motor. Through horn-rimmed glasses, Judge Masterson's falcon-eyed gaze followed her.

Denver Steeple stood next to an empty client chair in the overpowering vapors of Brut. In his pinstriped suit he looked like a man rooting for the Yanks in Ranger territory.

She pushed through the shutter door separating the bar

from the gallery, with Marina clinging like a barnacle. "Your Honor, may I approach?"

Steeple opened his mouth but Masterson, a burly man with a rumbling voice, silenced him with a glare. His gaze shifted to Raven, and he motioned her up to the bench. She thought her legs would buckle.

"What's the meaning of this, Young Lady? We're in the middle of a proceeding."

Blood pounded behind both eyes. Perspiration trickled down her sides and she whiffed her own fear. She took a deep breath and glanced at Ben Jennings for support.

Her voice trembled with the effort of speech. "Your Honor, there's been a grave injustice."

Steeple flipped through the Texas Penal Code. "Judge, this falls under kidnapping, pure and simple."

"You'll get your turn, Mr. Steeple." Masterson's head made a pendulum swing. "Deputy, did you take this child without her parent's permission?"

Raven considered the question.

He didn't say, "father." Prosecutors were all the time telling witnesses to answer only the question asked. So, it all boiled down to semantics and Masterson chose the word parent. Until the judge himself ruled otherwise, Marina's mother was still her parent. Maybe not the custodial parent at this exact moment, but a parent nonetheless. And on bended knee, Marina's mother had begged, "Get her back."

Masterson appraised her with a look. "Did you, Deputy?"

"No, Sir."

"Your Honor, my client, Mr. Sparks, did not—"

"Denver, be quiet."

Marina's arms tightened around Raven's neck. Tears teetered along red-rimmed eyes. She stole a peek at the judge. In a stage whisper, she said, "Is this the Mister that's gonna gimme my mommy back?"

Raven's heart seized up. She felt the sting of a child's unreconciled grief. She fought for composure, not wanting to lie. "Yeah, Honey, he'll make everything all right."

Masterson watched, stone-faced. "Young Lady, don't go making my decisions."

A shot of heat went through her stomach. "No Sir, I'd never do that." She shifted Marina's weight to her other hip.

"Deputy, do you realize you could be charged with kidnapping?"

So far, the score figured Yankees One, Rangers Zip; Denver Steeple's ego inflated with confidence, chicken feathers turned into a peacock fan.

Marina whispered into Raven's ear. "Where's my mommy?"

"Shhh. In a minute."

Ben Jennings intervened. "Judge, I think I can explain—"

"I'm asking her, Counselor. You'll get your chance."

Raven swallowed the lump forming in her throat. "Your Honor, there were exigent circumstances."

"Such as?"

"Her father's a convicted felon. He served time in Angola for child molestation. And . . . he left her in the house by herself. The law states you can't leave a child alone longer than five minutes or it's abandonment."

Steeple came unglued. "I didn't know anything about prison, Judge. Mr. Sparks never said anything about doing time, and frankly, I don't believe this woman. And if Mr. Sparks left that kid alone, I'm sure he was outside—"

"Let her speak." Masterson stared through shrewd eyes. "Gave this a pretty good amount of thought, did you?"

"I'm one of those people who believes you can still find justice in a courtroom."

Above a phalanx of wrinkles, ageless eyes glimmered. "Where'd you get that foolish notion?"

"From my Sunday School teacher."

Marina played with a lock of her hair, and Raven felt a tickle climb her neck.

"I wanna go home, Mister." Doe-eyed, she melted the old man with a look. "I want my mommy back."

The judge got the bailiff's attention. "Get the mother up here." He rose from the bench. "We'll reconvene in a half hour."

Steeple's eyes lit up in wild protest. "Your Honor, what about—"

Masterson whipped around like Vampire LeStat.

"Denver, you used up all the equity you built in this court. My clerk will set you a court date. In the meantime, while we wait for this child's mother to arrive, I'm going to telephone my cousin, Eleanor, and say my good-byes before she returns to Beverly Hills."

Blood drained from Steeple's face as if invisible fangs pierced his neck and siphoned out a pint. He reached blindly for a chair. Wordlessly, he dropped into the seat, his fingertips trembling against the arms.

Grand slam, clear the bases, Rangers whip the Yankees.

The last fold of Masterson's robe disappeared out the door.

"The Mister's nice, isn't he?" Marina traced a finger down Raven's nose.

"He's a very good man."

She sat on a bench, rocking the little girl. Sinking deep into her thoughts, she wondered . . . what were the odds of two women named Eleanor from Beverly Hills, visiting Fort

Worth at the same time?

Twenty minutes went by. The child's eyes fell shut, her lips parted, and she took long, deep breaths through her mouth.

Ann-Jeanette Rice exploded through the doors. Marina's eyes opened. She slid off Raven's lap and flew across the room.

"Mommy, Mommy, Mommy."

Their weepy reunion echoed through the courtroom.

Ben Jennings swaggered over wearing his signature cartoon tie and slapped a handful of motions down on Steeple's table.

Steeple's eyes darkened. He gathered the papers and rose from his seat. "See you in court."

Jennings waved. "We'll be suing you."

The court coordinator, a petite lady with red hair and redder glasses, rushed in, breathless. "A couple of leprechauns with baseball bats are outside, bashing the hell out of a silver Jaguar."

Raven's hand fluttered to her open mouth.

Balogh.

Jennings sucked air. "I have a silver Jaguar."

Steeple sucked air. "Me, too."

They exchanged anguished looks. Jennings said, "Where'd you park?"

"North side of the courthouse."

"South side."

Eyes moved in a collective shift to the court coordinator.

She hunched her shoulders and winced. "It's the Jag on the north side."

Jennings almost passed out from relief. Steeple sprang from his chair and bolted for the door.

Raven cut her eyes to the ceiling. She tried to suppress a

guilty chuckle. "I thought that was your Jaguar, so I stuck a greeting card under the windshield."

Jennings said, "Mistaken identity?"

"Guess so."

"Think you'll tell Steeple about the gypsies next time you run into him?"

"I suppose I'll have to. When he reads what I wrote in that card, he'll probably end up on my front porch."

Dell filled the doorway. Mickey showed up, too. Raven gave them an embarrassed smile and moved into Dell's protective embrace. They shared a simultaneous thought.

Some days I love this job.

With any luck, the judge would still be on the line with Eleanor Thornton. She slipped out of reach and hurried to Masterson's chamber.

Poor Mrs. Thornton. She might look favorably on one of Jinx Porter's rivals. Perhaps she could give the nice lady a lift to the airport? Maybe work in some girl talk?

Chapter Twenty-eight

Ben Jennings phoned the newspaper. They sent a reporter, and after mugging for the photographer, Raven returned to an empty office. Chin up and walking on clouds, she deposited a bouquet of Tyler Roses on Georgia's desk. With her emotions under seige, she walked next door to the Fort Worth Police Department. If Dell was right and the chief offered to carry her as a reserve officer until the next police academy started, she'd be able to crank out a resignation letter as soon as she left his office.

And Dell was right. He picked up her commission on the spot.

She returned to the office to find Georgia puddled up and all hugs.

Gil sauntered in, suited up nice enough to be buried, and settled behind his desk with a copy of the front page. He dropped the paper just enough to peer over the edge. "Good lick."

Dell and Mickey stared, open-mouthed.

"I couldn't have done it without you guys."

Gil glanced up, expressionless. "Don't know what you're talking about. I've been at my Rotary Club luncheon most of the afternoon."

Mickey and Dell exchanged puzzled looks.

Still on an emotional high, Raven rummaged through her handbag until she found a computer disk sandwiched between her checkbook and ID. But when she booted up the *Buck-You-Fuddy* file, her fingertips shook against the keyboard. She tried to control her feelings when she typed in the date but the bad taste in her mouth persisted.

While the printer spat out her resignation, she packed her gear in a cardboard box. When she got up to retrieve her letter, her legs quivered under her weight.

She was about to hand it off to Georgia when Jinx walked in sporting a pink smudge on his collar, looking more relaxed than she'd seen him in weeks. A surge of heat shot through her and her legs turned to lead. The mere sight of him scorched her eyeballs.

"Any messages?"

Georgia gave him a hostile stare, slapped her romance shut, and handed over a fistful of telephone slips.

The Jell-O in Raven's knees melted away. Rebar took its place. "I have a message for you."

He turned, and a half smile angled up one side of his face.

"You gave me VD, Asshole. You and that toothless old whore-dog."

She balled up a fist and swung. The haymaker to the orbital bone smashed his head upward and sent him reeling. With a few hard shakes, she flicked the sting out of her hand.

Jinx's mouth rounded into a rictus.

The room sucked air like a wind tunnel. No one moved. It was as if they had all vaporized into thin air, leaving only her and Jinx in the room.

She slapped the resignation against his chest.

It fluttered to the floor.

"Next time you go screwing somebody's grandma, remember this," she said through clenched teeth. "A purple mouse under the eye lasts about a week. And a week's a helluva lot less than a close encounter of the worst kind."

Jinx massaged his cheek in stunned silence.

Raven checked her hand. A red thread on Jinx's orbital bone matched the "R" on her insignia ring. "And you're paying my medical, Tightwad. And if you try to weasel out of it, I'll have a thousand copies of the doctor bill printed up with an explanation. And I'll pitch them out the window of a Cessna at five hundred feet. Let them trickle all over the polling places."

Jinx blinked his good eye, the one that wasn't firing machine-gun teardrops. "You're fired."

"Too late. I already quit." She smoothed the hair back from her temples and picked up the cardboard box. "I believe that about covers it."

She glided to the door with the dignity of a Japanese empress. With a smile for Georgia and a little finger wave to the guys, she left Jinx with a parting shot.

"One more thing—good luck in the election, Sweetie. You're gonna need it."

On Raven's way to Shiloh Wilette's, she noticed a makeshift scaffold attached to Rudy Castro's billboard. A dwarf stood atop the shoulders of another dwarf, swiping a paintbrush across Castro's upper lip.

Raven made a calculated decision.

Either way the primary turns out, both of you guys are in trouble.

Chapter Twenty-nine

The last of a tangerine sunset filtered through a grove of pecan trees where Shiloh Wilette sat beside a rumbling stream. In a simpler world, far from Jinx Porter, she flourished.

"This is my spot," Shiloh said emphatically. "Anything bad happens, I come here."

Raven whiffed the sweet scent of wisteria. She joined Shiloh on a boulder next to the swollen creek bank.

Her new friend pointed at a leaf floating past. "It's kinda like glimpsing snippets of your life, isn't it? There's a pretty red oak leaf going by, and that represents something good. Helping the Coyote clean that Peacemaker, maybe." A piece of garbage appeared. "Yonder goes Jinx Porter."

Raven gazed across the pasture behind Shiloh's doublewide. The bewitching sight of wildflowers defined the horizon. Golds and magentas stood out like nature's jewels against the backdrop of a tanzanite sky. Another gust mingled the woodsy scent of old tree bark with clusters of rainwashed mint, and Raven drank it all in with a deep breath. At her feet, a tree root threaded itself in and out of the sandy loam with the precision of a Chinese dressmaker. Out of nowhere, a tuft from a cottonwood drifted into view like a comet to be wished upon.

"Even now, part of me still loves the bum. I can't believe I slugged him."

"Some people need a wallop upside the head to get their attention." Shiloh uncrossed her arms and leaned back, propped on elbows. She lifted a finger and pointed to a smashed beer can washing by. "There you go, that's Bubbles."

Raven chuckled. She'd come to adore Shiloh. This unsophisticated woman was a survivor. Jinx's ex would show her the way out.

"I can tell by your face you think it's the end of the world, don't you, Sugar? You scared you'll die over Jinx?"

"Scared that I won't."

"Do you really want to spend the rest of your life with a man who could wake up on any given morning with more spots on his dick than a cheetah?"

They shared a laugh.

Shiloh stared at the ladybug circling Raven's hand. "You told me a story last time; now I'm gonna tell you one."

"Okay."

"There was this guy, wanted to climb Mt. Everest. Now, everybody has something they want to do, but not everybody does it. This guy? He made it to the top. Before he could get back down, though, he got snowed in and was freezing to death. He had a radio with him so he could communicate with the rescue team, but they couldn't get to him 'til the blizzard let up. So, they talked to him. Coaxed him along."

Raven watched a blue-jay feather, carried past on a ripple. "That's nice."

"No," Shiloh snapped, "it's not nice. It's not nice because they kept telling him to get up and walk. To walk down the mountain since they couldn't come after him. He'd answer them. He'd say, 'I'm coming, I'm on the way.' After a piece, they'd call him again and he'd tell them the same thing. But you know what? After a few hours he hadn't made it down and they started to worry."

A styrofoam cup floated past. Loose-Wheel Lucille.

"The rescue crew radioed him again. Told him to keep walking. He said, 'I'm coming, I'm on the way.' When the white-out lifted and the rescue crew reached the summit, what do you think they found?" Shiloh's eyes narrowed ruthlessly. "*Him*. Sitting right where he'd been sitting the whole time, frozen to death. He was telling 'em he was on the way, but he never left."

Raven blinked.

"Don't you see, Sugar? I can be your radio, you can talk to me anytime you want. But it's you who's gotta get up and walk. You're freezing to death and I can't reach you. The only one who can help you is you."

Tears blistered behind Raven's eyeballs.

Shiloh hauled off and slapped her hard across the cheek. "Stop it, Raven. Stop it right now and get up and walk."

When the shock of the moment wore off, they fell into each other's arms and wept.

Chapter Thirty

Even before he lurched the Chevy into the Château's parking lot, Jinx saw the strobing emergency overheads of a MedStar ambulance, a couple of Fort Worth police cars—one with a head silhouetted behind the cage—and the crime scene van parked against the curb.

He took the stairs in twos. When he reached the top, a band of yellow tape with CRIME SCENE—DO NOT CROSS repeated every few feet in black lettering had already been used to seal off his apartment.

Paramedics rolled a gurney out the front door, with a sheet draped over a body.

Wheels clattered over the wooden decking as they rolled it toward the steps. The odor of betadine wafted up to Jinx's nose.

Amos had committed his first homicide.

A plainclothes detective with a metal clipboard filled the doorway and blocked Jinx's entrance.

"Crime scene," he said by way of introduction, and smoothed his sandy mustache. "Move along. You can catch the story in tomorrow's Star."

Jinx stood transfixed. "The Hell you say. You're in my apartment." Jinx nudged his way inside. His internal radar for media personalities kicked in. What appeared to be a female reporter dressed in a plaid mini-skirt, opaque tights, and a knit pullover shrink-wrapped onto her skin stood near the door, smacking gum and taking notes.

Jinx said, "Who're you?"

The crime scene detective kept the girl under his

watchful gaze. "Step aside, Cupcake, give the man room."
To Jinx, he said, "I'm Detective A. J. Heilman. I'll need
your full name."

"Jinx Porter, Constable. What the Hell's going on?
Where's my cat?"

The cub reporter wiggled over, bright-eyed. "You're Jinx
Porter?"

He liked her breathy voice. "That's me."

"Man-oh-man. How long've you been running a prosti-
tution ring outta here?" She poised her pen to write.

"What?"

Detective Heilman narrowed his eyes. "Pumpkin, I told
you I'd bring you along if you promised not to butt in. I'm
doing the questioning. You just write your little story." He
turned to Jinx. "How long've you been running whores,
Constable?"

Jinx's cheeks went cold and his palms clammy. But his
eyes, wide with fear, dried out. It was probably a good thing
the crime scene officer had already arrived since he intended to kill Amos himself as soon as Heilman's goons finished redecorating his white walls with fingerprint powder.

Heilman tugged a laminated Miranda card from his ID
case. "I'm going to read you a warning which spells out certain Constitutional rights you possess."

"Screw Miranda." He didn't need to hear the canned
speech. He hadn't done anything wrong. "Scoop's" pen
scrawled across the notebook at ninety miles an hour.

Evan Rainey.

Jinx checked his watch. He'd call Evan Rainey the instant Heilman stepped aside long enough for him to get to
the phone.

The plan went askew.

Like Elvis on stage, Amos rounded the hall corner, surrounded by an entourage of cops. Their eyes met.

"Jinx!"

A patrolman said, "Hey, A.J.—wait'll you hear what this kid has to say."

The cop unclamped his hold on Amos's elbow and the gelatinous blob broke free. He bounded over dripping in sweat, his eyes dilated with excitement.

"Whoa, Jinx, you won't believe what happened." Ivy's delinquent heaved the dramatic sigh of a starlet at her first premiere. "Oh, man, it was *so* weird. I was in my bedroom when—"

"What're you doing home?"

"I got to leave early 'cause the teacher got in the way of this spitball and had to get his eye looked at."

"I hope they haul you to jail and put you in lockdown."

Scoop scribbled furiously.

He noticed Heilman propped against the doorframe, watching the exchange.

"If we're lucky, the DA will find a way to certify you as an adult, and you'll get the needle."

"Me? What the Sam Hill are you yellin' at me for? I ain't the one killed Mr. Hardy."

Heilman said, "Is that his name?"

"You spell that H-A-R-D-Y?" Scoop checked her notes. Oversized glasses slid down the bridge of her nose, and she pushed them back up with the tip of her pen.

Jinx's eyes sizzled in their sockets. "Who's Mr. Hardy?"

Amos's grin plumped up his cheeks. He moved to the door and pointed. "The old coot who lives across the court-yard. The one with the Chihuahua that carries the can of oxygen."

"What the hell was he doing here? Did you let him in?"

"No way. But they were fumigating apartments, see?"

The angle of the mini-blinds shredded the afternoon sun. Jinx moved to a window, lifted a slat and peered out, beyond the trees to Hardy's apartment. He heard a drawer slam shut in his bedroom. Sons-of-bitches were pawing through his stuff. What if they found his cheesecake picture of Raven? Or the quadruple-X movies he'd hidden from the Unabomber?

Amos shone in the limelight. He braced his fat arms across his chest and spilled his guts. The paramedics packed up the last of their gear and tromped through the living room.

"Sorry about the mess," one said on his way out.

Another rounded the corner, grim-faced, carrying a small bundle wrapped in a blood-streaked towel.

Jinx's heart lurched. He unleashed a long, anguished, one-word plea.

"No."

Caesar. Dead. It couldn't be.

His insides gave a violent twist. In an unguarded moment, his emotions unhinged. His shoulders quaked and he fought valiantly to strangle a scream. Even the emergency medical technician wore the mournful expression of someone unaccustomed to such grisly crime scenes.

"Sorry, Sir. You want to see him before I take him away?"

Jinx's spirits sank to fathomless depths. Removing his jacket gave him something to do while he gutted up enough nerve to lift a bloody flap of towel. A tear started on the inside track of his left eye and his heart gave a joyous leap.

He might not have the cat's location vectored, but the sight of a mauled Chihuahua filled him with a rush of internal satisfaction. He cackled hysterically.

Caesar lived.

The paramedic scowled. "You're a sick-o, man. This whole scene is sick." He jerked the carcass away. "And that cat's vicious. He clawed the stuffing out of my supervisor. My boss's over at the ER getting his hand stitched up right now. I've half a mind to recommend he be put down."

He stalked out the door, leaving Jinx with a parting sneer.

The Siamese wandered in with his tail crooked into a question mark. He stationed himself in a corner and licked Chihuahua remains off his claws.

Jinx glowered at Amos. "You'd better start explaining."

"Like I said, I got expelled. So, I came home."

"He doesn't live here," Jinx said quickly.

Scoop made a notation in her spiral notebook.

"I was in my room."

"It's not his room. He's only staying here until his mother—"

"Let the boy speak." Heilman torqued his jaw muscles.

Scoop moved closer. "Mind if I get your picture when we're through, Little Boy?"

"Fine by me. Anyway, I was mindin' my own business, like I always do . . ."

Jinx rolled his eyes.

". . . when all a sudden, I hear somebody come in through the front door."

"Somebody broke into my apartment?"

"Nope. She let herself in with a key."

Jinx's breath caught in his throat.

Amos murdered Raven.

He lunged for the neck. "You little bastard, I'll put you outta your misery."

Heilman stuck out a boot. Amos ducked out of the way. Jinx sprawled across the carpet, certain the white flash came from a camera. He rolled over, sat up, and touched the rug-burn on his chin, momentarily blinded by another brilliant explosion from Scoop's flashbulb.

"I didn't do nothin', Jinx. I only watched. Oh, man, you won't believe the stuff I saw."

Scoop flipped the page and scrawled at breakneck speed.

In the back, a door snapped shut. Next, they'd be inventorying his closets. Jinx's chest tightened. He made a move to get up.

"Stay put," Heilman said. "You make me nervous. Go ahead with your story, Son."

"Like I was sayin', somebody came in and I heard people talkin'. Two of 'em. So I hid in the closet."

"I thought you said you were in your room," Jinx snapped. "You little bastard, you were going through my stuff again, weren't you?"

"I thought you said he didn't live here?" Heilman.

"Jesus H." Jinx gritted his teeth.

"The old lady from downstairs says somethin' about wantin' to wait here 'cause of the fumigatin'. Next thing I know, she's shuckin' off her clothes. Then Mr. Hardy got naked—"

"What old lady?" Heilman and Scoop, in stereo.

"Man, I never saw so much skin. Jigglin' like a couple of Chinese wrinkle dogs."

"Shar-Peis?" Scoop asked.

Heilman put a finger in her face. "Cookie, what'd I tell you? I won't let you ride with me anymore if you don't stop butting in."

The reporter shrank against the door.

"Can I hold your gun?" Amos asked, suddenly interested in the .45 strapped on Heilman's hip.

"No."

Laurie Moore

"My mama carries a gun. I handle hers all the time."

Jinx closed his eyes. Things just got worse.

"Hit the high spots," Heilman prodded.

"Them two got buck naked. Old Mr. Hardy said he'd pay extra if she took out her teeth. He give her ten bucks and she did things that made him keel over dead." Amos sliced his hand through the air with a flourish. "Right smack-dab on the floor. I gotta tell you, Jinx, it was pretty gross. Old geezer started gaggin'. I seen her doin' CPR on his wiener first. Later, she done it on his mouth. *Yuck-o.*"

"I get the picture."

So did Scoop. A flash popped, the shutter snapped, and she fled the apartment to meet her deadline.

Jinx turned his attention to Heilman. "Where's Lucille?"

"That her name? Lucille?" Heilman entered the information on his clipboard. "Cuffed and stuffed." Meaning seated in the back seat of the patrol car.

Jinx hoisted himself to his feet.

"So," Heilman asked, "what's Lucille's full name, and how long *have* you been running prostitutes out of your apartment?"

Chapter Thirty-one

This time, Jinx was sitting in the shadows, in his easy chair, when the maniac Mexican lobbed the newspaper over the balcony. It hit the glass and left a spiderweb crack in one corner, but Jinx figured a broken window was the least of his worries. He turned on the lamp, ripped away the protective plastic, and pulled out the Metro section.

Nothing about him anywhere.

A giddy laugh popped out and he collapsed into the easy chair. Tension drained from his shoulders.

Thank you, Lord. Didn't let me down.

He refolded the Metro section and shook out the front page. Two pictures made his spine go rigid. Muscles twisted like bedsprings.

Jesus H.

He lunged from the chair, letting the newspaper fall to the floor, and hurried to the bedroom to put on clothes. In a few minutes, his mother would be brewing a cup of foglifter; his father, scooching his chair up to the breakfast table and draping a cloth napkin over his lap. Kamille would be looking for news on her bridge partner, the fabulously wealthy Eleanor Thornton—a woman who would sooner see him castrated without anesthetic and left to bleed out than to consider that serving divorce papers went with the job.

He didn't bother to shave. Still buttoning his shirt as he trundled down the stairs, he had a crazy thought. Maybe he could just cut the pictures out and give them their paper with a hole in it.

Nah. He could do better than that.

He'd substitute yesterday's front page. He could reach into the dumpster—

Wincing, he rejected the idea.

By the time he got to the unmarked cruiser, he had his gun holstered and his belt buckled. His heart beat with a frenzy during the two-mile drive to their home.

Dan was flicking dewdrops off the plastic sleeve of the morning edition when Jinx rounded the block. He blasted the horn, but Dan shuffled inside the house before he could curb the vehicle.

Poor Kamille. He almost felt sorry for her. She was expecting to see a shot of her bridge partner in one of her famous beaded gowns, coming out of the premiere of Swan Lake with the new ballerina everyone at the club had been raving about.

Or expecting another story about the pipe organ acquired in memory of Van Cliburn's mother, Rildia Bee—a woman Kamille once said was the sweetest lady to ever grace a room, God rest her soul.

He stood at the door, pressing the bell for what seemed like a full minute when his mother's DNA-altering scream stopped him. The plaintive wail that followed made him wince.

His mother's shrill voice penetrated the thick wooden door. "Oh, good God. It's Jinx again. Will this never stop?"

"What's he done now?" Dan, barely audible. "Ugh." Much louder.

Jinx pressed his ear against the wood. Flattened his palms against the door like a suction-cupped plush-toy. In his mind, he saw Kamille pointing a French-manicured talon at the picture of him, openmouthed, at the uniformed knees of the Fort Worth Police. And next to a photo that could be taken totally out of context without the caption underneath, a close-up of the toothless smile of Loose-Wheel Lucille, taken through the window of a patrol car.

Jinx hoped his father didn't have time to put on his spectacles.

Dan's reassuring voice came through. "I know I was busy after the war and all, trying to build a business. And all in all, you've been a pretty good wife. So, I'll understand, since Mimzy's perfect—always has been, always will be."

"Understand what?" Kamille. In a voice so shrill it was meant for dogs.

"I'll understand when you tell me all those lonely nights you claim to have spent weren't spent by yourself."

"Dan Porter, what exactly are you implying?"

"I'm just saying, when a war's on, things happen. People can't be blamed. If Jinx isn't mine, I won't hold it against you."

"Well, hold on a second," Kamille shrieked. "The way you're talking, *you* had a fling."

"Honeybun, things are different in wartime. People make mistakes."

Jinx rolled his eyes, certain it couldn't get any worse.

Then came the sickening sound of Limoges china fragmenting against the wall. Kamille had come up with a unique way of clearing the table.

Obviously, his parents weren't coming to the door. Jinx stepped behind the holly shrubs and inched over to the window with needles piercing his slacks. His father must have rushed in from the bathroom with his pants half-up and his python dangling.

Kamille's eyes bulged. The newspaper fluttered to the floor like an injured bird, soaking up coffee splattered over the floor. Dan picked up the front page with a tremble in his fingers. His PJ bottoms fell to his ankles.

Kamille shouted, "You selfish crumb, I ought to divorce you and take everything you've got."

"I'm not admitting anything. I'm only saying I'll understand if you tell me you had a fling."

She gave her chair a violent push from the table and stood in front of her husband. Which placed the top of her perfect, spun-glass hair at chest level. Then she snatched up a piece of toast and threw it at him.

"You think because I just found out you had some left-handed honeymoon on the Left Bank sixty years ago makes it any easier? You're the one who insisted on getting married before flying off to Europe. Now you confess guns weren't the only things you were shooting off in France, and I'm just supposed to like it or lump it?"

His father stayed hidden behind the front page.

"If I just found out my best friend died last year and I didn't learn about it until just now, you wouldn't expect me to just get over it, Dan."

Dan Porter lowered the paper. "Kamille—Honeybun, what's past is past. There was a war, for pity's sake."

"You may have sole custody of the children."

"The kids are grown, Kamille. And I don't want a divorce, but I do appreciate the noble gesture. I know what a personal sacrifice you'd be making."

Jinx rapped on the windowpane. Neither so much as glanced over.

Kamille squared her shoulders. Regarded her husband's flaccid penis with disgust.

Dan talked fast. "All I was saying is, Jinx isn't like either one of us. He's just too—" He seemed to be searching for just the right word. "—peculiar. I'm only saying I can forgive you if Jinx isn't mine."

"Oh, he's yours, all right. It's Mimzy who's *not*."

Under cover of darkness and candlelight, on the east side of Fort Worth in an area known as Poly, gypsies gathered at the nondescript brick home Ivan Balogh shared with his parents, King Kos and Queen Ruta.

The exterior appeared unpretentious. It could have been mistaken for any other lower middle class tracthouse, if no one took into consideration the elaborately recessed pin cameras and laser beams at the exits. Inside told a different story. Walls of gold-flocked wallpaper gleamed beneath crystal chandeliers. Splendorous Italian furnishings rested on antique Persian rugs—all stolen, of course.

Concealed behind the shrubbery, dressed all in black, Raven whispered to Ben Jennings.

"Gypsy Kos, King of the Gypsies, called a Kris—a Romany council meeting."

"This was a crazy idea, Raven. We should call FWPD— or the Feds. Maybe get some directional mikes and a surveillance van. This place has cameras all over the goddam place."

"No. The cops don't seem to be all that interested in some piss-ant plot to kill me."

"Then the FBI."

"Those guys are morons."

"Yeah, but they have the best toys. All I have's my dick."

"Shhhhh." She peered through the glass beyond the slit in the drapery where the curtains failed to meet.

King Kos, withered and frail, led the menfolk into an opulent parlor where gold-threaded tapestries worthy of the most discriminating museums lined the walls. The King raised a gnarled, nicotine-stained finger, and motioned his guests to a round table.

Raven pointed. "See that old crone? That's Queen Ruta."

Jennings rasped, "You realize if we get caught, we'll probably go to jail—"

"We won't get caught."

"—I'll be disbarred—"

"Never happen."

"—or you'll end up with a bullet between your eyes, and I'll get my ying-yang blown off."

"Shhhh. They're about to start."

"Tell me again why we're here?"

"Because a confidential informant said Gypsy Kos called the Kris to plot how to do me in. Look—Ruta's placing a silver tray on the table. Jeez-Louise, that's Baccarat crystal. How'd they afford that? According to the IRS agent, Kos only claims an annual income of five thousand dollars."

"Maybe they stole it, you think?" Sarcastic.

Ruta left the room, pulling the door closed behind her. The lock snicked into place. Kos spread out the newspaper's Metro section, stuck his eagle beak nose inches from the photograph, and let out a demented screech.

Raven touched Jennings' hand. "Kos can't read. Neither can the others. They're illiterate."

"Yes, but he knows your picture when he sees it. By the way, if we're going to die anyway, I have to tell you how great you look in that picture. Marina's a cute kid. Too bad you won't live long enough to have your own."

"We'll see about that. Wait—Kos is about to say something."

The ancient man cleared his throat. His skin glowed yellow in the candlelight.

"This gadja—do you see her?" He held up the paper and

gave it a finger flick. "She is smiling. Her eyes jump off the page to mock us. To paralyze us. She has become a formidable opponent."

Murmurs of Yes rumbled around the table. Along with considerable head-bobbing.

"It is time to put an end to this-this-this . . . merry chase. The IRS is breathing down my neck."

An ugly troll with jet black hair held up a sausage finger. "Surely you do not suggest we retreat? Baloghs do not run."

Kos spread his arms. His gold robe, edged in ermine pelts, glittered in the candlelight. "We must consider the number of casualties." Nods of agreement. "The gadja's bullet zigzagged across Ephram's scalp. Though lovely Ruta closed the wound with sewing thread, the whiney-boy still staggers into our valuables and complains of ringing ears.

"And Estv, even with the advantage of height—still locked in jail.

"Ralph? Nursing a broken arm, falling from the dump truck.

"Viktor?" Gypsy Kos pointed to a man propped against the wall wearing a body cast and cervical collar. "This is from the gadja's bodyguards, wielding their tire irons."

A squatty man with his back to the window said, "What of Mikel?"

"Mikel? Our Dallas relatives hide this mangy coward. And Georg? Well, you have only to look at him." Kos motioned the family's snappiest dresser to stand.

The one called Georg was still sporting the same two alligator shoes, two cashmere socks, two nugget cufflinks, two black eyes—

Seemingly weary, King Kos searched the candlelit faces of old men Raven had yet to meet.

"Yanni, Pietro, Laszlo, Karl—" He rattled off a roll call

of names. "—we can afford no more losses. The streets we once had exclusive control over now crawl with IRS agents. By day, G-men drive past in tinted cars, their eyes shaded with sunglasses. They write our license plate numbers. Take pictures of our houses. Follow our children, and our children's children.

"At night, my son, Ivan, Prince of the Gypsies, watches from his bedroom at the top of our jade staircase. They come in vans, in sports cars, always a different automobile. And the men working on the telephone lines—I think they are not actually repairmen, but IRS agents trying to discover the money-making, fortune-telling, one-nine hundred lines Queen Ruta runs out of our home."

A withered little man with dark, wizened skin spoke. "What shall we do, King Kos?"

"The gadja has grown much too beloved. It is time to rid ourselves of the gadja curse."

"Do we have anyone left we can send to kill her?"

Raven's breath caught in her throat.

With tears glimmering in both eyes, Kos made his decision. "I have given it much thought. There is no other way. In order to continue our livelihood—"

Tears sluiced down his jaundiced cheeks.

"—to be prosperous—"

He gnashed his teeth.

"—to make the gadja leave us in peace—"

King Kos wailed in anguish.

"—My eldest, Ivan Balogh, Prince of the Gypsies, must die."

Chapter Thirty-two

The primary arrived.

For Jinx and his supporters—mostly consisting of staff pressed into service as poll watchers—election day started before sunup and lasted until the polls closed twelve hours later. Jinx checked each polling place to ensure Skeeter sent volunteers to hold yard signs or hand out pushcards as voters filed in to cast their ballots.

It didn't take long for Jinx to cement the notion he never should have put Skeeter in charge.

It wasn't the Vietnamese pot-belly pig with REELECT JINX PORTER bumper stickers slapped all over its bristly hide that created the Barnum & Bailey atmosphere; if Georgia was too wimpy to stand up to Skeeter when he insisted she walk the pig around the junior high on a leash, then she deserved to have her arm jerked out of its socket.

Hot Pants Hattie, an old friend of Loose-Wheel Lucille's he glimpsed parading around in short-shorts and one of Skeeter's "Rudy Castro" T-shirts, wasn't a problem either—especially since the oozing sores on the exposed parts of her arms discouraged people from accepting Castro's pushcards.

The eye-scalder came at the polling place Skeeter staked out for his own. The used car salesman hunkered near the driver's window of a lime green Camaro, a Slim-Jim in his hand—while Castro's girlfriend stood nearby passing out pushcards.

Jinx bailed out of the patrol car and sauntered over to his treasurer.

"What'n the hell's going on?"

"Pod'na." Skeeter brushed his flyaway hair back and gave him a cheesy grin. "I'm helpin' a damsel in distress."

"I can see that. Why didn't you just ask the little pip-squeak if you could be *his* treasurer instead of inflicting yourself on my campaign?"

"You got it all wrong, Pod'na. Castro's girlfriend locked her keys in the car. I told her I could rectify the problem, but she'd have to pass out your cards."

Rudy Castro's squeeze was passing out JINX PORTER pushcards.

Sonofagun. Skeeter finally got a testicle transplant.

For the first time in six months, the used car salesman made him chuckle.

With a twinge of excitement, he drove the mile over to the elementary school Raven should have been working.

Would have been working, if he hadn't fired her.

What he saw stunned him.

She stood with her back to the street, decked out in a broomstick skirt, matching green boots, with the brim of a Lady Texas High Roller tilted low on her forehead. In one hand, she held a rope with a donkey at the other end. Huge ears poked out of a black Constable ballcap she affixed to its head, and on its back hung a multicolored serape with Jinx Porter bumper stickers stuck on it. A line of pre-schoolers waited to pat the silly-looking beast. Worse, streams of voters filed past empty-handed, while his pushcards lay untouched in a box, sloughed off to one side.

"Be gentle," she said in that endearing drawl. "Don't hit the donkey. Let's not stick any fingers near his mouth, either."

Hee haw.

In a slow blink of ultimate trust, the animal fanned her with its spidery lashes. Children approached single-file to

272

caress the velvety nose or run a hand across its glossy rump.

Hee haw.

Jinx cleared his throat.

She jerked her head. Forced a smile. But her gray eyes stared from cold depths like a couple of ice cubes.

He said, "How's it going?"

"Good. Great, in fact."

He wanted to laugh. Raven always was a bad liar. "I didn't figure you'd show."

"I'm not the one who has trouble keeping promises," she said archly.

"Where'd the donkey come from?"

"Your idiot treasurer dumped him off. Here, hold this. I want a picture." She handed over the rope and lifted a camera strapped to her wrist. "I'll have a blow-up made for your office," she said gleefully, then lowered her voice and muttered, "so people can play Find-The-Jackass."

"That'd be nice." He handed over the tether.

Let her have her fun at his expense. He had it coming. In the meantime, she made for a good advertisement, and it gave him another live body to pass out pushcards. When the election was over, he'd rehire her. Talk her into giving him one more chance. He'd promise to give up other women, now that Lucille agreed they should meet at a motel.

The smell of cafeteria food drifted out the school doors, mixing with the scent of a freshly deposited donkey patty. The last of the kids headed back to the classroom.

"We need to talk."

She dropped the tether and favored him with the stunned expression of someone who had just been electrocuted.

"I know it's too early to ask you to forgive me—"

"Forgive you?"

"—but if you can't, you're not—"

"I'm only here because this position should go to a person with law enforcement credentials, not some dumbshit, candy-ass, lazy-boy politician who's just using it as a stepping stone to a higher office."

He wanted to finish. To tell her not having her around had left him with a hole in his heart and a gnawing ache in the pit of his stomach.

But Raven's eyes narrowed into slits.

He took a step backward in case she tried to give him a matching shiner.

She pointed across the school yard. "Your ass's dragging—"

He looked over.

"—the harness across the playground."

The campaign donkey trotted fifty feet away, churning crop circles in the school's flowerbed. Jinx stomped off after it, and the jenny broke into a run.

When he returned, Raven was gone. He tied the beast to a tree limb and left the box of cards where they sat.

On the way over to check the polling place Gladiola Brooks volunteered at, Jinx took a detour. He slowed the car long enough to see Glen Lee and the Munsch brothers decked out in full regalia. By the time he whipped the car into the parking lot, slammed the door hard enough to shatter the windows, stalked over to demand they take their sequined, feathered, spike-heeled asses home, they stopped him in his tracks.

Glen Lee and the Munsch brothers were passing out Castro's cards, alienating the few conservative Democrats still left in the precinct, with their affected, exaggerated, effeminate bullshit.

"Come here, you big stallion," Gerald said to Harold. Or vice versa.

When they dressed up like Judy Garland in the *Wizard of Oz*, he couldn't tell them apart.

"Give that gorgeous hunka-hunka burnin' love over there one of Rudy's cards."

The old man they targeted crumpled the card, dropped it on the ground, spat on it, and shot them the finger on his way inside.

"Litterbug." Glen Lee.

"Perverts," the man shouted over his shoulder.

Jinx muttered, "Keep up the good work," and trudged across the lawn where the Unabomber sat, sulking.

The kid acted like he had the weight of the pyramids on his shoulders.

"What're you doing here?"

"Glen Lee said I had to help."

"Don't do me any favors."

A good looking middle-aged lady strolled toward them.

"I'll handle this," Jinx said.

Before he could whip out a business card, Amos stepped in front of him and pressed a Rudy Castro card into her hand.

"Gee, you're a knockout," he slobbered.

"Why, thank you." The woman's eyes crinkled. The corners of her lips turned up.

"You always wear your skirts that short?"

Her mouth went slack. Wide eyes flickered to Castro's card. She folded it in half and torqued her jaw.

"You sure got nice tits."

"How dare you."

"Okay, you got great tits," Amos said, seemingly unapologetic.

Bingo.

The woman glared at Jinx. "Are you with him?"

"No, Ma'am. I'm Constable Jinx Porter. I'm running for reelection." He turned to Amos. "I ought to haul you to Juvenile Detention."

"I'm just passing out my daddy's cards. You know Rudy Castro? The guy running for constable?"

Jinx balled up a fist. He wanted to shake Ivy's little pervert 'til his insides rattled.

Amos carried on in his boorish way. "I know my daddy don't have no law enforcement experience, but he told my mama he'd marry her if he got to be constable—even though he got those other women pregnant and that last girl's due any day now—so you've gotta vote for him. Besides, he'd make a good one. He's got a hard-on for guns, and he quick-draws pretty good, and if you're constable, you get to wear a hogleg and shoot people."

Jinx turned in time to see the woman's face mold itself into a grotesque mask of contempt.

He set the hook.

"Excuse me, Ma'am. I'd like your vote. And I'm not so busy I can't do something about this little recidivist."

He pressed his business card into her hand. With any luck, she'd call to thank him. He'd tell her to let him know if there was anything he could ever do for her, and if Raven didn't come back home, he'd be able to knock off a new piece of tail by the end of the week.

When she promised him her vote and strutted inside, Jinx collared Amos, jerked him up on tiptoes and pulled him around the side of the building for a Come-to-Jesus meeting.

"I was just trying to help."

"How many times have you done this today? And don't lie."

Amos gulped. Scuffed the toe of his PF-Flyer against the

gravel. " 'Bout a hunnerd, I reckon."

"Keep it up. When it's over, I'll pay you a buck apiece, providing the totals match when the votes are counted."

Amos brightened. "Really? Fine-o, albino." He dug into his pocket, pulled out a crumpled wad and handed it over.

"What's this?"

"Report card."

Jinx flattened it out. In a crude forgery, Amos had almost erased a hole converting a forty-nine into a ninety-nine. "When I tried this, my parents threatened me with reform school."

Amos bucked up. "Sign it. You're my guardian."

"No way." He handed it back. The little thug shrugged, and it disappeared inside the pocket of his unwashed denims.

Jinx hurried back to the car. He needed to check by Gladiola's polling place.

Dressed like Jackie Kennedy on the morning of the assassination, Ola was in the throes of a passionate argument with Cupid.

"That's my dress," she hollered.

"Is not." Cupid matched Ola's squinty-eyed glint.

"Is."

Jinx sauntered over. "How're we doing?"

An angelic smile settled over Ola's face. She shouted as if he were deaf. "We got six hundred absentee ballots."

Cast for him. She should know. He suspected she did most of the counting.

By seven o'clock that evening, the courthouse buzzed with wannabes, are-nows, has-beens and never-weres. Incumbents and challengers alike crowded to see the television monitors set up to post the trickle of county-wide

277

ballots. Jinx hovered in a far corner, flanked by Skeeter, Ola, his office entourage, and Amos, freshly reunited with his ditzy mother.

He had a good feeling about the election.

For no particular reason, he broke into a tune. "I call my baby Candy, 'cause she makes my peanut brittle—"

Things turned to shit.

Raven glided in, arms linked with Ben Jennings, and the social butterflies flitted around the room like they were cross-pollinating.

First, she planted a sloppy kiss on old Judge Masterson's face and congratulated him for having sixty-two percent of the votes in his race. Then she sidled up to the huddle of Party Chairmen and whispered into their delighted ears.

Gil said, "You think she misses you?"

If she missed him, she didn't let on.

At eleven o'clock, with five minor boxes still out, whoops and squeals of "Congratulations" echoed through the room. Positions occupied by Gil, Dell, Mickey, Ivy, and Georgia were spared for four more years.

Rudy Castro skulked out of the courthouse as if he'd just been indicted on bestiality charges.

No one seemed happier for Jinx's victory than Raven.

She glided over with that engaging smile. "Good lick. I'm absolutely thrilled. You deserve it."

Jennings looked snappy in his navy blazer, khaki Dockers and Bally loafers. "Way to go, Constable."

"Could we talk?" Before Raven could put up a fuss, Jinx took her by the elbow and steered her under a stairwell, away from the madness surrounding them.

"You should have worn your violet pinpoint oxford." She eyed the purple coon-ring behind his glasses. "At least it would match."

"You should've been home to pick out my clothes."

Raven's eyes darted around. She seemed to be looking for an escape route. "Okay, Jinx, why so cloak-and-dagger?"

"I'll change." He hated his tone. For the first time in twenty years, he found himself begging.

She raised a hand to caress his swollen cheek. "Just be yourself. That'll help me the most."

"I can't tell you the misery I've gone through."

"I'm glad you won. Things wouldn't be the same if you weren't the Democratic winner."

"What do you mean? I'm the winner, period. There's no Republican in the general election." But Raven only smiled. "Look—I'll rehire you tomorrow. We can forget the whole thing. I was under stress."

"Oh, I'll be back, don't you worry." She winked. "You haven't heard the last of me."

He had a bad feeling she meant something else.

Georgia's bold scream hushed the room. She flung herself through the doors and rushed inside with a news bulletin.

"Come quick," she cried. "There's two midgets letting the air out of Jinx's tires."

Chapter Thirty-three

Maybe Dell hadn't heard the news buzzing through every Westside residence with a property value over a million bucks. As they sat in his patrol car, in front of her house, Raven wondered why he reached across the seat and took her hand.

"There's something I have to tell you about me and Nicole." Tiny lines around his piercing eyes relaxed.

"I have something to tell you, too."

"You first."

She took a deep breath and outed the news. "I did something irreparable. That's why I asked you to come over. I wanted to say good-bye."

"What?" Dell came alive. Sat up so straight his head barely cleared the roof liner. Aqua eyes turned stormy. "You're leaving?"

"The day we left the courthouse, after the Rice hearing, I drove Eleanor Thornton to the airport."

"You what?"

She could almost smell his fear. "It's true. I told her I knew how she felt. We had a nice long chat while we waited for her plane. I told her about Jinx and Loose-Wheel Lucille."

"You didn't."

Raven nodded. She opened her handbag and pulled out a piece of paper. Unfolded it. Held it up for him to see. Slitted eyes nearly popped out of his head. She could tell by the way they bulged with intensity that he was counting zeros on the check.

"A hundred thousand dollars," she said, in case he misread. "Enough for billboards." Dell's eyebrows knitted in confusion. "A campaign contribution. For me. And that's just the beginning."

"I don't get it. The election's over."

"No, it's not. There's still the general election in November."

"But you're not even on the ballot."

"I will be." His face contorted in disapproval. "Don't look at me that way. Jinx stole every shred of dignity I had. I'm just evening the score."

For an eternal moment, they sat locked in each other's gazes. Dell still didn't get it.

"I'm taking Jinx's job. It's a fair trade-off. Say something."

His answer came in the form of a head banged against the headrest.

"You think I'm wrong, don't you?" The silence stretched into minutes. "I lost what I loved most. Now it's Jinx's turn. I'm evening the score."

With each sweeping blink, Dell's pulsing black pinpoints seemed to say, You're nuts. "Does he know?"

"Not yet."

"He wants you to come back to work for him. I want you to come back. It's not the same without you. You don't really want to be constable. Forget this crazy idea and just come back where you belong."

"I'm not coming back."

Dell made another point. "If he finds out, your goose is cooked with that office. He won't let us talk to you."

The deputy was right. When Jinx took a gander at the billboards going up on either side of the freeway, he might not peg Eleanor Thornton for her benefactor, but he'd durned-sure think she juiced somebody out of money.

Dell said, "When are you gonna tell him?"

"I'm on my way in to see him. He thinks I'm coming to pick up my badge and ID. Want to give me a lift?"

"Can't." Dell refused to make eye contact. "He signs my paycheck."

She studied his face, shadowed in the darkness of a thousand Hells. He pulled at the brim of his hat until it dipped low, shading his eyes from view.

Then it dawned on her. "What'd you want me to know about you and Nicole?"

"Nothing." He reached across her and opened the latch. The door swung open and he looked away. "Not a thing."

For a fleeting instant, she thought Dell's eyes misted. But she had to be wrong. Because when he turned to face her, the icy depths of his eyes numbed her spirits with bone-chilling cold. Without another word, she got out and watched him pull away.

Imagine.

She hadn't even announced her candidacy for Jinx's job and she couldn't help but feel she'd already lost the vote of her biggest supporter.

Jinx sat at his desk with the drawer slightly ajar, studying Raven's photo. He discouraged his growing hard-on with a thump. It had been, what?—three days without sex? Served him right. Should've figured if he kept on with Loose-Wheel Lucille, he'd get stuck holding the Old Maid.

He should set the black-and-white glossy back out on display where it belonged. After all, she'd helped him win. If it hadn't been for her knocking on doors, giving people his pushcards, and charming voters with that stupid-ass donkey, Castro might've squeaked by. It was a cinch nobody else lifted a finger to help.

Sure was pretty.

A lump formed in his throat and he swallowed hard.

Maybe lost the best friend he ever had.

He strolled into the front office and propped himself against Mickey's desk. Georgia was searching the obituary section like it was a movie guide, no doubt looking for a funeral to attend, in another cheap ploy to leave work.

"These people are lucky," she said with conviction. "I bet every one of them's up there, sitting on Jesus's knee."

"And I suppose you wish you were, too?"

She stretched in her chair, yawned, and cut her gaze in his direction. "I'm not afraid to go, if that's what you mean. Matter of fact, I'm looking forward to it."

"That's good, because I remind you—that's the only way you'll get a day off until you build back up all the sick leave and vacation you're in hock to me."

She scowled and went right on scouring death notices. "Goodness me. Here's the man who used to pump gas at the filling station down the street from where I grew up."

"No. You're not going."

"My daddy used to give me a nickel to get a Big Orange from his soda machine."

"Forget it."

He wandered into the computer room and found Dell running a teletype on an ex-con he suspected his seventeen-year-old daughter was slipping around with. Dell wanted him arrested and sent back to the penitentiary.

"Any Blue Warrants on your guy?" Jinx asked.

"Not yet. But I can hope."

Jinx returned to Georgia's side. Like an alligator peering over a log, she lowered the paper and gave him a hostile stare.

"If you wanted to send somebody flowers," he whispered, "what would you get?"

She arched her brows, interested. "Well, Honey, I guess that depended on who I wanted to send them to."

"If you had some making up to do, what would you buy?"

She clapped her hands together in an enthusiastic clench, and delivered her answer without hesitation. "Tropicals. A big birds-of-paradise spray with those waxy-looking red things and maybe even a few African violets stuck in. And that's just what I'd have sitting here at the office," she continued, before he had a chance to butt in. "I'd have them waiting with plane tickets to Hawaii."

"No trip."

Georgia snorted as if to suggest she'd wasted her breath. "Why not? The primary's over, you don't have an opponent in the general and you need a vacation."

But Jinx knew she was really thinking, So do we.

The secretary's eyes sparkled. "I'd have a hundred roses set up for her at home. And maybe some balloons. With mushy stuff written on a card—more than just Thanks for the help."

Jinx sighed in surrender. Georgia beat him down with his own guilt and her enthusiasm.

"Get the flower shop on the phone."

The cowbell clanged. Mickey strolled in, with Ivy in tow. He slung his briefcase on the desk, nearly dislodging Jinx from his perch. His face registered utter disgust.

"I was looking forward to a little time off. Thought I'd head for the coast and go fishing."

Georgia snapped her fingers in an attempt to garner Jinx's attention. She covered the mouthpiece with her hand. "They want to know what you want to order."

"What we discussed." He didn't much care for the rest of the office tuning in to hear he was about to do some blue-ribbon groveling. To Mickey, he said, "If you want off, put your name on the calendar."

Mickey's eyes bulged. "But you said as long as you were running for reelection, we couldn't take vacation."

Ivy jabbed her colleague in the ribs. Said, "I don't reckon Jinx knows," in a stage whisper.

Jinx pushed himself off the desk and folded his arms across his chest. "What don't I know?"

Georgia slipped her hand over the mouthpiece again. "They don't have any birds of paradise. Pick something else."

He held up a hand for silence and glared at the weakest link.

Ivy smoothed the wild print shirt bunched up at her thick waist and tattled. Spilled her guts about Eleanor Thornton and the money.

"It's true," Mickey said. "Ask Dell. She's the one told him."

Jinx could almost feel his blood clot. A lightheaded rush went straight to his eyeballs, and a scary numbness enveloped the rest of his body.

"What do I tell them?" Georgia again, seemingly oblivious to Ivy's upending news bulletin. "They want to know what kind of flowers you want."

"Ask them if they've got any dead ones."

Chapter Thirty-four

To be on the safe side, Raven scanned the rearview mirror of Joe-Bob's cootie for miniature people driving large cars. Even though the King of the Gypsies said they should leave her alone, she made her way over to Sonny's Auto Hospital wondering if the gyps were recruiting a bunch of tall homeless people to bushwack her.

She rounded the final corner and saw the mechanic, sitting on a fender, sipping from a paper cup.

"Go away." He stepped into the sunlight. Thick eyebrows met in the middle of his frown and formed a dam that held back the reservoir of sweat beading up on his forehead.

Joe-Bob rolled out from under a Toyota, pulled himself to his feet, and squinted against the sun. His wrench clattered to the concrete. He let out an anguished wail and sprinted out of the bay to inspect what was left of his car.

Sonny glanced over mournfully. "See what you done? You made Joe-Bob cry."

"Where's my car?"

Sonny's face creased with pain. He continued to watch Joe-Bob, writhing against the back windshield.

Raven lost patience. "Shouldn't you tell him to stop making those spooky noises? He's scaring the paint shop guys across the street."

With the speed of a slug on a December sidewalk, Sonny turned his head and stared down his nose at her. "What's it gonna take to make you leave?"

"Fix my BMW."

"It ain't running."

"I want my Beemer."

"People in the ghetto want Swiss bank accounts." He looked her over. "You been wrestlin' hogs at the Stockyards?"

Raven tilted her chin. "Don't give me any flack. I've had a rough day. Just give me a loaner and finish my car."

"I reckon you know what's on the lot for you to drive." He squinted into the horizon. Settled his gaze on the Lincoln.

"I hate you."

Sonny shrugged and went back to work.

"Not so fast."

The wrench thudded to the ground. He jammed his fists against his paunch. "Now you lookie here, Missy. Everything don't come to a screechin' halt just because you want somethin'."

"You get paid, don't you?"

"Yeah, but—"

"That's what it's all about. I've got a problem with my car, I pay you to fix it."

"Find somebody else. I ain't workin' on it no more."

"What?"

"You just want too much fixed. Go on."

"How am I supposed to get it out of here? It isn't even running."

"That's what I been trying to tell you." He reached in his pocket, fished out a set of keys, and tossed them to her.

"Two weeks," she said. "I mean it."

The Lincoln's barbecued seat crunched under her weight. She fired up the engine and dropped the car into reverse.

After casing the precinct for billboards, the best location

appeared to be next to Al's AAAA Aardvark Import Auto Salvage and Repair.

Grudgingly, Raven shifted gears and pointed the Lincoln toward Al's.

On his first day back at work after the primary, Jinx only had two things to do. The first was to patch things up with Raven. The second, to figure out how to keep Lucille.

A memory of Loose-Wheel Lucille's satisfied smile popped into mind and he shuddered. Why Raven hadn't killed them both, he'd never know.

Raven.

He turned the car stereo up loud, but even George Strait couldn't drown out the woman's presence. Damned Loose-Wheel Lucille, anyway—always demanding sex. Always begging for a handout.

Here's twenty bucks, go buy you something nice.

But she always came back with a twelve-pack of beer and cigarettes—the long, skinny kind that stank like a buffalo's butt.

In a last minute gesture, he jerked the steering wheel and aimed the car at the freeway. On light traffic days, he could picture himself driving until the gas gauge settled on "E."

What a mess.

It wasn't as if he hadn't tried to discourage the old hag. But each time he said, "Let's just be good friends," Lucille's eyes would water and she'd let her fingers do the walking.

You don't mean that, Jinxy. Come to Mama.

He slammed on the brakes. Tires screamed against the asphalt and he pulled the squad car onto the shoulder. His eyes closed in the tight squint of disbelief.

When he opened them wide, the billboard on the

freeway still loomed large.

Against the backdrop of an ominous sky stood a larger-than-life shot of his girlfriend, favoring drivers with one of her sultry smiles. Words advertised her qualifications—

—informed voters she had the wherewithal to carry out an aggressive office—

—and let everyone know she was a serious candidate—

NOT JUST ANOTHER PRETTY FACE.

Raven drew first blood.

If the billboard stayed up for seven months, every voter in his precinct would know the correct spelling of her name when they filled in the blank under write-in candidate.

Even though her watch pulsed four-forty-five on the digital display, Raven knew Ali had seen her through the blinds because he ran to the door and flipped the OPEN sign to CLOSED. They grabbed the door handle at the same time, but she threw her weight against it enough to get a foot in the door.

"Let me in. I know you're open."

"I am pleased to say, my business establishment is closed. See you later, alligator."

She braced her hand against the doorjamb and forced her shoulder through the sliver. "It's not five o'clock. You're only doing this to be mean."

"Alas, there is no Mom in my Mom-and-Pop business. I am a sole proprietor. Today, I have given my best employee the rest of the afternoon off. Please to say good-bye and come again."

"I won't be back."

Ali's black eyes glimmered. "Do these ears deceive me? Or has Allah truly answered my prayers?"

Raven wedged herself halfway through the opening. "I'm

not coming back tomorrow—or ever, for that matter—if you'll do me a favor."

"Favor? What kind of favor? This is not a sexual request, I hope."

"Listen, Ali, if you want breakfast in bed, go sleep in the kitchen. I'm talking about a favor that will benefit both of us. Let me come in."

He glanced over his shoulder at the wall clock. "Thirteen minutes." His grip relaxed enough for her to slip through.

"I'm running for constable."

"You should consult your physician for a laxative."

"Not constipated. Constable. It's like being sheriff."

"But this is perilous employment, is it not?"

"Yes. It's often dangerous."

"You could be killed at any moment?"

"I suppose so."

"May Allah will that you should have this constable position. Eleven minutes."

With a narrow-hipped swagger, Ali moved around the counter and logged off his computer. Raven lifted a leg and slid onto a bar stool opposite him.

"Here's the deal." She pointed out the plate glass window. "I want that billboard."

"This is to advertise my business establishment."

"I'm prepared to rent it for the next seven months."

Ali smiled wide enough for her to see a missing back tooth. "This is exceptional. I shall accept your check. The rental is one hundred thousand dollars."

She glared across the Formica. "I'm not paying a hundred thousand dollars for that billboard. I'll pay ten. For seven months."

"I'm afraid Allah would be most displeased. Nine minutes."

"Ah—" She wagged her finger. "—I'm prepared to offer a bonus."

"What is bonus?"

She laid the groundwork for him to relinquish the sign. "In exchange for you letting me use that billboard for the next seven months, I'll pay you ten thousand dollars, and—" Raven injected cheer into her voice. "—I promise never to darken your door again."

Chapter Thirty-five

A few weeks after the primary, the cowbell clanged at the Constable's Office.

"Hi, there." Raven leaned inside the door enough to hold out a nosegay of wildflowers. "I thought you'd appreciate these. They're not store-bought, but I think they're better. I picked them myself at a friend's place."

"Honey, you're back." Georgia rolled her chair away from the desk and came around with outstretched arms. She took one look at the police cadet uniform and barely restrained a sigh. "Guess not."

Raven regarded the sea of unguarded faces. "Jinx in?"

Georgia's eyes cut to the door and she used her library voice. "He's next door, talking to the chief of police. I hope you don't aim to get him stirred up."

"I figure I owe it to him to let him know I intend to pull out all the stops. I just don't want him saying I did him dirty."

Mickey grabbed his Stetson. "Give us a chance to bail out, will you?" He jutted his chin at Dell, who grabbed his cowboy hat and adjusted the brim low.

Gil gave her a weak smile and went back to his newspaper.

"Heard a nasty rumor the queers at Jinx's apartment got you the Gay-Lesbian endorsement. 'Course, that like to have killed Jinx," Mickey deadpanned on his way to the door.

Across the room, Ivy hung up the telephone, vacuumed in air and reached for her shoulder bag. "I gotta get. Amos just called. The trailer next door to our house caught fire and burned to the ground."

All eyes locked on Ivy.

Mickey was first to speak. "Where's Amos?"

"That's sweet of you to ask. He's just fine. He's home, talking to the fire marshal."

"The fire marshal," Mickey echoed.

"Yep. I was mad as all get-out when he got expelled from school, but now—" She stared up in philosophical wonderment. "—All I can say is, thank goodness. If he hadn't been at home, our house could've burned, too. God works in mysterious ways."

"No mystery to it," Gil muttered behind the front page. He rescued Georgia from the bleating of the telephone. "Ivy, it's the principal. Something about a bomb threat."

Jinx walked in and freeze-framed the room. His voice was controlled and polite, but his eyes blazed white-hot. "Something we can help you with?"

"Got a minute?"

He motioned her back to his office, closed the door, and thumbed at a chair.

Raven said, "I'd like a cease-fire. I wanted you to know—"

He silenced her with an upraised hand. "I already know. Anybody who puts their name on the ballot can get twenty percent of the vote, so it's not like you wouldn't get any at all."

She kept her cool. Feigned interest. Hung on every condescending word, the way she used to before she developed a backbone. "Is that right?"

"You were having a tantrum. You knew you couldn't win when you started this nonsense, so it's just as well you drop out now."

She could almost hear her blood reach the boiling point. Her first impulse was to ball up a fist and make his eyes match, but she let the silence speak for her.

"Here's what I'll do. I'll pick up your commission and we can go back to the way things were. Besides," he added, "those uniform pants are too tight. You look better in jeans."

She kept her voice even and metered. "You talked to the chief about me, didn't you? That's what you were doing at the PD." She dragged in thick, stale air. "You were bad-mouthing me, trying to get him to yank my peace officer commission."

He looked at her slitty-eyed. His expression hardened. "Not that it's any of your business . . . I went to see about my bus sign."

"What about Lucille?"

"I called her this morning. Told her we could be friends, but it was over."

She studied him carefully. "You're dumping her because of me?"

"You could say that."

"This is your way of stopping me from running against you."

Jinx shook his head.

She had to remind herself that the battery acid eating away at her stomach lining was nothing more than carnal panic. "Pick up the phone and call Lucille. I want to hear you tell her."

"No. And I'm not worried about you running for this office because the voters in this precinct won't stand for a woman constable. It's good you figured it out before you embarrassed yourself." The worry lines in his face relaxed.

Raven's eyes sizzled in their sockets.

"So, how about it? You bringing your stuff back home, or not?"

"Got your checkbook?"

His face lined with confusion. "Yeah, why?"

"We're going to the jewelers," she said, tempering her voice to cloak her anger. "You're buying me a three-carat diamond, and I'm picking it out."

She rode in silence, unable to get a word in edgewise with Jinx filling her in on the office doings. When they arrived at the jeweler's, Raven beat him inside.

"That one." It wasn't three carats, but it looked big and gaudy, and could double as a weapon if the need arose.

Jinx wrote out the check. "Sure you don't want something else?" Facetious.

"Actually, I'd like matching earrings."

When he dropped her off at her house, she leaned in the passenger window and gave him one last chance to save his political skin.

"Do you love me?"

"Not the way you want me to."

You get what you settle for.

She twisted the ring on her finger.

"I'm not coming back. I'm keeping the ring. And I'm still in the race."

That evening, when Jinx showed up at Harry Fine's Auto Mall to strongarm a financial report out of Skeeter, the car hawker delivered the bad news.

"Well, Pod'na, we got just enough cash to stamp mailouts to the Tarrant County Bar Association, begging donations."

"I hate asking for money. There's got to be a better way."

Skeeter propped his elbows on the desk and rested his head in his palms. His jowls stretched like Silly Putty. "There is one way to neutralize her." His voice trailed.

Jinx waited for him to detonate the verbal landmine. It didn't take long.

"Eleanor Thornton's backing your girlfriend because Mrs. Thornton hates your guts. So, I was thinking, Who hates Eleanor Thornton's guts?" Laughter flickered behind his eyes. He settled back in his chair, slapped his hands against his thighs, and answered his own question. "Alexander Thornton III, Pod'na. We could ask Thornton for the money, get them two to bickering. You know, smear your ex."

It could work. Jinx went quiet and sank into his own thoughts.

"So, whatcha think? Should I call Thornton?"

"No."

Skeeter cocked his head. "But Pod'na, we're down to the wire."

Jinx scooped his new gray Stetson off Skeeter's desk, put it on, and adjusted the brim. Nobody played dirtier than Trey Thornton. If they took the money, Thornton would see to it he won.

"It's a great idea," Jinx admitted. "But we're not asking him."

Call him crazy, but he wouldn't tarnish Raven's name.

Skeeter slid open the desk drawer. "All right, Pod'na, I didn't want to have to do this, but you leave me no choice."

His hand disappeared momentarily and came out with a cheesecake photograph of Raven taken on their trip to Hawaii. Jinx heated up.

"Where'd you get this?"

"Lookin' kinda green, Pod'na."

"I'm wondering whether a grand jury would indict me if I actually do what I'm thinking about doing to you. You got that picture from Ivy's little serial killer, didn't you?"

Skeeter beamed. "I've got a great idea."

"Don't make me come over the desk."

"We'll turn it over to the gypsies—"

Before Skeeter could finish, Jinx ripped the snapshot out of his hand and stuffed it in the pocket of his sportcoat, headed for the exit, and said what he should have said a year ago.

"You're fired."

Chapter Thirty-six

Having returned from one of his penitential trips to Kamille's speechless with rage, Jinx was doing his best not to listen to Georgia fretting over a newspaper article on mass suicide. Instead, he concentrated his efforts on admiring himself for not venting his spleen when his mother outwardly admired Raven's billboard, and his father dared ask outside Kamille's presence whether Raven was hot in the sack.

They never snapped to the fact she was running against him, merely thought she was running for a similar position. And worse, both expressed discontent they weren't in the proper precinct to cast votes for her. The fact that Eleanor Thornton was financing Raven's candidacy never came up.

They didn't seem to give a rat that on the cusp of one of the hottest summers predicted, he would spend every weekend until the first Tuesday after the first Monday in November knocking on doors until his clothes were wringing wet.

With sweat trickling down his sides, he threw his brief-case into the nearest chair and took stock of the room. Perched against Mickey's desk, Jinx watched Dempsey near the water cooler, wrestling with a trash liner.

He said, "Hey, Dempsey. How about some water?"

"Sure, Mistah Portah." The janitor took the last cup, filled it until the bottle gurgled, and downed it where he stood. "Mind if I have another?"

He was about to tell Dempsey he could drown in it for all he cared, but Georgia thumped the newspaper with her finger.

"This is awful. Don't people know if you kill yourself, you can't get into Heaven?"

Unless she had bona fide proof God had a few thousand absentee votes up there for him, he wasn't about to be suckered into another one of her religious discussions.

The custodian said, "That's sad."

Mickey agreed.

Georgia jumped on the deputy like a bum on a baloney sandwich. "I figured you'd be the first to argue with me."

"Not me. Suicide rankles me. Always has. For one thing, I never understood it. I mean, if somebody makes you unhappy, kill them, not yourself. After all, they're the ones causing trouble."

Dell stared, a hint of approval settling in his eyes.

Jinx caught himself nodding. He sat there thinking of ways to kill himself, and decided eating a couple of pints of Ben and Jerry's Chunky Monkey every night for the next five months might work.

"You people are jaded." Georgia sucked in a deep breath and blew dust off her plastic Jesus statue. "If you don't start changing your ways, you'll all be taking the tour bus to Hell."

The door clanged open.

Ivy pushed her way in, eyes scouring her phone bill, her lavender polyester slacks rustling at the thighs, happier than a hog hip-high in mud.

Angling over to her desk, she halted in her tracks. "Sweden? We don't know anybody in Sweden."

All eyes moved in a collective shift.

"Dadgum phone company." She reached for the receiver. "We'll just see about this tommy-rot. Bunch of morons can't even fill out an invoice the right way. Sweden. Did you ever? And what the hell's this? Brazil?"

The entire crew exchanged knowing looks. No one uttered a word. They didn't have to. They were all thinking the same thing.

Dempsey rolled his pushcart to the door. With a mournful look, he said, "Is Miss Raven ever comin' back?"

Georgia drew in a sharp intake of air.

At the mention of Raven's name, the deputies remembered they had things to do. Dell bent his head in concentration and pecked on the computer keyboard. Mickey smoothed his mustache, while Gil retreated behind the paper.

"You never know," Jinx said with a noncommittal shrug. His stomach went hollow, and he snatched his briefcase off the chair and headed back to his office.

"She sure looked pretty on TV this mornin'." Dempsey's words stopped him cold.

Jinx whipped around. He caught Dell watching him with the intensity of a cheetah.

"Raven was on television?"

"Yessuh. Cuttin' a ribbon over at the Women's Shelter with a pair of big ol' scissors. Looked real nice in her red suit. And I heard the newsman say tomorrow she'll be on Oprah with some rich lady from Beverly Hills."

All stressed out and no one to pistol-whip.

Every time Jinx thought about Raven flitting around town, charming his constituents while he tended to business, it galled him no end. She wouldn't think it was such a great job if she had to engineer the day's strategic battle plan.

He didn't need any more bad press. And taking on a pocket of screwballs who called themselves members of the Republic of Texas wasn't exactly the kind of thing he looked forward to, given that his decrepit parents would probably stroke out if they saw another negative story about him.

That afternoon, he mustered Gil, Mickey, Dell, and Ivy, and laid out a plan for the following morning's eviction.

"I need y'all here about four o'clock. We'll set up on them and hit the door about five. Agreed?"

Ivy whined. "It can't be later? Does the landlord really want to bring us a key that early?"

"His key won't fit. They changed the locks."

Mickey alerted with the enthusiasm of a drug K-9 in an airport baggage terminal. "Do we get to crowbar it?"

"Dell can kick it. Or use the battering ram. We're not taking any guff off anybody, either. I don't want this turning into a Waco deal. I want this to work like a 'quickie.' Get on, get in, get out."

Everyone nodded.

"The longer it takes, the harder it'll be to get these fruitcakes out. The harder it is, the more chance somebody'll get hurt."

Gil said, "Will Channel Eighteen be there?"

He huffed in disgust. "Lord, I hope not. This isn't the time for free publicity. If the move-out works, more power to us, and I'll wish I'd called them. But if something gets screwed up, the last thing I need is my mother phoning."

At four-thirty the next morning, patrol cars filed out of the drive, headed for the eviction site.

Jinx's thoughts turned to Raven.

He missed her sense of humor. Missed hearing her hum "Flight of the Valkyries" over the PA system. Oh, hell, who was he kidding? He missed her in the sack.

In far south Fort Worth, they passed the mouth of a long driveway and parked in the next block. Mickey toted the battering ram, just in case Dell didn't kick the door in on the first try.

They crept to the house.

Ivy caught up even with Jinx. "Don't you think we should've asked the sheriff's department for reinforcements?"

"One riot, one Ranger." He wondered if she could make out his murderous glare through the darkness.

With Jinx and Dell on the porch flanking the front door, Mickey and Gil at the rear, and Ivy off by a side window, Jinx gave Dell the go-ahead.

The deputy reared back.

Planted a size twelve-double-D to the side of the knob.

Wood disintegrated in a powerful explosion, ripping away one of the hinges. Like a loose tooth, the door dangled open wide enough to stampede the house.

Dell hit the wall switch, flooding the room with light.

Mickey shattered the back door with the battering ram, and the house crawled with deputy constables.

Jinx and Dell burst into a bedroom. A man scrambling off a cot lunged for the night stand.

Dell grabbed a hunk of undershirt, wound it around a fist, and raised him to his tiptoes. "Where d'ya think you're going?"

Dawn came, and the movers hauled out the last stick of furniture and dumped it onto the curb. A carpenter stood by, waiting to board up the gaping exits with plywood.

The sky revealed itself in layers of purple and streaks of pink. As a tangerine sun popped up on the horizon, a pair of headlights rocked up the drive.

Channel Eighteen.

Ivy flinched under Jinx's glare.

"I did it for you," she said.

"It could've turned into a fiasco."

"But it didn't. The only one who doesn't have faith in you, Jinx, is you."

A reporter and cameraman bailed out of the news van. A beacon of light lit up the shadows and a man with hair that looked as if it had been freeze-dried and shellacked shoved a microphone under Jinx's nose.

"They say they're going to sue . . . that you can't do this kind of thing in the Republic of Texas."

He let out a bark of laughter. "They may think they're in the Republic of Texas, but this is still my precinct."

Sonny tossed an empty candy wrapper into the trash and stared at the underbelly of a jalopy on a lift. To Raven, he seemed to be paying homage to the great chassis-god.

"Where's my car?"

"Go away."

"Are you finished with her?"

He jutted his chin in the direction of the parking lot.

Raven drew a hand to her lips. An opal on wheels glittered in the sunlight.

"She's got new parts, but she'll never run the same."

"At least we have something in common."

"Want my advice? Trade it."

Raven shook her head. "She may have gotten a little beat up, tangling with that big old truck, but that car has a lot of heart. Next time, it's the truck that better watch out."

Chapter Thirty-seven

The first Monday in November rolled around.

For Jinx, the previous week had been one continuous gut-cramp. A family named Pérez moved into the apartment next door and lost no time hammering Christmas decorations into the brick mortar outside his window. The twinkle lights that covered the side of the building induced a seizure in an epileptic in the corner apartment; but the lights were merely annoying compared to the live nativity scene *la familia Pérez* set up outside his bedroom window overlooking the front lawn—complete with donkey droppings.

Jinx even thought he could endure the carnival atmosphere until a transformer blew. Caesar poked his head through the slats in the Venetian blinds, and when Jinx tried to extricate the Siamese, a crowd of people gawking at the livestock pointed to the cat and cried, "Jesús!" Now, pilgrims appeared in droves each evening, praying for a glimpse of the apparition they believed to be *El Niño Cristo*.

And that morning, the Mexican newspaper carrier almost rendered him unconscious when he opened the door and the morning edition struck him between the eyes. By the time he stopped seeing double, it was too late to read it.

Even worse, Gladiola Brooks came down with pneumonia and checked into a private room at Our Lady of Mercy. According to her doctors, she couldn't be released before Wednesday, which meant she wouldn't be released in time to vote in the general. When he tried to find Skeeter to see if the campaign chest had enough money to hire an ambulance to transport Ola to the polling place and back, Harry Fine took diabolical delight telling him Skeeter took the week off and flew to Cancún.

The only good thing about the last few months was that he'd built up an immunity to Raven's TV and radio spots. Even the indignity of having her show up at the Rotary Club with Gil didn't leave him with a queasy stomach, as long as he ate bland food and stayed away from anything spicy.

He drove to the mall with Raven haunting his thoughts.

He hadn't seen Loose-Wheel Lucille since that horrible afternoon—even though she was giving him the hard-sell, trying to lure him back into the sack. Once he made it clear he wanted to patch things up with Raven, he screened out her phone calls and ignored her pages, even when she punched in nine one one after her number. He finally saw her through Raven's eyes.

Jezebel.

Finding a parking place near the front entrance surprised him. Maybe his luck was about to turn.

When he beat Raven hands down, he'd ask her to marry him.

No kids, though. He didn't need kids.

Maybe one.

Then he could make up for the botched relationship with his own daughter.

Midway through the crosswalk, his ears pricked up at the sound of a roaring engine. A flatbed pickup full of swarthy short guys zoomed past and shot him the finger. He returned the hand gesture of the terminally pissed, then lost sight of them in the crowded lot. If it turned out gypsies were after him, he'd have no trouble screwing the barrel of his .38 in their collective ears. When he reached the mall entrance, he checked over his shoulder, watching until the door closed behind him.

He took a deep breath and forced himself to make the Bataan Death March into the toy store. A smocked clerk who appeared to be too young to vote sauntered up with pep in her walk and offered assistance.

"I'm looking for a present for a little girl. I guess she'd be about five. Do kids that age still want Barbie Dolls?"

The answer pleased him.

"Does King Kong like big bananas?"

Bubbles.

Raven's eyes widened at the obituary. She slumped against the down-filled pillow and stared at the timeless photograph of a go-go dancer named Lucille "Bubbles" Graham. Apparently the previous day, the old lady departed more than just the Château Du Roy and Jinx Porter's bed. According to the two-inch notice, Loose-Wheel Lucille had no survivors.

She grabbed a pen off the night table, circled the name of the funeral home, and cleared her schedule. It might be interesting to see who showed up at the graveside service besides her. Especially since they were planting the old woman on Election Day.

You picked a fine time to leave me, Lucille.

With only one day to go in the political pressure cooker, the old alkie's pickled liver gave out. Jinx begged her to vote absentee, but she liked it when he rode her around in the car. Looked forward to him hauling her down to the polling place. At least if she'd voted early, he could've counted on two votes.

Stinking women never listened.

Jinx sat in his recliner with the obituary page folded in his lap, reflecting on their relationship, mindful of the downpour pelting the roof.

He'd brought home a pound of spare ribs—guaranteed to burst the hearts of laboratory rats—but settled on a bowl of oatmeal, hoping it would calm his queasy stomach. Even brooding over Lucille, he managed to eat a few bites, until a weevil crawled up the side of the dish.

He searched the refrigerator to see if he could identify anything edible, but the stuff either turned out to be as hard as granite or covered with tundra. After sifting through a couple of ripe containers that hadn't been opened since Raven took off, Jinx gave up.

With Caesar in his lap, he sank back into the recliner and flipped through the TV schedule. The erotic sound of flesh slapping against flesh filtered up from the Munsch twins' apartment.

"Give it to me, Big Stallion."

A sensual moan sent Jinx grappling for the volume control.

The Cowboys drowned out the debauchery downstairs. Texas had the ball five yards from the goal. They would T-D, of course, and for the first time in weeks, he felt a smile of satisfaction spread across his face.

Unexpectedly, the Baltimore Ravens sacked the quarterback. He blinked in disbelief. Squinted at the instant replay. Sure enough, the ball shot out from under the pile like a remote-control goat pellet.

Jinx groaned. But not enough to mute the exciting crescendo of hungry grunts from the transvestite sex fiends.

"YES, LLAMA-BOY, YES."

He upped the volume and gritted his teeth.

The Ravens were picking *Da Boys'* bones. Caesar wound

into a tight coil and placed a paw over one eye, but Jinx took in every painful play.

What sounded like a meteor hitting the apartment roof sent the Siamese flying to the safety of the bathroom. The next thing Jinx knew, he'd gone blind.

Unless that was a chunk of sheetrock wedged between his face and eyeglasses.

Water poured in through the ceiling. Sections of drywall avalanched onto the computer, furniture, and Jinx himself. The roof might as well have been a sieve. With the indignation of a dethroned king, the cat crept back in and explored the damage while Jinx tried to squeegee his glasses clean with the edge of a sopping wet T-shirt.

The Ravens snapped the ball, and some spider-legged sonofabitch ran like he had Jet Assisted Takeoff Rockets strapped to his ass. The score no longer mattered—even thermometers didn't go that high.

In the corner of the living room, the lightbulb from an overturned lamp sputtered, then exploded in a blinding burst of blue glitter. He relaxed against the chair cushion, unpuckered his sphincter and conducted his own instant replay of the last few minutes.

For him and the cat, life boiled down to a broken home.

Momentarily, he turned his attention away from the ruins and wrangled his way out of the recliner. With his feet suctioning the carpet like a couple of plungers, he headed for the phone. The floor creaked underfoot, but it was the ominous pop and twiglike snap that made him jump reflexively. Without warning, the living room shifted in the concave beginnings of a sinkhole.

The sounds that followed took on all the characteristics of the Fourth of July. The center of the floor drooped, pulling the coffee table and TV down with it. The carpet metamorphosed into a furniture-swallowing hammock. Jinx dropped the receiver and made a wild grab for the cat.

Downstairs in the Munsch brothers' apartment, dual screams filtered up. The macaws reacted with delight.

"Bite me."

Chapter Thirty-eight

The day of the funeral, Raven got an early start. First she cast her ballot. Then she saw Dempsey leaving the polls.

"You vote, Dempsey?"

"Naw. I'm here with my mama."

"You're not a registered voter?"

"Naw. I just brought Mama."

Raven nodded glumly. "I sure could've used your help."

"Don't fret, Miss Raven. Tough times never last. Tough people always do."

She left him fifty dollars and a box of pushcards to hand out.

At eleven, she drove through the oak-covered back roads to the Reverend Willie Lee Washington's Celestial House of the Dove.

A hundred yards from the freshly turned earth, she staked out her position behind a large tree and watched through binoculars. She scanned the treeline—

—and her jaw dropped open.

Fifty yards away, Shiloh Wilette was hiding in a stand of live oaks, doing the same thing.

Jinx's ex lowered her field glasses and lifted her hand in a feeble wave. Raven blinked. They'd both come to make sure the woman who'd ruined their lives was really dead. A shiver zigzagged up her spine and she tightened the belt to her camel hair overcoat and lifted the collar to break the chill.

A white limousine pulled up behind a horse-drawn caisson. A grim-faced old black man in a dark suit opened the door for the lone attendant. She raised the binoculars.

Ohmygod.

Why's he here? He promised he wouldn't have anything else to do with her.

A team of workers heaved a red coffin off its platform and placed it next to a gap in the earth. When Jinx turned to the old man to wave him away, the contours of his face were lined with pure, uncontrolled grief. A young boy snapped the reins on a midnight stallion and the horse clopped off. Taillights from the sleek limo brightened, and the car slumped forward and disappeared from view. The old man slipped out of sight and reappeared beyond the grove of trees with his top hat in hand and his head bowed in respect.

Jinx dropped to one knee and wordlessly stared off into space. From the tilt of his head, Raven suspected he was recapturing a memory.

His lips moved.

His shoulders shook.

Is he crying?

Jinx rose. He removed a flower from his coat and laid it on the casket with reverence, then gave the grim-faced Negro a somber nod.

Whereupon the old man walked over to a cage.

Pulled a lever.

The latch clinked loud against metal, and the door dropped open.

Five hundred pigeons ascended for the Heavens.

While Jinx Porter ran like Hell.

The political custom on the Tuesday following the first Monday in November was for the candidates and their entourages to convene at the courthouse while votes were being tallied. But Raven stunned supporters. Not only did she inform them she wouldn't be at the courthouse when the final ballots were tallied, she politely declined the ride downtown in Eleanor Thornton's limousine.

Home alone, she washed two sleeping pills down with an eight-ounce glass-bottled Coke, killed the lights, screened her calls through the answering machine, and wondered how Jinx was doing.

And who he was doing.

Along with where they were doing it.

She smashed her fist into the pillow and yanked the eiderdown comforter over her head. By nine o'clock she couldn't take any more well-wishers. She unplugged the phone with such dread she could almost hear the sucking sound of her life circling the drain.

By ten-thirty, the unexpected crying jag finally waned and she drifted off to sleep with images of Jinx surrounded by toothless hula girls with picket-fence hair.

She awakened to the sound of a fist thundering against the door. The digital readout on the clock flashed electric blue numbers. She squinted fiercely and made out the time. Five-thirty.

What kind of idiot showed up on a person's doorstep this time of morning?

She sat bolt upright.

Gypsies?

Nah. Then, again. . . .

Cinching her robe, she grabbed the Glock off the night stand and padded, barefoot, to the living room in a fog. She sensed movement behind the front door and rose on tiptoes to look out the peephole.

Jinx.

She put down the gun, turned the knob, and was treated

to a view of him adjusting his crotch.

Raindrops dotted his head and sluiced down his neck. Wire-rims sat, cock-eyed, on the bridge of his nose.

"Congratulations," he said dully.

"What in God's name happened to you?"

"Got caught up in a little home improvement project at the Château Du Roy." He stuck a hand in his pocket and jingled his coins the way he always did when he wasn't quite finished, but didn't know how to continue. "It really is your lucky day. I guess you saw today's newspaper?"

She shook her head. "The paperboy doesn't come for another half hour."

"You know how Georgia's always looking for funerals to go to? Well, she found one that might interest you."

She stared in stricken silence. Had he seen her at Loose-Wheel Lucille's?

"Ivan Balogh. Looks like you're free of the gypsy curse."

Balogh? Dead?

Raven slumped against the doorframe. It wouldn't do to squeal with delight, so she settled for a more innocuous response. "I can't tell you how sad that makes me."

"Reckon I better get going. You'll be having company soon. I'm surprised they're not already here."

"What're you talking about?"

He rocked on his heels. Pressed his lips together until they made a gray line. "You got what you wanted."

Her gut sank. She stepped aside, hoping he would come in.

"I thought I'd be a sport and drop by. I told Dell you wouldn't be at the courthouse and I was right."

"Dell's a great guy."

"So are the others." He kept his eyes firmly averted. "Just do me a favor, Raven, and don't fire any of them. Especially Ivy. I know y'all haven't always seen eye-to-eye, but she needs that job."

He turned his back on her and headed into the night.

Maybe the best man hadn't won.

Jinx could think of only one other time his life took such a nosedive—when Shiloh left with their girl. Ironic, how the two most important women in his life—women he trusted— gutted him.

He parked the patrol car several houses down from Ann-Jeanette Rice's, and studied the surroundings. He hadn't expected to see lights on. Would she open the door this early?

And if she did, would she slam it in his face?

What if she wouldn't let the kid accept his gift?

He tiptoed up the cracked sidewalk. A board on the rickety porch creaked under his weight. The aroma of crackling cedar permeated the air, filling his nostrils with the same smells of winter he loved as a child. Through the sheers he saw Marina in her mother's lap, wearing her fuzzy-footed PJs, pointing a chubby finger at an open picture book. They shared a laugh. The girl's shrill giggle echoed like windchimes.

Instead of tapping at the door, he leaned the brightly wrapped present against the frame.

At the last second, he removed the card and left.

Chapter Thirty-nine

The wake for Ivan Balogh lasted three days and three nights. Over two thousand gypsies showed up to pay homage, some living out of their cars, others pitching tents on the funeral home grounds until the lawn was reduced to a green stain.

Raven sat behind the wheel of Eleanor Thornton's limousine, wearing a tuxedo from Gil's brother's dry cleaners and a fake beard glued to her skin. She twisted in her seat and was momentarily blinded by Gil's Liberace cape.

"We look stupid. This'll never work."

Gil fluffed the lace on his shirt. "It'll work."

"I'm going in with you. It's the only way I'll know if he's really dead."

"I've seen a picture. I can tell you if it's him."

"Not good enough." Raven pulled out a wicked, pearl-tipped hatpin from the carnation boutonniere secured against her lapel. She held the point up for him to see. "I want to prick the corpse to see if it twitches."

"You're sick."

"Just playing it safe." She powered her window halfway down. They were treated to the ripe smell of filth, body odor, and human excrement, and she quickly closed the glass. "I guess it's true—they don't perform the Three-S ritual until the heir apparent is deeply rooted underground."

Gil tried to talk her out of going inside. "You don't think they'll notice a man with breasts?"

"Lots of men have breasts—"

"Maybe fat guys."

"—besides, I tried to flatten mine out with an ace bandage."

"Whatever you say, Marilyn."

"For God's sake, they've turned this place into Ringling Brothers. They're cooking a pig over a spit next to the chapel. Women are dressed up like fortune-tellers. I should fit right in."

But Gil posed another problem. "At least I'm Mexican. I'll blend in fine, but you? Too pale." He shook his head. "Too risky."

"Too late." She popped open the door, swung out a leg, then walked to the rear door and opened it. With the command of the King of Prussia on coronation day, Gil stepped out.

Her stomach clenched. "Oh, shit. Here comes Steve Balogh."

They made eye contact and he passed her by. She caught up with Gil, and narrowly escaped through a side door.

Gypsy mourners transformed the funeral home into an internment camp. Raven started to slip inside the women's restroom, then caught herself. When she opened the door to the men's room, three young gypsies were removing the brass fixtures from the sinks.

To accommodate the overflow of mourners, the funeral home shut down business and opened its biggest rooms. Ivan Balogh's remains were presented in a mahogany casket, lacquered to a high gloss, left open for visitors to view a corpse veiled in traditional white lace.

With hatpin in hand, Raven moved stealthily through the crowd, humming along with "Camptown Races" piped in through the speakers. A "suit" standing beside a huge archway constructed with seasonal flowers caught her attention. She suspected the IRS had sent one of their agents, hoping to close an open file for tax evasion.

Dozens of floral arrangements lined the walls. She stared at a Cuban cigar fashioned from bronze crysanthemums; a replica READER AND ADVISOR sign made from a background of marigolds with letters in red rosebuds; a garish "Texas Cactus" lotto ticket crafted from carnations sprayed with green and silver paint. By far, the most impressive display was the telephone keypad for the Balogh's one-nine hundred psychic hotline, sculped from zinnias.

Since most of the flower arrangements took the shape of vices, she didn't want to dwell too long on the red roses crafted into a pair of lips, wrapped around a tubular-shaped pink—

—someone bumped her hard enough to spin her around.

Instinctively, she felt for her wallet, and remembered she had the good sense to store it in her breast pocket.

"Bad, Bad Leroy Brown" blasted over the speakers but no one seemed to notice. Then came "Texas Our Texas." Ten feet away from the coffin, Raven positioned the hatpin to strike.

A couple of midgets tossed silver dollars and hooch into the coffin. The line moved forward. A tinny brass band with a flat trombone and a sharp coronet struck up a melody. It took a few strains before Raven recognized "Happy Trails To You."

She gauged the distance between the dead gypsy and the nearest exit. If things soured, she could hurdle a couple of kids, and be nothing but a black streak in under ten seconds.

Six feet away, a middle-aged woman threw herself onto the body and howled.

An old crone with her head covered by a long scarf whipped around unexpectedly. Wagged her finger in a "no" motion, and cast the evil eye. "The curse is not so easy to lift with the enemy inside these walls."

Raven's eyes got big. The shrieking woman writhed against the corpse. Dozens of short guys appeared out of nowhere, as if the Jolly Green Giant had suddenly peed on an antbed.

The crowd parted.

Ephram and Georg ushered in Queen Ruta.

Mikel and Ralph walked behind them.

Raven held her breath in self-defense. The place stank like an outhouse.

Without warning, King Kos popped up in front of her. The dwarves peeled the weeping woman off the corpse and Kos slammed down the lid to the coffin.

He raised his hands above his head.

A hush fell over the room.

Beady eyes scanned the sea of faces.

Could've heard a hatpin drop.

"It is time to leave his family alone with him," Kos announced in an eagle screech. "Soon, we feast, for the curse will be lifted."

Raven was pushed outside in a wave of smelly gyps. With her hand to her mouth to conceal a lopsided mustache, she met Gil at the limousine.

"I didn't get to stick him."

"That's okay. We'll watch 'em shovel dirt on him."

En route to the cemetery, the motorcade of the century created a traffic jam of wailing gypsies unlike any Fort Worth had ever seen. Cars with license plates from as far away as Illinois and New York City fell in line and crept to the gravesite like a bloated anaconda.

Raven parked the limousine near a stand of trees.

Gil pointed. "Uh-oh."

Two men in black suits jumped out of a dark blue Crown Victoria with heavily tinted windows. They rushed the car.

"Oh, shit."

"Be cool."

Raven repositioned the fake mustache and powered down the window. Deepened her voice. "Help you?"

One of the men bent over and peered into the vehicle. The other moved to the right rear quarter panel and stood where he had the advantage of sight. She knew at once they were lawdogs, and suspected they were probably feds.

The one by her window said, "Move along."

"Free country." She tried not to look directly at him, but he whipped out a badge case and her eyes strayed on their own volition.

The evening sun glinted off his shield and temporarily blinded her. "U.S. Treasury. Beat it."

She assumed her regular voice. "I'm a cop. So's he." She thumbed at the back seat.

"You're female."

"I'm reaching for my badge, so don't cap me."

"Hey, Pete. U.C. cop. A female."

She presented her credentials and he scrutinized them. "Why're you here?"

"The SOB tried to have me bumped off. You?"

"Money laundering."

Heads bobbed all around.

Raven peeled off the mustache and beard. "Want to team up? We've got a nice wet bar in the back and a color TV. I could put some Fleetwood Mac in the CD player and we could compare notes." Without his sunglasses, the guy looked pretty cute.

"No, thanks. We have a directional mike."

Gil practically launched himself into the front seat. "Can we hang with you fellows?"

The feds swapped looks. "You'll have to ditch the car."

Raven flashed her best beauty pageant smile. "No way, Dude. Yours has twelve antennae. I made you for law enforcement right off. You get rid of yours. Besides, we have barbequed brisket. Show him, Gil."

The feds stashed their car behind a pump house and set up the directional mike where they could blend into the trees. From time to time, the agent with sandy-colored hair would identify one of the Baloghs in the buzz of voices.

Raven lowered the field glasses. "Which one are you after?"

"There isn't a paddy wagon big enough to collect them all."

The dark-haired agent agreed. "You wouldn't by chance know any of the Szabu clan, would you? Andor Szabu would be a nice one to filet, flour, and fry."

She shook her head. Gil curled up in the back seat for a nap. Before long, he was snoring like a harp seal.

Several hours later, Raven shook him. "Wake up. Something's happening."

He climbed out of the limo, yawning, and joined the agents behind the trees.

"I don't get it." She watched the hubbub through a pair of binoculars. "No reputable funeral parlor would let gyppos con a burial out of them."

Gil wiped the sleep from his eyes. "This one's teetering on bankruptcy."

"It's all clear to me." Raven inhaled the scent of freshly cut grass and ticked off her suspicions one-two-three. "The Balogh dynasty pays a ton of money to offset the aggravation, and before the gyppos scatter to the four winds, they gut the building and leave a skeletal mess free of plumbing fixtures, musical instruments, crystal chandeliers, drapes, chairs, and even patches of carpet. Look—"

Gil raised his hand and squinted against the afternoon sun. The sandy-haired agent repositioned the mike.

The coffin was opened for a final offering of coins, hooch, illegal smokes and jewelry.

Duda, Ivan's widow, dropped to her knees and screamed in anguish.

Abruptly, the finger-pointing began.

Such a disaster would not have happened if Estv had carried out his burden.

Honor demanded that Estv's mother hurl insults. It was not Estv but Ephram who fouled things up.

Ephram's father slandered Estv's brother. Three more families joined the backbiting. Ralph was the real knucklehead. Georg, too. And who could forget Mikel, the greasy little coward?

A shrill voice carried on a breeze. "Your daughter is a whore. My Vlad is too good for her."

Queen Ruta doubled up her fist and moved the air in front of the woman's face. "Your son deflowered Sabina. He is vile and unclean."

More blows were swung. Before Ivan Balogh was laid to rest, his cousin Mikel knocked Viktor into the coffin, sending the whole kit and caboodle crashing to the ground. Mourners leaped out of the way.

Ivan rolled onto the fake turf, cocooned in lace.

King Kos rushed to scoop up the corpulent corpse and shove it back into the casket; but not before gathering a handful of coins.

Ruta and Duda screamed. Kos opened his mouth and a hideous, rusty hinge screech pierced the chaos. Mourners fell silent and pugilists freeze-framed in mid-blow.

"Enough. The curse is lifted. We feast."

Ivan Balogh went into the ground.

The first clumps of dirt were shoveled into the gaping hole.

When the thieving gyps finally disbanded, they left in their wake a commercial holocaust.

The blond agent dismantled the mike. "King Kos probably pocketed enough gold to pay next year's taxes."

His partner agreed. "But that's not half as much as these locusts will steal by the time they return home." He turned to Raven and pressed a business card into her palm. "We're outta here. Call me."

Gil said, "Let's hit the road."

Raven shook her head. "Not me. I think I'll stay a little longer."

"Long enough to watch the backhoe cover him over?"

"Exactly."

"Remind me never to piss you off." Gil cupped his hands to his mouth and shouted to the Treasury agents. "Wait up. I need a lift."

The sun melted into the horizon like a glob of orange wax. Raven took off the chauffeur's cap and threaded her fingers through her hair enough to fluff it out.

The sound of a backhoe rumbled behind her. She looked over her shoulder in time to see it crest the hill. Cranked the ignition until the engine caught. Dropped the shift lever into gear.

Her eyelids fluttered in astonishment.

She stomped the brake.

Jammed the car into park.

Mouth agape, she stared in stricken silence. Drew in a sharp intake of air and felt a chill in her heart.

A stumpy ghoul climbed out of the pit. Ripped off its lace cocoon and threw it back into the hole. Ran like hell across the empty grounds, toward a flicker of headlights shrouded by trees.

"Son of a bitch." Her voice dissolved to a whisper and she uttered a vow. "I'll fix your ass, Ivan Balogh. When you're dead, you've gotta to stay dead. You can't show up at the 7-Eleven next week and resume buying lotto tickets."

Chapter Forty

December thirty-first.

Time to go.

Jinx checked his watch. Six-thirty, and nobody left but the cleanup crew.

First, he removed the pictures of the Dogs Playing Poker. Next, he took the photographs off the office wall. But when he emptied the last drawer and unearthed the photo of Raven, he couldn't bring himself to drop it in the trashcan. Instead, he left it on the desk. When he finished packing the last box, he telephoned a taxi, snatched up the eight-by-ten of Raven, and took it with him.

Having slammed the county car keys on Raven's desk in a final act of defiance, he hauled his boxes out to the loading dock behind the building. He helped the cabbie load the trunk in the driving rain, then yanked the door open, flung his briefcase inside, and slid in behind.

Once they rolled out of the parking lot, he peeled off his glasses and wiped the droplets off the lenses. When he decided they were clean, he slipped them back on. The driver came into focus.

"Where to, man?"

A robust, jolly-faced Negro in his late forties grinned over the upturned collar of his windbreaker.

"Know how to get to the Château Du Roy?"

"The fag place? Sure, man."

Jinx set his jaw. The cabbie's eyes rolled up to meet his gaze in the rearview mirror—the mirror with a tip glass prominently displayed underneath.

"Sorry, man. It's just . . . that place has a bad rep."

"Keep driving. By way of the Cosmo's Barbeque. You know the place?"

"Sure, man."

"Good. There's an extra five bucks in it if you don't try to make conversation with me."

At Cosmo's Jinx waited in line for ribs, something he'd never had to do in the seventeen years he'd been constable. By the time he returned to the cab, it was almost seven. Rain turned to sleet, and they navigated their way through the streets until they were within a mile of the Château.

"Yo, man. Over yonder." The cabbie pointed. "That's one bodacious fire."

Jinx lifted his tired eyelids. "It's not a fire. It's the Aurora Borealis."

"Whatchoo mean? It's an inferno."

"No, it's my apartment. The idiot next door strung up a bunch of twinkle lights to jazz up the dump."

"I don't think so."

In no mood to argue, Jinx slumped against the door, leaned his head against the freezing window and warmed his hands with the heated tin of pork ribs.

When they came within several blocks, he bolted upright in the seat. A flash of emergency lights reflected off the adjacent buildings.

He grabbed the headrest to the front seat and jerked himself within inches of the cabbie's ear. "Good God, it's my apartment."

The cabbie winced. "Does this mean I don't get the extra five dollars?"

"Ten, if you stomp on it."

"But the light's red."

"Twenty."

"Damn straight." Tires spun on wet asphalt. The cab shot through the light.

Jinx made a quick visual count. LIGHTNING, AUNT LILLIAN, PANTHER, and AUNT SUSIE. Altogether, four firetrucks.

A policeman stepped off the curb and halted the cab. The cabbie slid his window down. Shards of ice stung the driver as the cop stuck his face in.

"Can't go any farther, Guys. Real bad fire."

Jinx was out the door in a heartbeat.

"What about my money?"

"Stop! That's an order."

Jinx kept running.

Caesar.

He hurtled past fire hoses and pulled up short. His lungs stung from an ominous mixture of freezing drizzle and acrid smoke. High atop a cherrypicker, near Jinx's broken bedroom window, a firefighter began his descent. A wet, sooty mass plastered to the sparky's yellow slicker reached out a tentative limb *and serrated the man's face.*

The fireman screamed and let go. The blackened blur leaped across the engine's hood, banked off a policeman's hat, then streaked past the Pérezes. Huddled near what appeared to be Jinx's flaming sofa, the frenzied familia pawed through a plastic bag with undetermined contents.

The cat bounded over, ears flat against his head. His eyes glazed over and popped with fear.

"Caesar!"

The filthy hairball bristled. Jinx buried his face in the wet fur. He sucked in a relieved breath, hardly noticing the smell.

"Yo, man, was that your crib?"

Drenched and shivering, Jinx stared at the skeletal remains of his apartment. Stiff-necked, he managed a slow nod.

"Won'tcha get back in the cab?"

Numb with disbelief, Jinx stood anchored in place and gave him a slow headshake.

"Lemme take you anywhere you want to go, man. The drive's on me."

"I don't have anyplace to go. Nowhere that would take my cat in."

On the opposite curb, the Munsch brothers, dressed in frilly nightgowns, huddled under a blanket. Each held a birdcage.

The last time Jinx saw Glen Lee Spence dressed in anything close to Levis and a V-neck T-shirt was Halloween night when he surprised everyone by trick-or-treating as a man. With a boa of marabou feathers draped over one shoulder, he strutted anxiously about in reindeer boxers and a tank top, waving his cigarette holder with the frustration of a Philharmonic music conductor directing a brass band.

"I do not believe the Fort Worth Fire Department could not save these peoples' apartments. This is the problem with city government."

The Munsch brothers chimed in with their grievances.

"We don't have a place to stay. And our clothes—"

Harold broke into tears. "It took years, collecting those dresses."

The Pérez children stood over Jinx's smoldering couch, taste-testing skewers of blistering marshmallows. Other tenants ventured out of seclusion long enough to offer sanctuary to anyone game. Jinx avoided their sorrowful gazes, felt the pangs of longing at the sight of Loose-Wheel Lucille's darkened apartment, and turned to the taxi driver.

"Take me to a motel. Preferably one where I don't have to declare the cat."

No question about it, Jinx had walked away with his shoulders squared. Raven could still feel his strong presence, even as she read the blotter on his former desk.

December thirty-first.

The entry, written in Jinx's deliberate hand, read: TURN OVER KEYS.

She seated herself in front of his computer—her computer, now—and finished polishing the last chapter of a novel she'd spent nine months writing. The publisher's contract for *The Lonely Constable* had come from New York City that very morning.

He never gave her credit. Didn't regard her as his equal.

Only trouble was, while America would love the book, Jinx would probably sue.

She shivered. Her eyes drifted over the office where she would spend the next four years. She recalled the series of unlikely events that had led to her victory, and her gut snapped like an elevator cable. He'd hurt her.

She'd hurt him back.

Snatched the only thing besides the cat that really meant anything right out from under him.

She sank into a chair much too big for her, and smoothed her hand across the desktop. Tomorrow morning, her plants, the Coyote's picture, and other personal belongings would replace the things Jinx held dear.

She envisioned him in some remote outback in East Texas near the Big Thicket, churning out memoirs on a computer, spending days on end in front of a nineteen-inch screen monitor. There would be a woman, of course—another victim. Jinx Porter never went anywhere without leaving emotional cripples and lovesick casualties in his wake.

Unexpectedly, Georgia stuck her head in the door.

"I didn't realize you were still here. I don't mean to rush you, Honey, I just came back to shut off the lights. Jinx never liked us to waste electricity."

"I'm staying awhile. See you later?" At midnight, the county judge would swear her in.

"Goodness me, yes. I wouldn't miss it."

Georgia left her with her memories.

Raven didn't get to ask what she wanted to know most: whether Dell would show for her swearing-in ceremony.

She couldn't help but feel a little smug. Jinx was so full of himself, he never saw it coming.

For no reason other than instinct, she solved her potential lawsuit problem. If she just made one little change, everything in *The Lonely Constable* could be true, and Jinx would never even see himself.

So she did.

She scrolled back through the disk until she found what she was looking for—located the protagonist's attributes—*and gave her hero a little penis.*

She picked up Jinx's badge—her badge—from the desk, huffed a breath on it and shined the seven-pointed star against her sleeve. Then she pinned it to her waistband. She had his job, his office, his friends. Ever since the general, she had been on an adrenaline high. But once the excitement wore off, the tender feelings she once held for him still plagued her.

By the time she reached the door and saw where Jinx's name had been razor-bladed off, her heart ached.

On the short walk over to the Administration Building, tears blistered behind her eyeballs. At the double glass doors, she caught her reflection in the window pane. Irony struck, and she felt the first licks of genuine fear.

She still loved the jerk.

So, who, in reality, was *The Lonely Constable*?

Epilogue

A year after his defeat, in a log cabin on the outskirts of San Augustine, Texas, where he lived the existence of a hermit, Jinx hung up the telephone.

Ivy's voice still rang in his ear.

It seemed Raven had written a story about the constable race. Even more amazing, her novel had been published. According to the book review that came out in the Fort Worth newspaper that morning, it turned out to be a blockbuster, and Ivy hoped Raven would resign from office.

Outside, footfalls approached. The postman—his only regular visitor—dropped a bundle through the mail slot. As logs in the fireplace crackled, Jinx slipped on his Jiffies and shuffled to the door. He opened it a crack, enough to see where a layer of light snow covered the ground. Caesar stuck out his head long enough to decide to stay put.

In the mail, wrapped in brown paper and addressed in Raven's familiar script, was the book.

Against his better judgment, he opened a bottled Coke, eased into his recliner, and considered reading it. As a concession to curiosity, he opened the back cover and looked at her picture on the dust jacket.

Still pretty. And she owned a Siamese.

He closed the book and set it aside.

An hour later, he picked it up again and read the first chapter.

By lunchtime, he forced himself to take inventory of the refrigerator. He settled for a couple of links of dried-out sausage and a boiled egg, then went back into the living room.

Around four o'clock, his back pained him. He stuck the electric bill in the middle of the book to mark his place and snapped it closed. After a short walk to the Mom-and-Pop, he came back with a package of Oreos and an industrial strength bottle of aspirin.

By nightfall, he sandwiched himself between the covers and drew the cat close. When he finished the last page, he formed a conclusion: he could see why Ivy was pissed. The thinly disguised character Raven called "Flora" in her book pulled some pretty stupid stunts. And that kid Raven patterned after Amos—even Ivy believed the future serial killer set that apartment fire. While it was true there may have been similarities between himself and Jared Ponder, Raven had definitely not patterned her constable character after Jinx Porter.

So, when Ivy telephoned a few minutes before midnight, still insistent, he said what he'd wanted to say for the past eighteen years. "You're a frickin' idiot."

"Maybe you better go back and read it again," she said icily.

To put an end to the nonsense, he hung up on her.

The cat stood and arched his back into a horseshoe. He made two revolutions before flopping back down on the covers.

Jinx reached across the night stand, switched off the night light, and chuckled at Ivy's foolishness.

What a fruitloop.

He lay in bed, barely breathing, scratching the Siamese behind one ear, and listening to him purr.

Ivy either had to be stark raving mad, or on hallucinogens.

He rolled onto his side and scrunched his arm around the extra pillow, the way he always did now that Raven was gone.

What dingalings—Ivy and the Unabomber.

Outside frost-covered windows, a coyote wind howled. His eyelids grew heavy and he closed them. Took a deep breath and let it out slowly. Felt the lightheaded tingle of sleep about to descend.

What was that nitwit thinking, anyway?

No woman in Fort Worth would ever mistake him for Jared Ponder.

Jared Ponder had a little dick.

ABOUT THE AUTHOR

Merry Laureen Moore, "Laurie" to her friends, is a 23 year law enforcement veteran and attorney who currently practices law in Fort Worth, Texas.

Laurie spent seven years on police patrol in Austin, Texas, and worked as a Sergeant Investigator, Chief Investigator, and law clerk at four District Attorneys Offices in Central and North Texas. She graduated with a B.A. from The University of Texas at Austin in 1975 and received her J.D. from Texas Wesleyan University School of Law in 1995.

Writing is her passion. She is a member of the DFW Writers' Workshop and has a daughter at Rhodes, two bad Siamese, and a Welsh Corgi. She is still a licensed, commissioned peace officer.